Praise for
Such Sharp Te

"*Such Sharp Teeth* is wonderfully witty and wild. It's also heady and daring in how the story explores friend and family dynamics, the anger women aren't allowed to express within our culture, and the wounds that transform us against our will. The next full moon I see, I'll be rooting for Rory."

—Paul Tremblay, national bestselling author of *The Cabin at the End of the World* and *The Pallbearers Club*

"No one is writing horror that explores the intricacies of femininity like Rachel Harrison. This brilliant story is about accepting your identity, your past, love, friendship, and family . . . all wrapped up in a deeply satisfying and scary monster tale. *Such Sharp Teeth* is as irresistible as the pull of the full moon—I couldn't tear myself away."

—Mallory O'Meara, bestselling author of *The Lady from the Black Lagoon*

"At turns heartwarming, heartrending, and a little monstrous, Harrison's latest gives anything but your typical Big Bad Wolf story. *Such Sharp Teeth* runs slick with bone-crackling wit and cunning, but don't be fooled by that grin; this wolf has bite."

—Hailey Piper, Bram Stoker Award–winning author of *Queen of Teeth*

"Rachel Harrison's razor-sharp prose cuts straight to the bone. With its quick-witted dialogue and acutely human regard for its cursed characters, *Such Sharp Teeth* solidifies her spot as the alpha author of heartfelt horror."

—Clay McLeod Chapman, author of *Ghost Eaters*

"With prose as sleek as a wolf in full stride, *Such Sharp Teeth* feels at once like a classic werewolf story and something delightfully new. It's a breathless, poignant, blood-and-flesh-licking tale that asks: When our distractions and coping mechanisms are shredded away, who—or what—are we? And it confirms once again that Rachel Harrison is horror's poet laureate of quarter-life dread and existential transition."

—Nat Cassidy, author of *Mary: An Awakening of Terror*

"Darkly comic and modern . . . a story about rage, trauma, and leaning into one's wild side."

—*USA Today*

"Harrison is the master of pairing a horrific plot with fun and witty writing."

—*Mystery & Suspense Magazine*

"Harrison's latest is a rip-roaring, bloody adventure that also explores the wounds trauma can leave on both the body and the psyche . . . will appeal to fans of *Mongrels* by Stephen Graham Jones and *Her Body and Other Parties* by Carmen Maria Machado."

—*Library Journal*

"Known for her enthralling and eerie page-turners, Rachel Harrison delivers a darkly comedic love story in her new thriller."

—*Woman's World*

NOVELS BY RACHEL HARRISON

The Return

Cackle

Such Sharp Teeth

Black Sheep

SHORT STORY COLLECTION
BY RACHEL HARRISON

Bad Dolls

SUCH SHARP TEETH

Rachel Harrison

BERKLEY
New York

BERKLEY
An imprint of Penguin Random House LLC
penguinrandomhouse.com

ISBN: 978-0-593-54583-6

The Library of Congress has catalogued the Berkley hardcover edition of this book as follows:

Names: Harrison, Rachel, 1989– author.
Title: Such sharp teeth / Rachel Harrison.
Description: New York : Berkley, [2022]
Identifiers: LCCN 2022010996 (print) | LCCN 2022010997 (ebook) |
ISBN 9780593545829 (hardcover) | ISBN 9780593545843 (ebook)
Subjects: LCGFT: Novels.
Classification: LCC PS3608.A78368 S83 2022 (print) | LCC PS3608.A78368 (ebook) |
DDC 813/.6--dc23/eng/20220304
LC record available at https://lccn.loc.gov/2022010996
LC ebook record available at https://lccn.loc.gov/2022010997

Berkley hardcover edition / October 2022
Berkley trade paperback edition / August 2023

Printed in the United States of America
2nd Printing

Book design by Nancy Resnick
Postcard image by Callahan/Shutterstock.com

For my pack

I

Moths flutter around the fluorescent bulb as it blinks into the dark outside the bar. I lean back and lift my gaze to the night. There's no light pollution out here, and the stars are fierce. The moon is full, so I give it a wink.

"Did you just wink at me?"

Ian's so tall he blocks out the moon. When he's in front of you, there's nothing else. He's all there is.

"I did wink," I say. "But not at you. Sorry."

"All right," he says. "Glad we cleared that up."

"Apologies for any confusion."

He doesn't say anything else. He turns away from me to exhale, releasing a calm river of smoke toward the parking lot.

"Are you disappointed?" I ask him. "Did I give you false hope for a second there?"

"Well, yeah, but I've had false hope since we were thirteen, so I'm used to it," he says, turning back toward the light so I can see his good-natured grin.

It's been so many years since I last saw that grin. My heart begins to thump mutinously inside my chest. Maybe his hope isn't false after all.

All right, then. Time to go.

"I should head home. My sister will be jealous if she thinks I'm out having too much fun while she's stuck home. Sober."

"Tell Scarlett I say hello," he says.

"I will," I say, patting my pockets to check for my wallet, my keys. "Happy we ran into each other. Good to see you."

"Yeah," he says. "We should run into each other again while you're still in town."

I search for a cool, noncommittal response among the assortment I store readily under my tongue. I fumble. My lips part but offer nothing.

"Or not," he says, shrugging his massive shoulders. He pushes his glasses up his nose, the same squarish black Ray-Bans he wore in high school. Behind the thick lenses, his eyes are a striking, unusual blue. Cobalt.

"No, yeah," I stammer. "I mean, yes. Of course."

Horrifying.

"You good to drive? I can give you a ride," he says.

"I'm good. One beer. I can walk in a straight line for you, though, if you like. ABC's backwards."

"Could you?"

"I'm shy."

He laughs.

"All right." I take my car keys out of my pocket. I slip my index finger into the key ring and flip them around. "Good night."

"Bye, Rory."

I'm curious if he's watching me as I walk to my car. The restraint it takes to not sneak a glance over my shoulder. Shameful.

I'll leave this part out when I tell Scarlett.

If I tell Scarlett.

Despite her current situation, she seems to have retained her position as a hard-core romantic. She's like Mom. If I tell her I bumped into Ian Pedretti, forget it.

I get into the car and turn the heat on, thawing myself from the October chill. I pull out of the parking lot, stealing a quick look in my rearview.

Ian is still there, finishing his cigarette.

I forgot about the mist. There's an ever-present mist that skulks around here like a townie. It tumbles down from the mountain, seeps out of the woods, and slathers itself across the dull suburban landscape. It might be the only defining quality of my hometown. Persistent mist.

Even with my brights on, there's negligible visibility. I drive slowly around the winding curves of Cutter Road. I used to know it by heart. I could drive it in the dark no problem, but it's been a long time since I've been back. I didn't think it was something I could lose. I thought that the map of this place was etched into me, that I could navigate from muscle memory, but I guess time erases the things you least expect.

A yawn crawls out of me. It's dramatic about it. The heat has me sleepy. I need to stay awake and alert for the five minutes it'll take me to get back to Scarlett's. Doesn't seem like too monumental a task, but after years of being able to zone out on the subway, passively observing stops and the occasional kerfuffle, the additional attention required for driving seems like a big ask. I turn off the heat and crack open the windows, hoping the fresh air will keep me honest.

In comes the signature campfire smell of autumn, but also something else. Something more potent and less appealing. I sniff.

It's wet animal.

The distinct scent of damp fur.

It's overpowering. I consider closing the window, but then my phone chimes.

My eyes obediently flick over to the illuminated screen, and . . .

Thud.

Time leaps ahead, dragging me by the neck. It leaves me with my lungs convulsing, a hideous screeching in my ears. My seat belt is tight, at my throat like a knife.

My car is facing in the wrong direction. I inhale, and it's just burning rubber.

I hit something.

I hit something.

The sound, that grievous thud, replays loudly in my head. It's relentless, with a severe disorienting urgency.

I pull at my seat belt, attempting to loosen it, so I can breathe, but it's dead set on anchoring me in this hellish moment. I feel around for the button with a trembling hand. I find it eventually, and the seat belt releases with a fast snap. I open the car door and stumble onto the road.

The cold pulls me out of the fog of my shock. I do a quick examination of my body. Extremities seem to be intact. I feel my face. Aside from the wide gape of my mouth, there's nothing concerning. I move my neck side to side.

I'm fine.

Car? Not fine. My front bumper, the grille, whatever, is now so deeply indented, it's the shape of a V.

What did I hit? What could possibly cause that much damage? A deer?

I clench my teeth and take a minute to allow the reality to fully set in, as much as I'd prefer to hang out in the cozy palm of denial. I brace myself for the inevitable cycle of emotions. Anger at myself for being an irresponsible driver, frustration at the situation in general. Remorse for the animal I almost certainly killed.

I wasn't speeding. I was going only thirty, thirty-five at most. But if the sound and the state of my car are any indication, RIP. I guess I should check to make sure I don't abandon a concussed house pet, some freshly maimed family dog. If that's what I hit and there's a chance that it's somehow still alive, that means there's a chance I can save it.

I turn toward the road. Mist curls in all directions; it peels from the night like the skin from ripe fruit. There's a glittering black smear on the road, mostly eluding the reach of my headlights. I step toward it, holding my breath, preparing my apology to Spot or Bambi.

My presence disrupts the mist, and between my headlights, aggressive starlight, and a cruel, gawking moon, I can see the mess I've made.

I can't even tell what kind of animal it is. Or was.

It's inside out. The impact must have skinned it somehow because there's no evidence of fur. Giant worms of intestines unravel across the road. The wet abstract of organs contrasts against the pale shock of bone. It's a shapeless horror. An absolute massacre.

"I'm sorry," I tell it, searching for some hint of its identity. There's a lot of it, whatever it is. Too much. Guessing a deer? I scan for antlers.

There's a lump. I squint, stepping deeper into the haze. My eyes adjust, and I can see that the lump is fur. A neat mound of fur. Beside the mound, staring up at me with dead glassy eyes, is a head. I was right. It was a deer.

How is this possible? I was not going over thirty-five. And even if I was . . .

Something possesses me to reach out and hover my hand over the carcass. It's cold. There's no heat coming off it, no warmth at all. I just hit it. If it just died, wouldn't it still be warm?

I linger over the deer, wondering, until I realize I'm not required to turn in an autopsy report. It's not a mystery I need to solve. I killed it. I feel bad; that's it. My punishment is I'll likely never be able to stomach meat again. I'll be a vegetarian and a conscientious driver.

I sigh and straighten my legs.

I pause to listen. I hear something. Labored breathing. A sharp inhale followed by the slow rip of an exhale. It repeats.

I bring my hand to my chest. Its surf is steady. Rise, fall. Rise, fall. It contradicts the sound. But if I'm not making it, what is?

There's an onslaught of darkness, confusing me for all of two seconds before I realize something has passed in front of the headlights.

Until I realize I'm not the one who killed that deer.

I turn around.

It eclipses the headlights, concealing itself in darkness. I can make out a vague outline, trace an enormous mass sliced from shadow. It suddenly shifts between the headlights, uncoiling itself. The light scalds my eyes, forcing a brief retreat into the refuge of my head. I'm tempted to let them stay there, to leave my eyes closed and maybe just never open them again, never face whatever it is in front of me. But something else—maybe survival instinct or curiosity—wins out.

I open my eyes, and at first they struggle against the brightness. All I can see is that whatever's there, positioned between me and my car, it's standing upright.

A bear. It's a bear. It's the size of a large bear. It's got four limbs. A head. Fur.

I blink, and the scene comes into focus.

I've never seen a bear like this. Its proportions are weird.

It stands on the pads of its feet. They're not really paws. They're big but narrow, and they've got fur, only it's sparse, and where there's none, grayish skin is stretched tight over thin splinters of bone. Its toes are each about the size of my fist, and from them extend thick black nails, sharp, almost like talons. Its legs are long. Slim pale muscles slither around exposed bone, fur detaching in certain places, like around the knees. The legs have a disturbing bend to them. They're not straight. They won't straighten. They're hind legs.

It's slouched, concealing part of its torso. There's fur missing there, too. Its skin has been pulled too taut; there are obvious rips where the thing is fleshless. I can see a sickening twist of ribs and spongy insides, but most of it is shadowed by the curtain of its arms. The thing pulls them forward but leaves them limp. They dangle down past its knees.

Its hands are marred. Leathery tangled mitts. Bones peek through recessions of fur. Its giant knuckles are bald. Its fingers have way too many joints; they bend and unbend and bend.

I look up at its head.

A whiteness escapes its wide-open jaws. Froth pours through its fangs. Beyond its snout, two red eyes bore into me. The color of them, it's unreal.

It can't be real.

Did someone slip something into my beer?

I feel the skepticism creep across my expression, my eyebrows sinking, eyes narrowing as I study the thing standing in front of me. My doubt releases me from my fear, and for a moment the creature isn't real and I'm safe.

It must sense this, because it rears back, head up, opening its chest to the sky, arms wide. I can hear the awful creak of its jaw as it unhinges to an alarming degree, the separation between its teeth staggering. It begins to scream. The torturous pitch funnels ice into my veins. It's agonizing.

The scream splits, harmonizing with itself. It's like there's more than one voice.

Animals shouldn't be able to scream like that.

It's going on forever. I don't know if it'll ever stop. Should I run? Why haven't I already started running?

The thing finally stops screaming. It collapses onto all fours. It turns to me, and the clarity of its red gaze is unnerving. I understand.

It's angry. I hit it with my car. I interrupted its dinner.

And it's starving.

I run.

I take off into the mist. I'm a runner but this is different. Running for your life is different. It sucks.

I'm vulnerable on the road. There's nowhere for me to hide. If another car comes, it's more likely to hit me than be able to help me. I veer into the woods.

The wet carpet of moss swallows my footsteps. I dodge branches, hop over rocks. I know it's following me because it's not stealthy. It doesn't need to be because it's huge and fanged and fast. It's got that predator confidence. It knows it can catch me because it's the predator. And I'm prey.

It's not the first beast to see me this way. Might be the last, though.

My thoughts distract me. My run becomes increasingly reckless. A wayward arm smacks a cluster of low foliage. The rustle is thunderous.

I can't think. I can't think about what's happening. I can't stop to conjure the image of what's hunting me, pause to marvel at the horror of it. No time for *How?* or *Why?* or *What the ever-loving fuck?* Its snarls cleave the quiet; its hot breath is at my heels. Any hope of escape is obliterated. I'm not going to outrun the thing. I can't. I'm not getting home to my sister, who needs me. I can't go any faster.

Is this it, then? My final thought: *This is as fast as I can go.*

I spit dirt and blood from my mouth. The pain is disorienting. I'm facedown. The gentle creep of insect legs along my cheek is the only sensation I can decisively identify. The rest is just nebulous torment.

My ankle, maybe?

The brutal bloom of heat on my shoulder interrupts my analysis, and I'm flipped over onto my back. It's done easily, like I have no weight, like it's nothing, like I'm nothing. My body is not a factor, except right now I know it's the only factor. I go rigid.

It looms above me, the moon providing a direct spotlight, a wraithlike glow. Honestly, I could do without it. *Fuck you, moon.* I don't need my death by large inbred animal to have good lighting. Dark would be fine. Preferable.

I could close my eyes, but it's kind of hard when the thing looks the way it does.

I can almost hear the chiding of my future self, if there were to be a future self. Or maybe it's the chorus of outsiders who might someday read about what happened to me and wonder aloud, *"Why didn't she?" "Why didn't she wriggle away?" "If it were me, I would have punched it in the face!" "I would have fought back!" "I would have screamed!"*

Why didn't I? Why don't I?

Because I can't.

I can't.

It lowers itself down. It sniffs me, starting at my feet. It's removed my boots, or they've come off somehow. Not sure. I can see now that my ankle is twisted, bloody. My jeans are torn to shreds. They were my favorite jeans, too.

The soft twitch of my grin meets a salty wetness. I'm crying.

Scarlett.

I'm grateful we never had that special twin thing. We were disappointed as children that we didn't have that connection. She broke her collarbone at a soccer game, and I was across town having the time of my life sleeping over at Ash's. Double-fisting s'mores and dancing along to music videos on MTV. No phantom pain. No nothing.

Right now I hope she's on the couch reading, or sketching, or strumming absentmindedly on her guitar, feeling no pain. No twin telepathy. No inexplicable, all-consuming, utterly devastating fear.

As long as she isn't feeling what I'm feeling.

The soul-eviscerating terror of staring into the red eyes of this thing. It's so close to me now, its blood-slick snout pressed to my chin. It's definitely not a bear. Whatever it is, it's not natural.

In a swift, savage motion, it buries its face into my side.

The scream that escapes me is bloodcurdling, so monstrous that the creature unclamps its jaws and shoots me a look of what's maybe surprise. I can feel each puncture wound from each individual tooth with unfortunate lucidity. It stings, it burns. It's a shin on the corner of the coffee table, a bone you know is broken right away. It's a rally of all the pain I've ever felt, doused in acid. The hurt is transforming my mind. I can't stop screaming.

The thing is no longer deterred by it. It returns to slurp at the pulp of my wound.

"No!" I'm screaming. "No!"

Blood bubbles from my mouth. A sobering cold begins to inch its way through me. Everything darkens.

"No!" I sputter the word into multiple syllables. My mouth is flooding, tongue drowning in thick tangy blood.

It pulls away fast, taking some of me with it between its teeth. Strips of my skin dangle from its fangs. It stands and turns toward the sky, toward the dark of it. Fat clouds shroud the moon. It's completely lost, concealed from view.

My whimpering returns its attention to me. It looks down at me and cocks its head to the side. The movement has a certain innocence about it.

But then the clouds pass, and the moonlight returns with its menacing sheen. The thing growls at me, its thin lips rippling, gory fangs bared.

And just as it descends toward me, another animal decides to hurry by, maybe thinking the predator is preoccupied. Whatever the animal is, it must be more appealing, because the thing dashes after it, leaving me alone in the clearing, in a patch of bright silvery moonlight.

My breath collapses. I try to tilt my head down to see how bad it is. My entire side is covered in blood. It's been gnawed. Bitten. Butchered. The violence of it weakens me. Maybe it's the blood loss, or it could be the profound devastation over having had this done to me, having been vandalized in this way.

The carelessness, the disregard for my body, for my life. It's robbed me of my strength, my resolve. I let my eyes close without the faith I'll open them again.

I'm awakened by a rough pink tongue slobbering over my face. My drowsiness is slow to fade, my consciousness faltering.

A yell ruptures my stupor. I'm abruptly, terribly aware of my circumstance. There's a smiling spaniel panting just above me, and beyond it stands a woman in running clothes with her hands covering her mouth, horrified by the sight of me.

"Are you okay?" she asks, hysterical. "Are you okay?"

It's such a stupid question.

My voice is hoarse, but I manage to speak.

"I don't fucking know," I say. "Call nine-one-one."

11

Scarlett doesn't say hello. I don't see her come in. She just appears, her long blue hair in a perfect braid draped over her shoulder. Her roots are dark, her dye job growing out for the first time in forever. She wears all black. Patent leather jacket, coordinating combat boots with the buckles. Her bump is obscured by a flowy tunic. She looks me over, tapping a black coffin nail on her naked bottom lip. No makeup. That's the tell.

"You should see the bear," I say.

"I did. It's in the other room telling the police you hit first. Is that true?"

"Can neither confirm nor deny."

"All this over some honey," she says in her cool, enigmatic tone. I like to think that's exactly how I sound.

She lowers herself into the chair at my bedside, wincing all the way down.

"You feel okay?" I ask her.

She gives me one of her most disdainful stares.

"Just kidding," I say, hands up. "Honestly, I don't even care."

"You're the one in a hospital bed," she says. "Can we maybe talk for a sec about how I thought you were out getting laid and instead you were playing tag with a wild animal? What the fuck, Aurora?"

"I'm getting Aurora'd? How am I in trouble?"

"Why would you get out of the car?"

So it begins.

"Scarlett," I say, mirroring her cold stare. It's easy since we share a face.

She sighs, her head falling forward as she pinches the bridge of her nose. "What would I have done if I lost you? If you were killed by a *bear*?"

She doesn't know that's the wrong question. What would she have done if I had been killed by a monster?

It was a necessary lie. Had I told anyone the truth about what happened in the woods last night, that I was attacked by a massive fanged mystery beast, I'd likely be carted off to a mental institution. No one would believe me. I can't blame them. I barely believe it myself, and I was there. I know what I saw, and still . . .

It's a particular form of torture that I wish I were alone in, though I know I'm not. For some reason I can never fully trust my own experience. I'm always treating myself like an unreliable witness. I offer no empathy, only an endless cycle of interrogation.

Did I really see it? Or did I make up a fantastical creature to dissociate from reality? Wouldn't that make sense?

"Rory," Scarlett says.

"I was coming home from the bar and I hit something. I worried it was a dog. Some sweet golden retriever wearing a red bandanna and, like, a collar with tags that say, 'I'm loved.' I got out to check, and I guess maybe actually I hit the bear, or pissed it off somehow. Here we are."

"You've been back here for two weeks," she says. "Two weeks."

"I know," I say. "It could sense it. Bear was like 'Sweetie, go back to Manhattan.'"

"I'd understand," she says, tapping her nails on the arm of the chair. "If you want to go back. It's fine. I'll be fine."

"Hey. No," I say. "I'm not going anywhere. This doesn't change anything. I'm here."

"I woke up to the cops at the door. I don't ever want to wake up to a knock like that again."

I can't freak out because she's freaking out. One of us has to be calm. It's a rule.

"I'm sorry," I say. "Honestly, would rather be here. Rather be the one in the hospital bed than sitting beside it."

She stares at me for what feels like forty-five minutes.

"What?" I ask finally.

"You can't shrug this off," she says.

I shrug. It hurts.

"Aurora."

"Twice in one morning!"

"I'm serious. This is traumatic."

"You know what's traumatic? Is there anything worse than the moment before the disinfectant? You know it's going in. You know it's going to sting like a motherfucker. The anticipation. The worst."

"Yeah, well, I'm over here, knowing I'm going to have to give birth, so . . ."

It's been around five months since she told me, and I still can't figure out how she's feeling about it. Scarlett isn't one for sentiment, so it's possible she's concealing her excitement behind her typical nonchalance. On the subject of babies, both of us have always been a lukewarm I-don't-know-maybe. I wasn't totally shocked, especially considering how long she and Matty had been together, but it also didn't feel like good news.

It's possible his absence was impending, and that's why Scarlett was never keen to share sonogram pics and shop for onesies. She'll talk about it when she feels like talking about it, if she ever feels like talking about it.

"My favorite sisters."

Seth struts into the room in his white coat, clipboard under his arm, pen behind his ear, looking like the epic nerd he's always been.

"Doc," Scarlett says.

"Ashley wanted to come by, but she's stuck at home with the little guy," he says. "How are you feeling?"

"Amazing," I say.

"Me, too," Scarlett says. "Thanks for asking."

"I just really wanted to see you," I say. "Bear was an excuse."

Seth closes his eyes, something he often does when Scarlett and I are being ourselves. It's a technique he's developed over the years we've known him. He closes his eyes and takes a moment to fortify himself against our collective bullshit. His eyes were closed throughout the entirety of the maids of honor speech that Scarlett and I gave at his wedding. He married our best friend, and that lifelong commitment included us by default. He knew what he was getting himself into.

He opens his eyes. Courageously. "You're very lucky."

"Since I was a little girl, I hoped and dreamed I'd someday be the victim of a bear attack. And now here I am. Imagine?"

He shakes his head. "Minor cuts and scrapes. Could have been much worse."

It was much worse. The pain echoes in my side. The sound, I can hear it clear as day. The bite. Teeth breaking skin. The initial gnaw. I was torn open, mercilessly. Easily. And the smell of it. The smell of animal. The smell of blood. The taste of it in my mouth.

I can question what I saw, but I can't deny what I felt. A burning, raging hurt. It's not what it was in the moment, but it's still there writhing under the surface.

Yet somehow.

This morning, when they wiped away the dirt and dried blood, the damage wasn't significant. A constellation of shallow cuts. It wasn't a distinctive bite mark. It wasn't a distinctive anything.

They said most of the blood was from my head, from where I hit my head, but even that cut, just above my hairline, was measly. Didn't even require stitches.

My ankle is swollen, scratched, but the scratches are faint. Unapparent.

I don't know how I could invent pain like that, how I could conjure that type of suffering, those specific, unfamiliar sensations. But I don't have any evidence. Nothing to prove what I really went through or how it felt. Nothing visible, nothing tangible. I can feel it. The damage is there, but it's ghost damage, haunting my body like it's a goddamn Victorian manor. No one can see it but me. No one knows it's there except for me.

I adjust the neck of my hospital gown.

"Can I go now?" I ask.

"Yes, you can go. You can take some ibuprofen. Change the bandages tonight, or first thing tomorrow morning at the latest. This ointment on your head and your side," he says, handing Scarlett a white tube. "I can come by the house tomorrow afternoon and take a look. See how you're healing."

"Do you make house calls for all of your patients or am I special?"

"You're special," he says. "I'm very glad you're okay."

"Are you, though?" I ask.

He closes his eyes.

On the drive home, Scarlett and I stop for chai lattes at the shiny new Starbucks. We drink them at one of the tables outside, despite the drizzle. We enjoy our beautiful view of the parking lot.

"How long did they say?" I ask. We're talking about my poor car, the one I got just days ago.

"Three weeks," she says. "But who knows? You're welcome to share mine, but then you'll be trapped at the house while I'm at work. Might want to get a rental."

"Balls."

"Yep," she says, removing the lid of her cup to sip.

Usually, she does this to preserve her perfect red lip, but she's not wearing any lipstick. It's so rare to see her without it. I've been living with her for two weeks and this is the first time I've seen her face bare. It's the first thing she does when she wakes up. Washes her face, brushes her teeth, applies lipstick. Then the black cat eye, of course, her precision immaculate.

Sometimes she'll offer to do my makeup. Whenever she does, I always say yes.

"Is it like doing your own?" I asked her once.

"Kind of," she said. "It is but it isn't."

When I've got on the red lip and black eyeliner, we look the same. Except my hair isn't blue. I guess hers isn't either, technically.

"I thought of you last night," I say, watching the parking lot. A titanic SUV attempts to back into a space that is for sure too small. "About how I was relieved we don't have that twin thing. Where we can feel what the other feels."

"Yeah, I slept through the whole thing," she says. "I used to be a night owl. Lately I can barely make it past midnight."

"Midnight is late."

"No, it isn't," she says.

I can tell she doesn't want to talk about what happened last night, which is a relief, because I don't feel like talking about it either. I don't want to think about it. What I want is to enjoy my chai latte without reliving my suffering. To sit in this suburban parking lot on this overcast day with my sister and just be.

"You know who I ran into last night?" I ask.

She looks at me. "If you say a bear . . ."

"No, no," I say. "Ian Pedretti."

I get an instant grin.

"Ian Pedretti," she singsongs. "He was so in love with you."

"I know."

"I see him around all the time. He filled out. He was so gangly in high school."

"Yep."

"What did you guys talk about?" She rests both elbows on the table and bats her lashes at me.

"Politics," I deadpan.

"Hey," she says. "Please?"

"I don't know. Just caught up. Nothing earth-shattering," I say, hiding my face behind my cup. "I had every intention of enjoying a beer by myself, Scout's honor. He just happened to be there."

"You're squirming," she says.

"I'm not. I'm holding perfectly still."

The SUV has indeed successfully backed into that space. I crane my neck to behold its wizard driver.

"How'd you leave things?"

"What do you mean?"

"Are you going to see him again?"

I shrug, and it's that writhing pain. It hasn't gone away, but it had dulled to the point I could ignore it. Until now.

"What?" Scarlett asks.

"Nothing."

"Are you faking pain to get out of this conversation?"

"I wish."

"You want to go home?"

"No," I say. "I'm fine."

"You should go out with him. Really go out with him, not just to hook up."

The optimism. She gets it from our mother, who covets romance above all else. We were raised by a woman who honestly believes that men are the key to happiness, no matter how many times they've proven otherwise. No matter the fuckup. No matter how heinous the offense.

"Yeah, maybe," I say, instead of *Are you out of your goddamn mind?*

"Okay, that's a no," she says. "Why? He's super nice. Good sense of humor. Attractive. A musician. And he's not some rando you met out. You know him. He's a good guy."

"Ah, yes. A good guy."

She pops the lid back onto her coffee cup and begins to wipe the table, which is pointless because it's raining.

"I know what you're thinking, and I don't want to talk about it, but he isn't a bad guy."

"Sure. Matty is right up there with Mister Rogers. He's Clark fucking Kent," I say.

This is the first time she's brought him up since I've been here, and it's the first time I've said his name out loud since finding out he bailed on my pregnant sister. It leaves a sour taste in my mouth.

Pain ignites my side. It's so intense, the world blurs for a moment. It burns white.

"All right," Scarlett says, putting her palms flat on the table and pushing herself to stand. "I'm taking you home."

"But I want to stay in this Starbucks parking lot forever," I say, trying not to sound like I'm in excruciating pain.

It's not as bad as it was a second ago. It was a bizarre flare of absolute anguish.

Scarlett scoops up the cups and napkins and walks them over to the trash. I follow her to her car, a black Prius with a series of tarot card bumper stickers. The image of the moon card catches me. Two dogs bark at a stern moon; behind them, what's maybe a scorpion emerges from a river. I stop to study it further, and an invisible nail drags itself up my spine. I shiver.

"Coming?" Scarlett calls to me from the driver's seat.

"Yep."

We stop at the grocery store for ingredients, and when we get home, I sit at the kitchen island as Scarlett makes bread.

"You should be lying down," she says, violently kneading a pale slab of dough.

"I like watching," I say. "It's relaxing."

"You know what's relaxing?"

"Lying down."

"Very good."

I draw a smiley face in the flour on the countertop.

"Helpful," she says. "You know, you don't have to hang out for my sake. I don't need constant supervision. You being here is enough. Just knowing you're here. I've never lived alone. It was . . . I don't know. It was weird."

When Scarlett was eight, mom accidentally crushed her fingers in the car door without realizing. Scarlett cried quietly the entire drive to the mall, not saying a thing about it, cradling her injured fingers in her lap. I noticed only as we pulled up to Macy's. She'd spent twenty minutes suffering in silence.

Had I woken up alone in the woods this morning, and had I been physically able to get up and walk, I would have walked home instead of calling for help. It's how we are. I assume it's a trait inherited from our father, because it's certainly not from Mom, but it's not something I've ever been able to confirm since he fucked off to Florida when we were toddlers.

For Scarlett to call and ask me to come here and live with her for the next six months, I knew she must really need me. But I haven't seen any hint of need from her since I arrived.

I don't know why I thought I would. She, like me, suspects that exhibiting a sliver of vulnerability will cause the universe to implode.

"I haven't been here for that long," I tell her. "It won't be like this all the time. I'll figure out my own things to do. But it's been fun to hang out. I missed you. Missed this. We should get bunk beds. I feel like the time is right."

"Finally," she says. "I'm not trying to get rid of you. I'm just saying you're free to do what you want. You're not beholden to me."

"I'm here because I want to be here," I say. "That fast city life wears you down. I needed a break. Change of pace. This is as good for me as it is for you."

"Stars aligned," she says, smiling like she doesn't believe me.

She shouldn't. I'm not telling the truth. I love my life in the city. I love my job. I love business-development consulting, putting on suits and walking into posh conference rooms and telling C suite executives everything they're doing wrong. I love my apartment: a prewar walk-up with a beautiful but useless fireplace and a cute, pathetic little kitchen. I love staying out until four a.m. and doing karaoke in Midtown with tourists. I love trying trendy new restaurants and getting handsy with strangers in the bathroom of a seedy Lower East Side bar. I love complaining about the subway and brunch at Balthazar and the Union Square farmers market and the occasional trip to Coney Island to ride the Cyclone and cheat death.

I would only ever leave this life for my sister. And only temporarily. I didn't move out of my apartment; I sublet it. I didn't quit my job; I took a leave of absence. I have every intention of going back after the baby's born and Scarlett's settled.

"All right," I say. "I guess I will go lie down. Maybe take a nap. I like the idea of waking up from a nap to fresh bread."

"Sweet sleeping," she says, flicking some flour in my direction.

I hop off the stool too quickly and my side screams. I shuffle slowly toward the stairs. Scarlett doesn't comment.

I go up the stairs on all fours because it's easier that way.

Scarlett has always called the guest room "Rory's room." She painted it a muted blue and hung vintage postcards on the walls. The bed has a pretty wrought iron headboard; the linens are hotel white. The antique double dresser we shared as kids is in this room, above it the silver-framed mirror I saw my reflection change in as I grew up. There's a tweed armchair in the corner by the window, next to it a teetering stack of unread books and a small parlor palm. On the nightstand sit a squat lamp and a classic alarm clock. The rest of the house is colorful and cluttered with eccentric artwork and knickknacks and taxidermy and oversized furniture. The rest of the house is Scarlett. This room is me.

I'm too afraid to change out of the clothes that Scarlett brought to the hospital for me—a pair of my Columbia University sweatpants and a long-sleeved Grateful Dead tee, the only article of clothing she and I ever fought over as teens. If I were to undress, to change out of these clothes, I would see.

I don't want to see the bandages. I dread the bandages.

These clothes don't smell like hospital, but I do. I smell. They cleaned me up this morning, but I haven't had a proper shower since yesterday. Since before.

Bad things have a way of severing your life into "before" and "after." It's really annoying.

"After you" is never quite the same, so I've learned.

Fuck it. I climb into bed as is. I can always wash the sheets.

I wake to the smell of bread and the drum of rain on the windows. I yawn. I'm alarmed by the click of my jaw. It's not so much a click. It sounds like tearing paper, like breaking down cardboard. My chin descends, my mouth opening, opening, opening. The parting is unnatural. There's a cave in my face.

I sit up in bed, mashing my elbows into the pillow behind me. I look directly in front of me, into the mirror above the dresser. I'm there, inside the mirror, but I can't see myself because all I can see is the thing on the floor. The mass of matted fur crawling next to my bed, silently creeping on all fours. I can see the bend of its hind legs, the considerable hills of its shoulders. I can see the back of its head, the sinister sharpness of its ears. It's almost graceful in its movements, careful and calculated. But it's a predator, so it can't be graceful, because grace is a virtue, and predator's virtues all serve a violent purpose, so they really aren't virtues at all.

I watch as it reaches up to me, as it begins to extend its long, ugly fingers toward the mattress, up over the side. I want to scream for my sister, but I don't want her to come up here. I don't want her to be a part of this. I don't want her to see.

I check my reflection and connect with eyes that aren't mine. Red eyes, set back in a face that isn't mine, perched on top of a monstrous body that also isn't mine. But it sits where I sit. Unmoving, with a wide-open mouth. Vicious jaws salivating, a slowly extending snout.

The realization is pure heartbreak. Last night changed me. I'm going to be different now.

Its nails dig into my thigh.

I'm not going to be the same.

There's snarling and gasping, and it takes me a minute to understand that I just had a nightmare.

Having a nightmare during a nap seems particularly cruel. Regular sleep, fine. But to be betrayed by a *nap*? Uncool.

I wipe the sweat from my forehead.

Reaper, Scarlett's disgruntled old Jack Russell terrier, growls at me.

"What? What do you want?"

He barks twice. He's got the ugliest bark.

"Reaps!" I hear Scarlett call from downstairs.

The dog ignores my sister, committed to mean-mugging me.

"Reaps, you want a treat?" she calls up.

He narrows his eyes, abandoning his post only at the sound of the treat bag opening.

I groan and roll out of bed. I sniff my sheets, myself. Hospital, with notes of wet dog. My new signature fragrance.

"I also want a treat," I whine, clomping down the stairs.

"She wakes! Perfect timing," Scarlett says, slicing the bread to reveal a perfect swirl of black poppy seeds.

"Cut me one thick."

"Mm," she says, obliging. She slides it onto a pretty glass plate. "Milk?"

"Yes, please."

Poppy seed bread is a comfort food for us, a childhood treat for days off from school or birthday breakfasts. We'd eat it and then smile at each other, modeling the black specks stuck in our teeth.

"Ash called," Scarlett says. "She wants to come over tomorrow."

"All right, good by me," I say.

Not like I have anything else to do. I'm two weeks into my leave from work and starting to get bored.

Scarlett sits on the stool beside me. "I told her about Ian."

"What about Ian?"

"That you saw him and that you should go out with him."

"I already said I would," I say, shoving a piece of bread into my mouth.

It tastes weird. There's something off about it. It's gummy. Acrid. But I'm not going to say that to Scarlett, and I didn't realize how hungry I was until right this moment, so I swallow it anyway.

"Why are you tag-teaming me on something I already agreed to?"

"He's had a crush on you forever! You have to admit it'd be a great story."

"I was never interested in him like that," I say. "How is it a great story? The world beat me down, so finally I was like 'All right, guess you'll do.' "

"You're impossible," she says, sighing. "Let me live vicariously through you."

"I'll hang out with him but I'm not promising anything else," I say, mouth full.

I don't know why I keep eating this bread. What I could really go for is a burger.

"Fine, that's fair," she says.

She holds up her glass of milk, and I meet it with mine.

"What are we cheers-ing?"

"Your impending marriage to Ian Pedretti."

I roll my eyes so hard, I get dizzy.

"On to more important things," I say, leaning toward her. "How bad do I smell?"

She generously lends me her nose. She gives me two sniffs, then says, "It's not great."

"I should shower but I'm being lazy. What should I do about the bandages? You think I can take them off?"

"Text Seth," she says. "You might need to wrap them in plastic. I can help if you want."

"I don't want to Saran Wrap myself like a cheap sandwich," I say. "Besides, that sounds like too much effort. I'm over it."

"I'm sorry," she says. "That this happened to you. I'm sorry."

It's too direct. It unleashes something inside me. I'm in danger of tears.

I clear my throat. "It's not a big deal."

She reaches over and covers my hand with her hand.

Desperate to change the subject, I go for the low-hanging fruit. "Honestly, Ian does look pretty good. Aged into himself."

Later, Scarlett falls asleep on the couch while we're marathoning episodes of *The Twilight Zone*. The dog is also asleep, paws on Scarlett's lap. I get up quietly and sneak out to the back patio to vape. I sit on the concrete, surrounded by dying flowers, letting the silk-soft rain slowly soak my clothes.

I admire the night. The rain clouds amble away, leaving behind an exceptionally clear sky, an extravagance of stars.

I'm used to the sky above the city, where there's so much light pollution the stars are just rumors. When their shine finally finds you, its authenticity is impossible to determine. Through all the haze it could be an airplane or a sparkle in your eye, courtesy of your last sixteen-dollar cocktail.

Not here. Here when the stars shine, they shine beyond doubt, with diamond clarity. There are so many of them. Who knew?

It's a beautiful sky. It's the sky that I grew up under, that I must have taken for granted. One of the few redeeming features of this place that I swore I'd never come back to.

Not that I'm *back* back. It's six months.

I puff on my vape, and when I exhale, I follow the smoke up, up, and there's the moon, high and silver and smug as a motherfucker. The sight of it rattles my bones with such violence, but I can't look away. Because I can see its face. And it can see mine. It sinks itself into my eyes and it drags me toward it, demanding obedience. A mad mother.

I'm standing now. My side stings. There's a sudden fuming beneath the bandages. It shouldn't hurt like this. Why does it hurt like this?

There's a sound somewhere. The neighbors rolling their garbage bins down the driveway.

It distracts me from the moon. I shake her off.

I hit my vape pen again, then head back inside. I stand at the kitchen sink, drinking water straight from the tap. I don't know why. I should really get a glass.

I'm too thirsty. I drink and drink.

I pull away and wipe my mouth with the back of my hand.

I notice my phone charging on the counter. I have no idea how it got there. I guess someone recovered it from my car. Maybe the cops? I'm not happy to see it. We're fighting. If it hadn't distracted me, none of this would have happened. Why accept any responsibility when I can blame this evil pocket computer?

I flip it over and see I've got too many messages. From Ash, from Seth, from my mother, whom Scarlett must have informed about last night's misadventure. From Ian.

I offered to drive, his first message says.

How does he know?

Thinking of you. Heard you're okay but let me know if you need anything.

Heard from whom? I always hated this small-town-grapevine nonsense. That's something I love about the city. The anonymity. No one knows who you are, and no one gives a shit about your business. It's a beautiful thing.

Thanks, I respond.

I want to add something clever, maybe vaguely flirtatious, but my side is aching so badly, I can't think straight.

I unplug my phone and take it upstairs with me. I drop it on the bed and get a pair of pajamas out of the dresser, then head into the bathroom.

I slip out of my rain-damp clothes and kick them into a wet heap behind the door. I flip on the fan. Its dull, melancholy hum seems an appropriate soundtrack. I begin to pull at the gauze on my forehead. The tape is stuck to my hair, and its apparent there's no removing it without scalping myself.

I move on to my side. It's a pain I don't understand. A pain consistent with what I experienced last night, not what I saw this morning. In the stark hospital light, it was just a scrape. An anonymous pink smear. I've had nastier carpet burns. Even Seth said it wasn't that bad, and he's a doctor, so I should trust him and let that be that. Only I can't get away from the memory, or vision, or whatever.

I was bitten. I was chewed through.

I get my nails under the tape at the top of the dressing and yank it back.

"Ow, fuck!" I mutter into my neck.

I let the gauze hang there like a dead petal, the tape on the bottom still adhered to me.

My heart stops at the color. Against the white of the gauze is a mess of silver. Iridescent silver puss. It oozes from my side, from what previously appeared to be ordinary, innocuous cuts. My skin is discolored, unlike any bruise I've ever seen. It's an alarmingly vibrant purple.

It's an infection. It must be. A horrible, disgusting infection.

I turn toward the mirror.

Behind me, it's there. The massive animal with the frothing snarl and the red, red eyes.

I collapse onto the floor, curling into myself, grabbing my knees and breathing erratically into my chest.

A few minutes pass before my fear subsides, before logic returns, rolling its eyes.

I peer over my shoulder. There's no animal. Only me, naked on the cold tile.

I reach up to the vanity and pull myself to stand. My side wails. It's no wonder it hurts so badly. It looks terrible. What happened? How is this even possible?

I examine it in the mirror. It's such a gnarly bruise.

And the ooze. I'm watching it escape me. It bubbles out from depressions of skin, cuts that pucker like eager lips. I bring my hand toward it, let my index gently swipe against it, curious about its consistency.

It's thick and sticky, like honey.

I rub it between my thumb and index, lift it up to the light for a better look at the color. My breath catches in my throat, and I make a weird squeaking noise, like a mouse in a trap.

Yep. It's silver. It's like liquid metal, like mercury. It's concerning.

Shit.

I use my elbow to turn on the faucet, squirt an excess of foaming soap into my hands and lather up. I look at myself in the mirror. I'm ashen. My lips are white.

I can't pass out. If I pass out, Scarlett will find me, and the silver puss, and she'll tell Seth, and then . . . ???

I need to keep this to myself. This is freakish. Not normal.

Or maybe I'm not seeing what I think I'm seeing. Maybe I'm imagining things.

It was dark last night. The shock and panic of hitting something with your car is enough to slip you out of lucidity. And what I felt last night, that helplessness . . . it's not the first time I've felt it. Maybe this time, my body knew what to do. Maybe the creature was a construct, an illusion, an invented overlay to conceal the real animal. An escape into fiction.

I don't know if that would be better or worse.

I turn away from my reflection. I start up the shower and wait for the water to get hot. I rip off the gauze hanging at my side.

I take another quick look at the wound, now fully exposed, free of any bandaging. A pearl of laughter rolls up from my throat and off my tongue, entering the world luminous. Up comes another.

I'm laughing. I'm losing it.

On the shower curtain, there's the image of a kraken drowning a ship, its tentacles tangled in the sails.

I stare at it.

Yeah, okay. Monsters are real. There are creatures out there, discovered and undiscovered, named and unnamed. Just because I can't identify what bit me doesn't mean I wasn't bitten.

I could continue to ponder the nature of trauma, overanalyze, drag up my past, search for connections like a basement-dwelling conspiracy theorist. But that feels like a lot of work. Like pushing a boulder up an endless incline.

Denial is hard to sustain. It requires constant effort. The truth might not be pleasant, or logical in this case, but it's easy. I don't need to assign myself to it. It just is.

And the truth is, I was bitten. It happened. I know it happened. That's it.

I could go to Seth, be honest with him, but I'm pretty sure that would just punch my ticket to a psych evaluation. And even if it didn't, what could he do? It's not like he could treat me. I don't think they cover monster attacks during residency.

I'll just wait it out. I was better this morning. Maybe I'll get better again. Maybe this is my body purging itself of germs. Is that science?

"All right," I tell myself. "One thing at a time."

I step into the shower. I use the fancy shampoo Scarlett set out for me. It smells like coconut. It smells so good, it's all I care about for now.

It's heaven to be clean.

After my shower, I put on my pajamas and go downstairs to search for the ointment and extra bandaging Seth sent us home with. Scarlett is awake, drinking lavender tea and painting her nails.

"Water is still hot," she tells me. She's stenciling a pretty pattern on her left ring fingernail.

"Thanks," I say. "Where are my medical supplies?"

"Oh, I think I left them in the car. Sorry. I'll get them."

"No worries," I tell her. "How'd you get my phone?"

"Cops," she says. "Guess I forgot to mention that, too. I've been so scatterbrained. It's not me. It's the fetus."

"Should put that on a T-shirt," I say, pouring myself a cup of tea.

I sit down next to her. I want to tell her the truth, even though I know I can't. Or shouldn't. It's a lot to keep to myself, a grenade under my tongue. But she's dealing with enough.

Besides, even if I did tell her, there's no way she would believe me. I couldn't blame her. Still . . . I fear her disbelief. Nothing is worse than her doubt. It's the thing that scares me most in this world.

More than fucking monsters. I laugh to myself.

"What is it?" she asks me.

She doesn't break her concentration, doesn't look at me, doesn't slip up. She's a tattoo artist, so I guess it's a good thing that nothing can unsteady her hand.

"You okay?"

"I'm golden," I lie.

When I close my eyes, it's there. When I blink, it's waiting. The crimson blaze of its eyes, the threatening gleam of its teeth.

So I keep my eyes open. I don't blink. I watch my sister work. I watch her create something beautiful.

III

It's the next morning, and we're on our way to Ash's because Luca refused to wear pants.

"I made scones," she said, her defeat tangible even over FaceTime. "I can't bring them over, because I can't leave the house, because he won't wear pants, and if I let him out of the house without pants, he'll never wear pants again."

"It's fine," I said. "We'll come to you."

"No, no. You were just in the hospital," she said to me. Then to Scarlett, "And you're pregnant."

"Yes, and thus incapable of leaving my house."

"I just meant I should be the one coming to you guys," Ash said.

"We'll see you in fifteen," Scarlett said. She hung up and turned to me. "I really resent the implication."

I didn't say anything, just nodded and went to put on my shoes.

She's still annoyed. I get it. I also don't like to be treated like I'm fragile, even when I am fragile. Like now.

I did a shitty job taping my gauze. It's pinching my skin. Also, I can feel the stickiness underneath. The seepage. I adjust my seat belt.

The wound was, unfortunately, not better this morning. In fact, it was somehow significantly worse. Absurdly oozy.

"Luca is intense," Scarlett says, breaking the silence. "Shades of Damien."

"You think?" I ask, yawning.

We both slept in late and then Ash called before I could make coffee. I'm too wary of my sister's mood to request a stop at Starbucks.

"I don't know what I'll do if my kid is like that."

"I think a frank discussion. Sit it down and say, 'Listen. This isn't going to work for me.' "

"I'm being serious."

"So am I," I say. "It is *your* kid. It's of you. You respond well to candor. So do I. So will it."

I don't like referring to Scarlett's baby as "it," but she doesn't have a name picked out.

"He's just a lot," she says. "I like to think I'm patient, but I don't know if I'm *that* patient. I don't know how Ash does it."

"I don't think Luca is Satan spawn," I say. "He's just testing the limits. To be fair, I also hate wearing pants."

That cracks her. She laughs.

"Fair," she says. "Fair."

We pull up to Ashley's. Her lawn is a cemetery. There are plastic skeletons everywhere, foam headstones, fake spiderwebs. There's a giant jack-o'-lantern inflatable, and beside it a friendly ghost.

"Subtle," I say.

"Wait until Christmas."

We walk up the path, which is lined with petite pumpkins. Zombie hands reach up from the shrubbery.

"Nothing better jump out at me," I say, the exact moment a witch's cackle rings out from somewhere above me.

A wart-covered green face glares down from the front door, half hidden inside an ugly Halloween wreath.

"I hate it," I say. "Hate it."

Ash opens the door.

"Hello, hello! Come in," she says.

Luca, wearing a pair of Batman underwear, bursts between her legs with a throaty bellow.

Scarlett takes my hand and squeezes it.

"Luca," Ash says. "Can we please say hello to Aunt Scarlett and Aunt Rory?"

He continues to yell, like he's sustaining a note. Kid's got the lungs of an opera singer. Baby Bocelli.

Ash sighs, shrugs, then scoops him up under the armpits and drags him back into the house.

I step through the door, pulling a reluctant Scarlett behind me.

There are plastic bins overflowing with Halloween decorations in the foyer.

"Do you have enough decorations, Ash? Lawn's looking a little sparse."

"Those are my indoor decorations," she says, not understanding.

She's distracted by the wriggling toddler in her arms. She sets him down on the couch and hands him an iPad. Luca gives a triumphant, hiccupy giggle as his little finger begins to tap away at the screen. Ash shuffles into the kitchen. By the time Scarlett and I make it to the table, she's already set out a spread. Scones and bagels and cream cheese and lox and mixed fruit. Sausage and bacon and some kind of hash brown bake with a crust of bubbling brown cheese on top. There are carafes of orange juice and cranberry juice and iced tea.

"I can make some coffee," she says, reading my mind. "I've also got lunch stuff. I could make sandwiches, or salads, if you prefer."

"I don't prefer salad, no," Scarlett says, helping herself to a scone.

"Coffee would be great, thanks," I say, reaching for some bacon.

Half of it is crisp and the other is fatty and limp. I shove it into my mouth. It's the most delicious thing I've ever eaten.

"You look great, Rory," Ash says, pressing a series of buttons on her fancy coffee machine. It looks like it belongs in a lab, not a kitchen.

"Thanks," I say.

I suspect she's lying, but I haven't looked in a mirror today, so maybe? But if I look anything like how I feel, she could put me out on the lawn, and I'd fit right in. Passersby would shudder at the sight of me, without the slightest clue that I'm actually human and not a Halloween decoration.

A belligerent pain claws at the seam of my side. It's so explicit, the feeling of it under my skin, the strain of it against my bandages. It's an alive thing, this pain. A hurt with arms and legs, hands and feet. A hungry, anxious mouth.

I'm sitting here all casual as repulsive silver goo spills from me. Maybe I am a Halloween decoration.

"Oat milk?" Ash asks. "I've also got pumpkin spice creamer."

"I'll take the pumpkin spice," I say. "Not above it."

"Are you feeling all right?" she asks, setting the coffee down in front of me. It's in a giant white mug shaped like a ghost. It's got two black eyes and a gaping black mouth painted on it.

"Boo," I tell it, before taking a sip.

"I mean, we don't have to talk about it if you don't want to," she says, sitting next to me.

"Rory is going to date Ian Pedretti," Scarlett says, forking a strawberry.

She thinks she's saving me, but honestly, right now I'd rather talk about my ooze than Ian. It's becoming too big a deal and it's making me itchy and anxious, making me not want to see him again to spite the pressure.

"Really?" Ash asks, clapping.

"I perhaps might go on a date with Ian," I say. "A date, maybe. But I don't do relationships. You both know this."

"Still?" Ash says.

"I value my independence. I don't have boyfriends. I have fun," I say with a wink. I add a few sausage links to my plate. I stab one and begin to nibble on it. "This sausage is delicious, Ash. What is it?"

"Just the generic breakfast sausage," she says. "How did this Ian thing come about? We love Ian."

By "we" she means her and Seth. It makes me queasy, this "we." This is why I'm forever single.

"This morning you acted like it was too much for me to come over. Now you're ready to pay my dowry."

"Sorry," Ash says, clasping her hands together as if in desperate prayer. "I just love the idea of you two together. He's coming to our Halloween party, you know. Or we invited him, anyway. He usually comes to our parties."

"Great."

I forgot about the impending Halloween party. A bunch of young suburban parents getting drunk from punch with rubber eyeballs in it. Should be a blast.

I look over at Scarlett and can tell she's thinking the same thing. Worse, she'll have to suffer through the party sober. Ash will expect us to be there.

At the very least, there will be good snacks. Ash is an exceptional host. I grab another piece of bacon.

"Do you have costumes yet?" she asks us.

Scarlett snorts.

"Girls. Come on! It's gonna be fun!" Ash says. "I know you think you're too cool for costumes, but you're not."

"That legit hurt my feelings," I say, clutching my chest.

"Me, too," Scarlett says. "Sincerely."

"Oh! I meant to tell you. You'll never guess who else is in town and definitely coming to the party."

"Uh, Guy Fieri?" I ask. "The cast of *Friends*?"

Scarlett raises her hand. "Satan himself?"

"Mia Russo."

"I was right!" Scarlett says. "What do I win?"

Ash shakes her head. "I thought you liked Mia! We were all friends. Right, Rory? You and Mia were close."

"Sure. If you consider participating in a threesome close, yeah, we were close."

"I forgot about that," Scarlett says. "Now I need to forget again."

Mia Russo was a late addition to the friend group. She hung out with us the latter half of high school. She was fun. Mischievous. Loud and reckless. Treated attention like magic coins in a video game. She'd chase it, get it wherever she could, soak in the super glow.

For a time, we really were close. Close enough it caused vague tension with Scarlett, who once told me she thought Mia was a bad influence. I suspected she was jealous. Or Mia suspected. I can't remember.

"Scarlett always thought she was corrupting me," I say, "but who's to say I wasn't the one corrupting her?"

"Was the senior prank your idea?" Scarlett asks.

"Oh, my God, the senior prank!" Ash giggles.

"Almost got you suspended. You would have lost your scholarship. Not that Mia cared. She barely graduated," Scarlett says. "What's she doing back here? I thought she was in California?"

"Her dad died," Ash says.

"Could have led with that. Now I feel like an asshole," Scarlett says, looking guilty for approximately two seconds before popping another strawberry into her mouth.

"Look who it is!"

Seth has appeared, and his presence has stirred Luca, who is now windmilling his arms as he runs laps around his dad. Yelling, of course. Always yelling.

"Hey, little man," Seth says, ruffling Luca's curls. "How you feeling, Rory?"

"Fine," I say. "Changed the bandages. It's all fine."

"I can take a look," he says.

I clear my throat, "No. That's all right. I'm good. Nothing concerning."

I'm curious to see their faces, to search for any hint of skepticism. I want to know how obvious it is that I'm lying. But I know if I look at them, try to read the room, that'll give me away. So I just keep eating.

"You sure?" he asks. Luca is now climbing him, scaling his

body like it's a piece of gym equipment. "Want to make sure it doesn't get infected."

"Hey, your wife was wondering, do you have a spare cow to give to Ian Pedretti in exchange for my hand in marriage?"

"To Ian?" he asks.

"Yeah. Maybe a piece of fertile land. Any goods or property, really. Not sure if he'll take me otherwise."

"Ignore her," Ash says, waving her hand.

I grin at Scarlett, who rolls her eyes at me. Not having it.

We spend most of the day at Ash's, trading gossip, telling new stories, or retelling old ones, until Scarlett has to leave for work. She drops me off at home, tasking me with walking Reaper.

"You don't need to go far. A few blocks," she says. "Only if you feel up to it."

"I'm up to it," I say, even though I'm exhausted and in pain. I'm the soldier marching forward despite the arrows in my chest.

Scarlett thanks me and drives off.

When I open the front door, Reaper is there waiting for me, scowling.

"You want to go for a walk?" I say, attempting a peppy, animal-friendly tone.

He barks, and it sounds remarkably like a firm no.

"All right. Well, I'm not jazzed about this either, buddy."

He nips at me twice as I attach the leash to his collar, then warily follows me outside.

Once we're out, he's less salty, trotting ahead with only the occasional glance back, just to let me know I'm still on notice.

It's a sweet autumnal evening with a light cinnamony breeze

and a violet sunset. I forget where I'm going until I'm there. Until I'm here. At the edge of the woods.

A sudden gust of wind batters the trees. There's the shimmy of leaves, twigs snapping. An unsettling.

It's getting dark so fast, the night panting at my back.

My body goes cold.

What if it's still out there?

Telling the truth seemed futile because I knew no one would believe me. But I never considered the potential harm of the lie. It somehow failed to occur to me until this moment that whatever attacked me might still be out there roaming the woods and might go on to attack someone else. Or with my luck, me again.

I stare ahead, searching the ambiguous dark for some evidence of danger. Some validation of this fear I'm feeling. The threat may be invisible, but it's there. I know it's there. Somewhere. And now I'll always have to wonder: What if the hunt isn't over?

"I'm making an executive decision," I tell Reaper, who is busy eating a leaf. "Time to go home."

He ignores me.

"I'll give you so many treats. A bounty of treats."

An ear perks.

"Treats beyond your wildest imagination."

The other ear.

Additional bribery and a few tugs of the leash and we're on our way. I lead us at a brisk pace, afraid we're being followed.

That I'm being pursued by a monster only I know exists.

When I finally get us inside, I slam the door closed and lock it, then collapse onto the couch, trying to steady my rebellious breath.

Reaper snarls at me, unsympathetic, forcing me to make good on my promise of infinite treats.

I am safe in my bed. I am asleep.

But I am also in the woods.

Barefoot. The ground is soft from evening rain.

There's a crimson tint to everything, like the world is soaked in blood. Like I am soaked in blood.

I lift my hands and see they are not my hands.

I scream, but it's not my scream.

You're dreaming, *I think.*

Suddenly, I'm behind myself, staring at the back of my own head.

It's not me, in this other body. But it doesn't matter. All that matters is the hunger.

A limb. An ear. The neck.

I wake up in the morning ravenous.

Scarlett and I roam the aisles of a sad, dirty Party City, searching for last-minute Halloween costumes. It's been two weeks since the bite, and though I'm desperate for distractions, this particular outing isn't doing it for me.

"I want to be . . ." I start, scanning a wall of culturally insensitive plastic bag costumes, "invisible."

"Aw," Scarlett says.

"I was kidding," I say. "Kind of."

We take another lap around the store, passing an arrangement of large animatronic monsters. An evil scarecrow with eyes that glow neon green. A broomstick-wielding witch wearing a pointy hat. A truly horrifying sinister clown. And, of course, a werewolf. It howls whenever anyone walks by.

I know it's there. I saw it as soon as we came in, then promptly looked away. My heart's been on a rampage ever since, beating so loudly, I'm afraid Scarlett might hear.

On this pass, I take a deep breath and face it.

Well . . .

It looks a hell of a lot like the creature in the woods. It looks a hell of a lot like the beast that bit me.

The proportions aren't exact. My monster was bigger. Lankier. Less fuzzy. More haggard. But overall, pretty close! Disturbingly close. Especially the eyes. Big red eyes.

Looking up at these eyes, I'm gripped by this stomach-sinking, gut-twisting, throat-constricting dread.

Was I bitten by a fucking werewolf?

A quick Google search confirms it was a full moon that night. I let out an accidental gasp.

"Hm?" Scarlett asks.

I shake my head. "No, nothing."

She raises an eyebrow.

In the time that's passed since the attack, I've managed to keep my shit together. Aside from the persistent oozing of my wound, and the fact that the bruise there has marbled a truly morbid shade of purple, and that whenever Scarlett's at work, Reaper follows me from room to room growling, and that I've had intense cravings for meat, and wake up every morning sweaty and starving—aside from all that, everything's fine. I busy myself by answering the consistent stream of work emails from my team (who are "So sorry to bother you on leave!"), by cleaning the house and attempting to cook, and by doing anything else I can possibly think of to make Scarlett's life easier.

I learned young how to pretend like bad things never happened. It's scary how easy it's been to dissociate from the strange new reality of my body, the bizarre injury that seems insistent to fester. Still, about once a day, I open my browser and type in reported monster attacks or giant crossbreed species, then break into an instant sweat and X out before I can see any results. Then I clear my search history and go on with my life, abandoning the curiosity that I know doesn't serve me, the what-ifs that won't do me any good.

But staring up at this Halloween werewolf, listening to it howl, I can't default to avoidance. I can't distract myself or dissociate. And I feel certain I'm about to vomit in this Party City.

Bile bubbles up my throat.

"This is stressing me out," Scarlett says.

Right. *She's* stressed.

I laugh, and the bile almost leaks out. I swallow hard.

"What's up with you?" she asks.

"You already know," I tell her. "You know everything about me."

I realize for the first time that this is no longer true.

"I don't want to dress up as anything," she says, huffing. "I don't even want to be in my body right now."

"Same."

She gives me a look.

"I know it's not the same," I say. "But I'm still recovering."

She nods, letting it go. She hates talking about it just as much as I do. She wants to forget it ever happened, same as me.

"I've got a cloak at home," she says. "It's black velvet. Maybe I'll just wear that and do ghost makeup. Skull makeup."

She picks up a black-and-white makeup kit.

"That could work," I say. "Wait. Why do you have a cloak?"

"I'm Goth," she says, shrugging.

"Well, what about me?"

"I only have one cloak," she says.

"Brutal. My own sister leaving me in the dust."

"You're still hot. Be Catwoman or something."

The bile rises again. I can't be Catwoman. I don't want to be Catwoman. I don't want to be any kind of animal-human-hybrid anything. I want to be 100 percent human. Extra human. The most human.

"I'm not going," I say. "We don't have to go tonight."

"It's Ash," she says. "We do have to go. Just pick something."

"You pick."

The look on her face when I say this lets me know I've made a grave mistake.

She sashays through the store, whistling a pretty tune, as I follow behind, chewing off my fingernails. I would tell her that I've changed my mind, that I'll find my own costume, figure something out, but this is the happiest I've seen her since I've been back, laughing maleficently as she flips through the plastic sacks.

Eventually, she chooses "Adult Lady Archer Supreme."

"So, sexy Robin Hood?"

"Come on," she says, smiling wide. "We need to get you a bow and arrow."

On the way home from Party City, Scarlett sends me into the liquor store to get a bottle to bring to Ash's. She refuses to come in with me.

"I'm not putting myself in a position to be judged," she says. "I'll wait in the car."

"All right," I say.

I get my wallet out of the cupholder and start to button my coat.

"Can you be quick? I have to pee."

"Okay, okay," I say, leaving my coat unbuttoned.

It's cold and windy out, bitter for October. I hurry across the parking lot as my coat blows open, exposing me to the elements. A wet leaf adheres itself to my chest. I wait until I'm inside the store before trying to peel it off.

"Need help with that?"

I look up. It's Ian. He wears a black beanie, a navy flannel, dark jeans, and Doc Martens with hot pink laces. He's got stubble that wasn't there the last time I saw him. I can't tell if I like it or not. We've texted a few times, made casual conversation, but it's different standing across from him. There's something about his presence. He smells good. Not his cologne. *Him.*

"I'm all set, thanks," I say, flicking the leaf onto the floor.

"I'm bringing bourbon," he says, lifting the bottle in his hands.

"I can see that," I say. "Are you planning to share?"

"No, I'm not sharing it, no. This is just for me, so if you want to drink bourbon, better get your own."

"Okay, noted," I say.

It's hard to maintain eye contact with him. One, because he's so tall, it puts a strain on my neck to look up at him, and two, the lighting in here is weirdly great, and it makes his eyes appear even bluer. I forgot they were so blue. I kind of hate it. Looking into his eyes feels like eating something delicious you can't totally enjoy because you know it's really bad for you. His eyes are fucking me up. Giving me high cholesterol.

I've known this guy forever. How is he throwing me off my game?

"I see you're already in costume," I say.

He laughs. "Cute."

"All right, I got to hurry. Scarlett's in the car."

"See you later," he says, stepping out of my way.

"Yep."

I wander over to the vodka and pick a bottle at random. I peek out to make sure he's left before heading up to the register.

When I get back to the car, Scarlett asks what I got.

"Oh, um," I say, looking down and reading the label. "Looks like I selected Salted Karamel Stoli."

"Are you seventeen?"

"Hey, you're not drinking it."

"Neither are you," she says. "You won't drink that."

She's right. I don't like dessert-flavored liquor, and I don't really like vodka.

"I was rushed!"

"Sure," she says, turning out of the parking lot. "Blame me, your only sister, your blood, who has a tiny human living inside her, using her bladder as a punching bag. All my fault. Nothing to do with Ian Pedretti."

"Nope."

"He waved to me."

"How gentlemanly."

"I rolled down the window and said, 'Are you my new brother?' Wait. What are you doing? That's for the party."

I remove the plastic from around the top of the bottle.

"Not if you keep this up it's not."

She sighs, and the rest of the drive home is silent.

"I'll do your makeup, if you want," Scarlett says, kicking off her shoes. "I'm going to shower first."

"Okay," I say. "Let me know when."

I decide I should probably shower, too, because I smell like wet dog again. It's faint, but I can smell it. I choose to blame Reaper, even though I know it's me. I undress, removing the gauze that is, once again, soaked in silvery goo.

I had to order more bandaging off Amazon, then sneak the package inside so Scarlett wouldn't notice. I told her I have lingering scrapes, but she obviously doesn't know the gory details. Every day, I put the soiled gauze into a plastic bag and carry it down to the bins outside. I can't risk Scarlett finding any evidence. That's the last thing I need.

I stare at the wound in the mirror. The cuts remain, and the skin around them has gone stiff and pale. I'm holding out hope they're just scabbing over funny. They seep varying amounts of the thick iridescent discharge. Some days there's more than others. Some days there's barely any.

I remember when Scarlett first got her period. I cried at the kitchen table because I knew I would be next.

"It's not that bad," she said, eating Nutella straight from the jar.

"You get used to it," Mom said.

"I don't *want* to get used to it!"

I thought it was so disgusting, I couldn't get past it. It seemed so horrifically unfair, like a wicked curse.

I got mine two months later, and it was fine. I was shocked how fine it was, how quickly I was able to accept it and adapt.

I step into the shower and scrub myself clean. I thoroughly shampoo and condition my hair. After I dry off, I coat myself in scented lotion. Then I spritz perfume on my wrists, behind my knees, on my neck and ankles. I put on some fresh gauze and make sure to get it as flat as possible on my skin so it doesn't show under my skimpy costume.

I put on my bra and underwear. They're black, generic. I pause to contemplate the possibility of sex tonight.

I doubt there's going to be anyone at the party I'd consider sleeping with aside from Ian, and I don't really want to sleep with Ian just yet. Maybe a few drinks will change that, but this gauze isn't sexy, and what's underneath it definitely isn't sexy. So unlikely anyone's seeing my underwear tonight.

I get my blow-dryer and plug it into the outlet. I flip it on, and it purrs at my ear. I turn to face my reflection.

It's behind me. The monster. It's vast shadow hovering at my back.

Its long fingers prowl over my shoulder. I feel them. I can feel them.

I reach up, spinning around, ready to scream. But it isn't there.

I whip back to the mirror. I'm alone in it.

I turn the blow-dryer to the cool setting and aim it at my face. I keep it there until I've calmed down, until I have the strength to grip the round brush.

"There's nothing in this bathroom," I tell myself as I blow out my hair. "No one. Just you."

My hair turns out stupidly good. Maybe the magic product I've been missing all these years is distress? Or maybe it's the water here. My hair has been extra glossy lately. Glossy and voluminous.

I open the door to the bathroom, and Reaper is there waiting for me. He goes beyond his usual growl, peppering in some vicious barks.

"Reap!" I hear Scarlett call from down the hall. "Reaper!"

"Fuck off," I whisper to the dog, darting into my bedroom and locking the door behind me.

I check my phone, which I left charging on my nightstand. I have no new messages, no emails, no notifications, nothing. This leaves me a doomed opportunity to do the thing. I open Google and type in werewolf attack.

What comes up is a series of images and movie clips. I scroll through the images. Some of the renderings are eerily accurate.

I follow a link to the werewolf Wikipedia page.

I can't believe I'm on the werewolf Wikipedia page. Is this really where I'm looking to get my information? Am I really doing this?

What else should I do? Go to the library? The only books they'll have on werewolves are teen romances and horror novels.

I skim the page and my big takeaway is that apparently if you're bitten by a werewolf and you survive, then you are now a werewolf.

This, unfortunately, might explain some things. My weird ooze. My meat cravings. My lustrous hair. My aggravating Reaper. My smell.

I guess I have no way of knowing for sure, not unless I sprout a fucking tail during the next full moon.

"Hey."

Scarlett knocks on my door. I startle, and my phone flies out of my hands.

"Just a sec," I say, recovering my phone and promptly deleting my search history. "I still have to get dressed."

"Okay. Put on your costume and then come to my bathroom."

"Yep," I say.

I take a deep breath and reach for the plastic sack. I open it and take out the dress. Honestly, it's generous to refer to this amount of fabric as a dress. There's a little cape thing, also a faux leather belt and gloves. I put on a pair of stockings so I can feel a little less naked.

I tear up my closet, searching for my brown leather boots, before remembering I lost them the night of the attack. I *loved* those boots. I got them at a vintage shop in the Village. I could go look for them, but even if they're still out there, they've been left to the elements for the last two weeks, and I'd rather not revisit that particular patch of the woods, for obvious reasons. Tragedy on top of tragedy. I let it go, complete the getup with my suede boots instead.

When I walk into Scarlett's bathroom, she full-on cries, laughing.

"With the bow," she squawks. "I can't wait to see it with the bow."

"All right," I say. I'd be pissed, because I look ridiculous, but Scarlett's so tickled by it, I can't help but be amused. "Give me a smokey eye or something. Might as well lean in, right?"

She puts on a classic-rock playlist and tells me to hold still when I sing along to "Wild Thing."

"Your hair looks incredible," she says as she brushes out my eyebrows.

"I was thinking about braiding it. Better for the costume."

"No, leave it," she says, taking a strand and gently running it through her fingers. "My hair is so oily right now. Ash said her hair grew something outrageous with Luca. Like a foot. Any of the good things I was told would happen haven't happened. Just all this weird, awful shit no one warned me about. Sorry. I don't mean to be negative."

"You're fine. No one wants to be honest about the ugly stuff," I say.

"Yeah."

"We live in a society that wants us to be ashamed of our bodies. It's hard not to internalize that."

"You're right," she says, coming in with the mascara. "Open. Look up. And I don't know. I feel like if I say anything bad about my pregnancy, suddenly I'm Casey Anthony."

"That's crazy," I say. "You're way prettier."

She snorts. "Thanks. Thanks for that."

"You can always talk to me. I might not understand, but I won't judge you."

"I know you won't," she says. "Close your eyes. I'm gonna hit you with the setting spray."

She mists me and then moves out of the way so I can see myself in the mirror. I turn from my reflection, too afraid of what might appear behind me.

"I look gorgeous," I say, "just like Scarlett Morris."

"Ha-ha," she says.

I watch as she does her own makeup, turning her face into a beautiful skull. She puts on her cloak, hood up, and looks truly amazing. If I fuss too much over her, she'll think I'm bullshitting, so I give her a thumbs-up and keep my compliments to myself.

We get into the car, are about to leave, when Scarlett says, "I have to pee again. I'll be right back."

While she's in the house and I'm alone in the garage, wiggling impatiently in the passenger seat, I open my phone and search How many days until the next full moon?

It's fifteen.

Fifteen days.

IV

There are approximately forty million cars in front of Ashley's house, which is too bright to look at directly. The place is absolutely decked with orange string lights, so many it can likely be seen from space.

Scarlett finds a spot down the street, and we walk arm in arm along the rain-slick sidewalk, careful not to slip on any soppy fallen leaves. I stay alert, hyperaware of my surroundings. I've been looking over my shoulder so much lately, I think I'm developing neck problems.

As we approach the front door, I get a sense of just how loud it is in there. I can hear raucous laughter over the blare of Michael Jackson's "Thriller." It's eight seventeen p.m.

"What time did this start?" I ask Scarlett.

She shrugs. "Six?"

"Six?" I ask, incredulous. "Are we parties-start-at-six years old?"

"Don't," she says, lifting a single finger to me before opening the door.

I have a quick vision of her performing this gesture with her kid someday. The stone-cold single-finger "Don't." I know she'll be a good mother. Better than ours was.

We step inside and are met with a blast of hot air and pumpkin-scented something. There are a lot of smells at play here, but it's really the pumpkin that's king smell.

In the foyer, there are two men dressed in those plasticky dinosaur suits and a woman dressed as a cave person, or maybe one of the Flintstones. I'm not sure. They smile politely to acknowledge us and return to their conversation.

I look at Scarlett. "Do you know any of these people?"

"I know a few of Ash's friends from these parties."

"Amazing she has other friends besides us," I say. "The nerve."

Scarlett nods in agreement. She takes my wrist. "I'm starving. Let's get food."

We push through the crowd to get to the kitchen, where there's an incredible amount of food. I've never seen so many Crock-Pots in the same place. I count nine Crock-Pots. Nine! There are little pumpkin place cards in front of each identifying what's in their respective pot—a variety of meatballs, sausage and peppers, pumpkin chili. There's a folding table covered in a Halloween-themed tablecloth that has an assortment of dips and platters with mummy hot dogs and mini pizzas shaped like ghosts with black peppercorn eyes. There's guacamole in a cauldron surrounded by purple corn chips.

The dessert table is equally impressive, but I'm more interested in the makeshift bar Seth has set up outside on the deck, where he appears to be serving Halloween-themed cocktails dressed as Gomez Addams.

"I'm going to get a drink," I tell Scarlett.

"Okay," she says. "I'll make us plates and meet you outside."

There are lights strung up on the deck. A few cocktail tables are arranged around a heat lamp. They're covered in plastic cloths with fake flickering tea lights and real tiny pumpkins. I walk over to Seth, who I can tell is confused by my costume.

"You look . . ." he starts.

"Ridiculous," I say. "Scarlett picked it. I'm being a good sport."

"You look good, I was going to say."

"Don't lie to me, Gomez." I set the bottle of Stoli on the bar. "For you."

"Salted Karamel. Nice," he says. "You want this? I've got a special menu."

He points to a small chalkboard on the corner of the bar. In Ash's perfect script it reads, *Dracula's Blood Orange Spritzer, Poison Apple Bourbon, Black Magic Margarita.*

"The bourbon one, please," I say. "What's in it?"

"Jim Beam Apple, ginger beer, dash of cider, and a cinnamon stick."

"Do I have to tip you?" I ask as he mixes my drink.

"No, but you could respond when I text you."

He's reached out a few times about how I'm healing, and I've either ignored him or replied using only random assortments of emojis.

"I'm fine, Seth," I say. "A mere flesh wound."

"Yeah, but—"

"I don't want to think about it, all right?"

"All right," he says, handing me my cocktail. "Cheers."

"Thanks, Doc." I gulp it down. "May I have another?"

His mouth hangs open.

I raise my bow and arrow. "May I have another, *please*?"

He closes his eyes for a few seconds. Finally, he says, "You may."

"Are you stuck out here all night?"

"Not stuck," he says. "I like playing bartender."

"Well, then, we'll be seeing a lot of each other this evening," I say, accepting my second drink with a wink.

I turn around looking for Scarlett, but she must still be inside. There's a couple dressed up like pirates whisper-fighting at one of the tables. I avoid them and head to the back of the deck to wait for Scarlett. I lean on the banister and scan the yard. There's an epic swing set with multiple slides, climbing walls, swings, monkey bars. Ash had it custom built. Scarlett told me it cost three thousand dollars, which seems insane, but I guess I shouldn't judge. I once spent close to that on a pair of heels.

I feel a hand on my shoulder, and I know it's not Scarlett because of the size of the hand.

It's Ian.

He's in the same clothes he had on earlier, only now he wears a set of alien antennae on his head. They've each got a giant eyeball at the end. They're pretty funny.

He's discreet. It's a slight nod of the head as he descends the steps and walks out into the dark, away from the party. I follow him across the yard.

He sits on one of the swings and starts to open the bottle of bourbon, picking at the plastic hugging the rim.

"You think I'm going to break this thing?"

"The bottle?"

"No, the swings," he says.

I shrug. He might. It's meant for children. Small humans. He is not a small human.

I wonder what it would feel like to be with him. To have him pick me up and throw me around. He could. Easily.

It's like a match has been struck somewhere inside me. It's attraction. Want.

He gets the bottle open. I down the rest of my cocktail and hold out my empty cup to him.

"I thought I told you I wasn't sharing," he says.

"Don't make me use this," I say, raising my bow and arrow.

I can't keep a straight face about it. I start to laugh; then he laughs.

"Did you lose a bet?" he asks, pouring me some bourbon.

"What makes you say that? Don't like my costume?"

"I prefer your cheerleader uniform," he says.

"How dare you?" I say, tossing my bow and arrow onto the lawn and sitting on the other swing.

"Do you still have it or . . ."

"No."

He takes a swig from the bottle. "Damn."

"To ask me such a question. The audacity."

"I'll go back to being the shy one," he says, smiling.

He's more confident now than he was when I first knew him. He's grown into himself. Is that what's different? Is that what's causing this shift? Or is it me? For years I've been fucking strangers, finding the obscurity exhilarating. There's something wildly liberating about being so close to someone physically but remaining unknown to them. Keeping myself a secret. I never considered it could feel just as good to be with someone who does know me. Who knows my history like Ian does.

"I totally forgot I was a cheerleader," I say, sipping the bourbon.

"Cheerleader, student council president, lacrosse . . . what else?"

"Debate."

"Makes sense."

"What about you? Band."

"Yeah, band geek."

"Not geek," I say. "Well, yeah. But you were in legit bands outside of school."

Ian was a touring musician for a while, before moving back here. Now he teaches guitar and works with his dad remodeling houses. Pretty sure he remodeled Ash's kitchen.

It's a nice kitchen.

"What was your band called again?" I ask him, picking the cinnamon stick out of my cup.

"If you don't remember, I'm not going to tell you," he says, adjusting his glasses.

"I'll just ask Scarlett." Scarlett's first boyfriend, Rich, was in the band, too.

"Is she here?"

"Yeah," I say. "I should probably go find her."

"I'll see you inside."

"You're staying out here?"

"I'm gonna smoke."

"All right," I say. I swing myself to stand.

"Wait," he says.

His fingers graze my wrist.

I turn toward him. He's still taller than me, even with him sitting and me standing. His feet are on the ground, knees slightly apart. I step between them, drifting my free hand over his knee.

My other hand holds my drink, and the plastic cup cracks at the tightening of my grip. His hands. One of them finds my face. The other, my hip.

"Can I kiss you?" he asks me.

The yes snags somewhere in my throat. The want of the moment has warped all sensation. I feel everything and nothing. I'm numb and on fire. I manage to nod, but he waits. He looks at me. This is the closest we've ever been, I think. So close that my breath fogs up his glasses. He runs his thumb softly along my jaw, and then his lips press to mine.

I don't think it's lost on either of us that he's waited fifteen years for this. Now that it's happening, now that I'm here inside this kiss with him, it's no wonder why it took me so long. This is a game-over kiss. It's an electric, world-stopping, heart-cartwheeling, you're-totally-fucked kiss.

Maybe deep down I knew all along. That if I allowed myself to feel anything for this person, the feelings would be too much, immense and unwieldy, impossible to contain, to control. I wasn't ready for this kiss when I was an idiot teenager. I'm not sure I'm ready for it now at twenty-seven.

He pulls back just a little, so we're still close but no longer in the kiss, which is good, because I forgot to breathe, and now I'm light-headed. I press my forehead into his and inhale.

I want to climb onto his lap, burrow into him. I've never wanted to surrender myself to someone, to just let them hold me and not think twice. My eyes are closed, and I can hear "Monster Mash" playing in the distance. My breath smells like cinnamon; we both reek of bourbon.

The first time he told me that he liked me, we were loitering outside the movie theater, waiting to get picked up. Scarlett and

Rich were making out, so Ian and I sat on the curb eating the candy we hadn't finished during the movie. I forget what movie, but I remember the candy. Sour Straws and Peanut M&Ms.

"Blue raspberry," I'd said, sucking on one of the straws. "A superior flavor."

"I don't like anything that changes the color of my tongue," he told me. "Freaks me out."

"What?"

"When I was younger, I had some blue candy, and it turned my tongue blue, and I looked in the mirror and lost it. I thought it would be like that forever."

"I hate to be the one to tell you this," I said. "But you were a really stupid kid."

He laughed. Then he said, "You know I like you, right?"

"I know," I said. I remember being mad at him for ruining the moment, for telling me something I already knew but didn't want to be held accountable for knowing. "I'm just really busy."

He nodded. We didn't say anything for a while; then he tipped the bag of M&Ms in my direction. I opened my palm to receive the candy. He looked at me, and I stuck out my tongue.

"You don't have to add insult to injury," he said.

"Is it blue? From the straws?"

He shook his head.

We never talked about it again. When he started dating Kelly Iwanowski in eleventh grade, Scarlett asked me if I was jealous, and I answered honestly that I wasn't. I remember thinking they'd break up eventually and he'd still like me. He liked me first. He liked me best.

"You still like me?" I ask him now, swiping the cold tip of my nose across his forehead.

"No," he says. "Not at all. Over it."

"Hey."

He leans down, holds my chin in his hand, and tilts my face so our eyes are lined up exactly.

"You know the answer to that question. You've always known. Don't make me say it just to hear me say it."

He's being honest with me again, like he was on the curb outside of the movie theater. The kind of honest I can't skate around.

"I can't make you do anything," I say, stepping away from him. "You're much bigger than I am."

"Yeah, but you've got weapons," he says as I pick up my bow and arrow.

"Damn right," I say, crossing the yard back to the party, butterflies eating me alive from the inside.

I can't believe I just kissed a guy on a swing set. I can't believe I just kissed Ian Pedretti.

I need to find Scarlett.

As soon as I step into the house, my post-kiss giddiness is demolished by the song that's playing.

"There you are," Scarlett says, removing her hood. "I got stuck talking to these rubes. What's wrong?"

"Nothing," I say as Warren Zevon howls over a jaunty tune. I start to laugh in spite of myself. "This song."

Of all things. Honestly.

"You don't like 'Werewolves of London'? This is the first good song that's come on in, like, an hour," Scarlett says.

"We definitely haven't been here for an hour."

"Listen, I made you a plate but then I ate it. Sorry."

"That's all right," I say. I grab a mummy hot dog from the nearest platter and wash it down with my bourbon.

"Let's go outside," Scarlett says. "Ash told all of her mom friends that I'm pregnant and now they're all coming up to me with advice."

I escort her outside, where Seth is no longer tending bar. I pour myself another spot of the Jim Beam Apple.

"Pace yourself," Scarlett says.

I clutch my imaginary pearls. "You'd shame your own sister?"

"I support you in all your endeavors," she says. "But I can't carry you home if you get blitzed."

"I'm fine," I say.

And it's true. I've already had a fair amount to drink, and I'm not even buzzed.

I look over Scarlett's shoulder to the pirate couple, who appear to still be fighting. Scarlett follows my gaze to them, then looks back at me.

"Eeks," she whispers.

"Okay," I say, screwing the cap back on the Beam. "So you want to hang out here, or . . . ?"

"Let's just say hi to Ash and head home."

"You want to leave?"

"You don't?"

"We just got here," I say. "We should stay a little longer."

"Oh. *Ian*," she says. "Is he here yet?"

"Yeah. I saw him. We kissed."

"What? When?"

"Like five minutes ago. On the swing set."

I anticipate a big reaction. Girlish squeals and poking and teasing and swooning. What I get is something far more restrained. Barely a smile. It's a sort of distant, misty-eyed look.

"You've been losing your mind over me and Ian, and now something actually happens, and you look fully unenthused."

She's flustered. She's doing these odd little sighs, opening and closing her mouth like a day-old goldfish. Her shoulders twitch.

"What?" I ask.

"I don't know," she says. "I'm emotional."

She's crying. Actually crying.

"Scarlett?"

"It's not me!" she says. "I'm not crying."

"Sure," I say, snatching a cocktail napkin for her to use as a tissue.

"It's not me," she repeats. She's genuinely upset.

"What's the matter?"

"Nothing," she says, wiping her eyes. "Let's find Ashley."

I stand stunned for a moment before following her inside.

By the time I get into the house, she's already gone. I've lost her.

I see Ian; he's hard to miss. He's the tallest person here, costumes included. He towers over the T. rex heads and bad wigs. He talks to someone out of view.

"Hey, you!"

Ash stands behind me, a convincing Morticia.

"You look amazing," she says. "Love it."

"I look like I'm about to get the train run on me by the Merry Men," I say. "You can't lie to me. I've seen this porno."

"I believe it. You watch a lot of porn," she says, giggling.

These are the kind of things old friends know about you. It's what makes them as dangerous as they are precious. They're plutonium.

"Anyway. You look beautiful," I say. "Have you seen Scarlett? I lost her."

"No, I haven't seen her yet," she says.

I wave her in close to me. "Okay, two things. One, I kissed Ian."

She screams.

"Shhh," I hiss. I wave her in again. "Two, I told Scarlett and she basically burst into tears. And I'm not sure they were happy tears."

"What do you mean?"

"She seemed upset! She kept saying, 'It's not me.' Whatever that means."

Ash scrunches up her face. "Maybe it's about . . ."

She doesn't say his name out loud. She mouths it.

Matty.

That motherfucker.

"I guess I didn't think," I say. "That's it, I guess. I didn't think."

"No, no," Ash says, digging some stray wig hair out of her cleavage. "She doesn't talk about it. It's impossible to get a read on her. You're the same way. I thought maybe you'd have more insight into the situation. With him."

I shake my head.

"I learned a long time ago it's pointless to try to get anything out of either of you," she says. "I can't believe you kissed Ian."

"You're acting like I've never kissed anyone before."

"No, I know. It's just *Ian*. How was it?"

"We'll talk about it another time," I say. "Werewolves of London" is on again. An itch awakens under my bandages. "I'm gonna find Scarlett. Maybe we should go."

Ash frowns. "Already?"

"We'll come by tomorrow. Will help clean in exchange for leftovers."

"Deal," she says.

We lock it in with our supersecret best friend handshake, developed at a childhood sleepover, perfected over years of committed practice.

I break off into the crowd, elbowing my way through clusters of strangers. I'm accosted by a drunk vampire near the stairs.

"Hi," he says. "I like your costume. I'm Mike."

"So weird. You look more like a Dracula to me," I say. "Sorry. I'm actually looking for someone."

"You're here with someone?"

"Yeah," I say.

He stumbles forward, and I can see in his eyes that he's gone. He stinks of liquor.

"Are you really?" he asks.

He's wilting, getting closer and closer to me. He's about to touch me, about to fall on me. I can't tell if it's on purpose or not. I put my hand up and push him back.

I swear I don't exert much force.

It was a light nudge. I swear.

But he goes flying. Literally. He gets some air as his body travels away from me. His head snaps back on impact with the front door. It's not quiet.

It gets the attention of everybody nearby, including Ian.

Mike groans. His legs crumple beneath him, his arms and neck go limp. His vampire teeth have fallen out. They glide on the narrow floor space between us in a blood-tinged puddle of spit.

Either that guy was already out on his feet or I'm much stronger than I realized. Pilates. Who knew?

"That guy's really drunk," I say to the members of Mystery Inc., who stand beside me horrified.

"Vampires always suck the life out of the party."

I know that voice. A natural rasp, the tone of good trouble. My former accomplice in mischief. My old friend. I turn around, and there she is.

Mia Russo.

She's wearing the same costume as me. We look each other up and down and laugh. Just laugh.

"It's been a while," I say, reaching for her long bottle-blond hair.

I can't remember the last time we spoke. She moved out to Los Angeles postgraduation to pursue acting, but Mia bores easily and was done after a few auditions. She was a spin instructor for a minute; then she started a fitness blog that turned into travel blog. Now she's essentially an influencer. She's had a string of handsome, square-jawed suitors who appear and disappear from her feed without much fanfare. Honestly, I haven't thought about her much in the years since high school. I never really missed her, not until now with her hair in my hands.

"You look fucking great," I tell her.

"You're terrible at keeping in touch."

"I know."

"You look good, too. Surprise, surprise," she says, leaning over and kissing me on the cheek.

Beside us, the woman dressed as Velma hands Mike a Solo cup full of what I assume is water. He promptly spills it and laughs. Velma throws her hands up and says, "I tried!"

"We always want to save the monsters, don't we? And it never works out," Mia says. "Come, sunshine. Let's go take shots."

"I'd love to, but I need to find Scarlett."

"No fun," Mia says, pouting a lacquered lip. "We should get together. Just us. Go out for a night of debauchery, like old times."

"Done and done," I say. "How long are you in town for?"

"Oh, you know. However long I feel like."

She kisses me on the other cheek, then slinks off into the crowd. I head upstairs in search of my sister.

"Scarlett? You up here?"

I check the bathroom, which is occupied by a French maid, who apparently doesn't lock doors. I apologize and move on to Luca's room.

Scarlett lies on his tiny bed, on top of rocket ship sheets, staring at the glow-in-the-dark stars on his ceiling.

"I just slayed Dracula," I say, swatting at the solar system mobile grazing my ear.

"What?"

"This drunk vampire was getting in my personal space, uninvited, so I went to push him back. A flat palm, you know, one of these"—I demonstrate—"and he went straight back. Hit the front door. Fell to the ground."

"Oh, well," she says. She's somewhere else. Deep in her thoughts.

"I saw Mia. Did you pick her costume, too?"

"Huh?"

"You were right," I say. "We should go. Pretty sure this playlist is just five Halloween-adjacent songs on repeat."

"I wasn't able to find Ash."

"I talked to her," I say. "Told her we'd come over tomorrow for leftovers. She won't care if we leave. She's got her hands full hosting. Wait. Where's Luca?"

She points to the closet.

I experience a moment's confusion.

Scarlett finds it hilarious.

"Very good," I say. "Very funny."

"He's with Ash's parents. Help me up."

She reaches out to me. I take her by the forearms and pull. It is strange to feel the extra weight of her. I wonder what it's like to carry it around, that weight.

When we get to the bottom of the stairs, vampire Mike is gone, but Ian isn't. He's there talking to Mystery Inc.

"Say your goodbyes. I'll be in the car," Scarlett says, already halfway out the door.

"Wait," I tell her. "I don't want you walking alone. I'll only be a sec."

I catch Ian's attention and he excuses himself from the conversation.

"I'm leaving," I tell him.

"Did something happen before? With Mike?"

"He was about to pass out," I say. "I tipped him in a different direction."

"Okay," he says, his brow furrowed.

"What?"

"Nothing."

"Scarlett wants to leave. I'd be happy to stay and listen to 'Thriller' again. I've always said 'Thriller' is better a hundred times in a row."

He doesn't say anything, just hangs a hand on the back of his neck.

"Okay, what?" I ask.

He offers me the bottle of bourbon.

"Why do you still have this?" I ask him. "Were you serious about not sharing?"

"I took a direct swig when we were out on the swings," he says. "I wasn't thinking. I was distracted."

"Mm. I remember. Being distracting," I say. I accept the bottle. "So why are you giving it to me? Because I don't mind your backwash?"

"No," he says. "I want it back. You can drink it. Or not drink it. The bottle can be empty. I just want it back."

I get it. An excuse to see me.

Not smooth at all, but I appreciate the attempt. I try to rein in my grin.

"Okay. When?"

"Whenever," he says. "Soon would be good."

"This week?"

He takes my hand in his and gives it a quick squeeze.

"Good night," he says.

"Night, Ian."

I'm so preoccupied by the tingle in my hand that I slip twice on the way to the car.

Scarlett won't look at me. She doesn't say anything, doesn't put music on. This continues for about ten minutes until we're almost home.

That's when she says, "I have to tell you something."

I assume it's Matty related. "You can tell me anything."

"Mom's coming up."

"What?" I'd have preferred a hard slap across the face.

"Yeah. Not this coming weekend, the one after."

"Uh, again, what?"

"Mom and maybe Guy," she says. "He might be working."

"For how long?"

"A week."

"A *week*? When were you going to tell me?"

Scarlett has a much less complicated relationship with our

mother. They speak on a regular basis. Weekly FaceTime sessions, consistent texting. I speak to our mother only when absolutely necessary. I see her only on holidays, and I avoid being alone with her.

The idea of having to be around her for a week . . .

"Why are you springing this on me?"

"It's not springing," she says. "I'm telling you."

"Are you pissed at me?"

"Believe it or not, this visit isn't to spite you," she says. "She visits sometimes. It's normal."

"It is to spite me," I say.

I was having a good night. The timing feels calculated. It's cruel.

"I was dreading telling you because I knew you'd react like this. We don't need to argue. It'll be fine. It's a few days."

"Right," I say, infusing as much venom into the word as possible.

"I'm sorry," she says, sighing as we pull into the garage. "What do you want me to do? Tell her she can't come? I've been in the middle for years now. I can't do it anymore, Aurora. Especially not right now."

"I see how it is. Blame the baby, huh?" I ask, softening a little.

She laughs. "Yeah, I guess so."

We go inside, kicking our shoes off in the laundry room.

"You want tea?" she asks.

"No, thanks. I'm gonna go to bed," I say. "Sweet dreams."

I'm almost to the stairs when she calls my name.

"Yeah?" I ask, turning around.

"I am happy, about you and Ian. I always rooted for him," she says. "I'm not sad. I don't know why I started crying. I don't have any control."

"What do you mean?"

"My body, my emotions," she says. "It's frustrating. I don't feel like myself. I'm not myself. And . . . I don't know. It's just weird to see you starting something, when I'm—"

"Yeah," I say. "I get it."

"You sure you don't want tea?" she asks, filling the kettle.

"I'm good."

"All right," she says. "And I didn't mean to spring it on you. About Mom. I just didn't know how to tell you. It's a tough spot."

"Yeah," I say, foot on the first step.

"Maybe it's good she's coming. Maybe it'll give you guys the time to talk things out."

"Right. I'm going upstairs now. Night."

I hold Ian's bottle of bourbon close to my chest as I climb the stairs. Reaper is there at the top, growling at me per usual. I'm really not in the mood.

So I growl back.

I don't intend for it to come out the way it does. I had no idea I was capable of such a sound. It's beastly.

It sends Reaper off whimpering.

I hide in my room before any more unpleasantness can occur.

I undress immediately, tossing my costume into the laundry basket, even though I'm tempted to put it straight into the trash.

What stops me from doing that is it's what I was wearing when I first kissed Ian.

Shameful. Gross.

I'd continue to bully myself over my newfound mawkishness,

but I'm distracted by my bandaging. It's so itchy underneath. I relent, peeling back the tape so I can scratch.

I haven't leaked much; there's only a little drip of silver clinging to the disturbed skin. I use the gauze to wipe it away. Then I scratch.

It feels so good, I keep going past the point when I know I should stop. I keep going until I feel the sticky wetness.

Until I feel the fur.

I look down. I've ripped myself open. My skin falls away in oddly neat spirals. There's no red, no blood. Only silver. I'm all oozy silver inside.

Silver and fur.

There's fur under my skin. Prickly gray fur.

"Uhhhh, what the fuck?" I ask, holding my breath.

I try to mash the shreds of skin back into place and then restore the bandaging, but they keep slipping.

I'm panicking now.

This is next-level disgusting. This is a problem.

This is a big problem.

I manage to get the gauze back in place and tape it down. Then I add another layer of gauze, more tape, more gauze, more tape.

I sit on the bed for a minute, chewing the inside of my cheek and anxiously plucking fuzz from my sock.

"All right," I say, my best attempt at a pep talk. "All right."

I open the bottle of bourbon and my laptop.

I Google what should you do if you were bitten by a werewolf? Then I chug some of the bourbon.

The first link I click on leads to a surprisingly earnest article that recommends I get a cage for my monthly transformations and perhaps also purchase some meat snacks, like whole chickens.

It also gives an unhelpful heads-up about the excruciating pain of the transformation.

Great.

I gulp some more bourbon.

I'm starting to suspect that werewolves can't get drunk, which just might be the most unfortunate part about all of this.

I continue drinking anyway.

I find some random forums to scroll through. None of them are particularly informative, and as the threads go on, the discourse often devolves into arguments. Most of these arguments have something to do with vampires: Who would win in a fight? Can they kill one another, etc.?

At the very least, they can take out drunk men dressed as vampires. I proved that tonight. As for real vampires, I sure hope they don't exist.

One thing at a time.

I scroll on until the bourbon is gone, until my eyelids are heavy and tired. I hold my head in my hands.

There doesn't appear to be any legitimate, trustworthy information on the internet about werewolves. I wish that meant I was wrong about this, but I can't bullshit myself. A creature that looked like a werewolf attacked me during a full moon. And now my blood is silver and I have fur? I just tore off my skin by scratching an itch. I animal-style snarled at Reaper. What I thought was a gentle push to vampire Mike might as well have been a baseball bat to his sternum.

I hear Scarlett's voice saying, *Maybe it's good she's coming. Maybe it'll give you guys the time to talk things out.*

She doesn't understand that there is no talking them out. Maybe they can move on, but I can't. It's part of me. I remember Mrs. Meyer telling me that day, *The things that happen to us are not who we are,* but she was wrong.

I knew it then, too. That I was forever changed. Just like I know it now.

I close my laptop and try to get some sleep.

V

The next morning, when I check under my bandages, four shreds of shriveled pale skin spill out onto the floor.

I gag.

Strangely, that's the worst of it. The skin has regrown overnight, and now the only evidence of the injury is slight discoloration, a series of faint scars like knots in wood.

I decide to leave the gauze off for today and see how it is. I wear a shirt I don't particularly care about and a pair of old khakis.

I use a plastic bag as a makeshift glove to pick up the skin pieces and flush them down the toilet.

Out of sight, out of mind.

Scarlett is where I left her, in the kitchen making tea.

"I'll put on coffee," she says. "Wasn't sure when you'd be up."

"What time is it?" I ask, yawning.

"Almost eleven," she says. "Ash called and said we could go over whenever. I don't have work until tonight. My first appointment is at eight . . ."

"Well, whenever sounds good," I say. "I'll have coffee there."

"All right," she says, getting out a thermos for her tea.

She's in a better mood now than she was last night. Still not great. It's like someone lowered the dimmer switch. She's not as bright as usual.

"We don't have to go over if you're not up to it," I tell her. "Ash will understand."

She shrugs. "Whatever you want."

We end up staying home, sitting on the couch for hours without much interaction between us. I read and answer emails, and she sketches. The day slips away. She orders us pizza for dinner, and we eat it straight out of the box while watching a documentary about elephants.

"Not hungry?" she asks me.

I'm not actually eating the pizza, only the pepperonis.

"Not really," I lie.

After I drop her off at work, I eat slices of deli turkey and leftover Bolognese by the spoonful, sans pasta. I'm microwaving some frozen chicken fingers when Ian texts me, asking if I'm free Thursday night.

Yeah, I say. I'm not busy.

"What do I wear bowling?" I ask Scarlett. She sits on the bed as I raid my closet.

"Why don't you wear what you had on the other night?" she asks. "You looked *super*cute."

"What other . . . Oh. Halloween." I flip her off.

She falls over onto a pillow, laughing.

"Frankly, that outfit worked in my favor," I say.

"I'm sure it did."

"All right," I say, combing through my usual going-out dresses, which are all too much for a suburban bowling alley. "My wardrobe is not functional. I've got, like, hanging-around-the-house-running-errands clothes, or going-for-cocktails-in-Manhattan clothes. There's no in-between."

"Did you bring everything you own?" she asks, peering into the closet.

"Not my work clothes."

"No power suits?"

"Nope."

They're all back at my apartment, which I sublet to my trusted friend Laura, a former coworker who now reviews bars and restaurants and various hot spots for a bougie New York City lifestyle magazine. Whenever I go out with her, I spend too much money and, more often than not, make out with someone low-key famous. There've been several New York Rangers. A few supporting actors on New York–based TV shows. If I'm ever watching TV, thinking, *Where do I know him from?* I probably know him from a night out with Laura.

"What do you usually wear on dates?" Scarlett asks.

"I don't go on dates."

"Right," she says. "Are you nervous?"

"What do I have to be nervous about?" I look over my shoulder at her. She's deep in thought. "What?"

"I've just been thinking. With Mom coming to visit, and I guess because I'm about to have a kid, I've been thinking about what Mom did right. She gave us a lot of confidence."

"Mm," I say, my stomach turning.

"She was never secure in herself, so it's wild to me that she raised us. She had her own shit, but she was always really encouraging with us. She didn't just give us mom compliments like 'You're beautiful.' She really saw us."

She's not wrong. "Yeah. I'll give her credit where credit is due."

As soon as I say it, I know it's not true. I can't. Can't do it.

"If only she paid more attention," I say. "Or I don't know. Listened to her children."

Scarlett sits up. "I'm having a girl."

"Really?" My heart might explode.

"Don't get all . . ." she says, gesturing vaguely in my direction. "You have to resolve things with Mom. I have to know you're not going to resent her for the rest of your life."

"Okay," I say, my joy deflating in spectacular fashion. "I don't want to talk about it right now. I'm about to go on a date. Why would you bring that up now?"

She opens her mouth to speak, then changes her mind. She stands up and comes over to where I am in front of the closet . For a second, I think she might hug me, but then she pushes me out of the way.

"Let me," she says.

An hour later, I'm scrutinizing myself in the full-length mirror in Scarlett's bathroom. My palms are sweating. It's not just the wolf haunting the fringe of my reflection, the wolf that I see every time I look in the mirror now, that I know isn't really there behind me.

It's that I'm nervous.

I'm actually fucking nervous!

Scarlett ended up lending me clothes. A pair of high-waisted black jeans and a lacy black blouse with ruffles and billowy sleeves. I protested the top as *too nineteenth-century widow* but was overruled.

"I can't wear my own clothes anymore," Scarlett lamented. "You have to wear them for me."

I put on some mascara and tinted lip balm. I brush my eyebrows out. I realize my neck looks naked and go to my room to find an appropriate necklace. I select a silver choker.

I hear a faint sizzling noise as I attempt to clasp the chain around my neck.

Then I smell it. Smells like woodshop. Like . . .

I gasp. The necklace falls from my hands as I hurry into my bathroom. I close the door behind me and lock it. I hesitate before looking into the mirror.

There's a slim dark line around my neck, like someone just tried to choke me with piano wire. It's still sizzling.

I reach up and carefully run my index finger across the line. I watch myself wince.

I button the blouse all the way, but the collar is too low. I try to cover it up with my hair.

A shadow creeps into my reflection, and I look away.

I lift up the blouse and check the status of my side. Lights off, the remaining marks won't be noticeable. But my neck?

How can I hide my neck?

Also, what the fuck?

I'm silver on the inside, so why did I have this reaction to silver against my skin?

None of those fantasy nerds covered this on the forums.

I hear knocking, Reaper barking.

Shit shit shit shit.

"Ian Pedretti," I hear Scarlett say. "How are you?"

I open the bathroom door and dart into my room to grab my bag. I briefly consider a scarf.

"I'm good. How are you? Nice to see you," Ian says.

Where are all my goddamn scarves?

"You sure you want to do this?" Scarlett asks, raising her voice to make sure I can hear it. "You know, I'm currently unattached."

Forget it.

"Hey," I say, hurrying down the stairs. "Hey."

Ian kneels in the foyer petting Reaper, who looks about the happiest I've ever seen him. Tongue out, tail wagging.

"Hi," Ian says.

"Hi."

Everything is sweating. I think my shins are sweating.

They are. My shins are sweating. These jeans are damp.

"I'll get my shoes," I say, shuffling to the laundry room to grab my heels. I stumble as I put them on, all my grace gone from me.

When I walk back to the front door, Scarlett sports a smug grin. Because she can tell. She knows.

I'm a mess.

Ian stands, and the disruption of pets really pisses off Reaper, who, rightfully in this case, takes it out on me. He growls at me, bares his teeth.

"All right, all right, I'm going," I say. I turn to Ian. "Ready?"

He nods, holds the door open for me.

"Have fun," Scarlett says, kicking my heel.

I look back at her before leaving, and she's smiling, but her eyes are wet. They tug at something inside me, and suddenly I don't want to leave her.

But then Reaper barks at me. I throw up the peace sign and step outside.

Ian parked in the street, and as we cross the yard, there are a few seconds of nothing before he asks me, "Where's the bottle?"

I look at him. He's serious. "I thought you were trying to be clever. I didn't think you actually wanted it back."

"Did you recycle it at least?"

"No. I smashed it and then threw all of the broken glass on public playgrounds."

"Oh, yeah?" he asks, opening the car door for me.

"Yeah. Then I went to the beach and shanked a few dolphins."

"Did you shout, 'Fuck the planet!' while you were doing it?"

"Of course," I say.

He laughs, closing my door and coming around the front of the car. It's a sedan, and it's too small for him. He makes it look like a clown car.

On the way to the bowling alley, we listen to music and don't talk much, and that's fine. I try to think back to high school, if he ever picked me up, if I've ever been alone in the car with him before. I guess he was dating Kelly by the time we could drive.

In the parking lot, he pops the trunk and procures a pair of bowling shoes.

He doesn't say anything, and I don't say anything. There are no comments to be made about the shoes, about the fact that he owns his own bowling shoes, which he apparently keeps in the trunk of his car. There are many comments that could be made, but none of them are. I don't really feel like making fun of him. I actually find it kind of endearing that he's got a pair of bowling shoes in his trunk, and that he doesn't feel the need to offer me any explanation.

When we get inside, I'm surprised and delighted by the griminess of the place. It's got tacky eighties decor and fluorescent lighting and smells like feet. It's authentic. All the bowling alleys in the city are dark and posh and have exposed brick and serve cocktails and fish tacos. Here, you can get pitchers of beer, hot dogs, soft pretzels, nachos, cheese fries, and probably a staph infection.

I get my shoes and we're assigned our lane. It's one of the good lanes against the wall, which I guess doesn't really matter because the place is empty.

I sit and take off my heels, then put on my wonderfully ugly bowling shoes.

Ian's busy punching our names into the computer.

"I'm gonna get us beer," I say.

I limp over to the bar, the bowling shoes pinching my feet. I order us a five-dollar pitcher of some very pale, very shitty-looking beer. As I'm walking back with the pitcher, trying my best not to spill it as it overflows with foam, I glance up and take in the image of him. This view of his back.

He doesn't look the way he did in high school. He's taken a different shape. He's a different person. He's grown up. It occurs to me that maybe I don't know him anymore. Maybe I don't know him at all.

Our dynamic, too. It's not what it was. I don't have all the power anymore. I'm not in full control. Because I care. Because I want him.

I sip some of the beer straight from the pitcher.

"You first," he says.

"Are you a good bowler?" I ask him. "Is that why you asked me to go bowling?"

"No," he says. "Not particularly."

I select a dark purple ball. I don't really love the idea of sticking my fingers in these holes. Who knows the last time these balls were sanitized? But I guess I've done worse.

"Then why'd you take me bowling?" I ask him.

"Seemed like your kind of thing," he says. "You don't like to sit still."

"Mm," I say.

It's true. Maybe I don't know him anymore, but he knows me.

I let the ball go, and it doesn't really roll so much as soar a few inches over the lane. When it smashes into the pins, the sound is loud and violent. I worry I broke something.

I turn around, wearing this worry on my face.

"Strike," Ian says.

He doesn't appear fazed by the aggression of my bowl. Both the teenager behind the front desk and the bartender are gawping from afar, so it was definitely not the average strike.

On my next go, I practice restraint.

"If I didn't know you better, I would think you started to hold back on me," Ian says, eyeing me suspiciously as I wait for the machine to regurgitate my ball.

"No," I say. "This is me trying my hardest."

Trying my hardest not to reveal that I now have legit supernatural strength.

I become so focused on not putting a hole through the back of the alley, the conversation withers, and by the end of the game we're barely talking, just taking turns bowling.

I pour myself more beer and realize I've finished most of this pitcher myself.

It's not going well.

When the game is over, Ian stares at the screen and says, "Do you want to go to my place?"

He's barely finished the sentence before I say, "Yes."

Ian lives in a two-story brick building on a busy stretch of East Avenue, with restaurants and coffee shops and stores that sell shit like knit hats and greeting cards and ornaments. He pulls down a secluded driveway and parks on a patch of gravel behind the building. He opens the car door for me, which is helpful, because my hands are busy catching all this bountiful nervous sweat my body has apparently been stockpiling for the last twenty-seven years.

"This used to be a bank," he says, letting us in through the back door.

He flips on the lights.

There's a kitchen to the left, with stainless steel cabinets and appliances. There's a long, counter-height wooden dining table with pipes for legs and stools underneath.

Beyond the kitchen is a living space with vaulted ceilings, wooden beams, exposed brick. Hanging Edison bulbs light the room. There are an enormous couch and a few worn leather armchairs. Many, many bookshelves, the same wood-and-pipe style as the dining table, jammed with books. There are framed pictures of album covers and concert venues. In the corner of the room is a collection of instruments, mostly guitars, a drum set, a keyboard, a bass. There's a record player sitting beside crates and crates of records.

A flight of stairs leads up to a loft space.

I spin around to give the place another look-over. He's got plants. They're alive. Thriving, even.

It's nice. Too nice.

I wasn't expecting it to be this nice.

I don't know what I was expecting.

He's not concerned with me and what I'm doing. He's cooking something. He's got a pot of water on the stove. I come over and sit at the kitchen table. He takes out a glass, fills it with ice, then sets it down in front of me, along with a can of root beer. We both love root beer. It's our soda of choice.

"Thank you," I say.

And that's it, nothing else, nothing cute or clever, because my brain seems to have been swapped with a blobfish.

He nods and goes back to cooking.

Music plays, but I don't know when it started or how. In my nervous fidgeting, I push my hair behind my ears and accidentally graze my neck. The mark is still there. It feels hard now, like it scabbed over. I hope it's not noticeable. If it is, I hope he doesn't ask me about it.

"I sort of figured if you ever agreed to go out with me, it'd be like this," he says, sprinkling some salt into the pot.

"Like what?" I ask, my voice weak and squeaky.

He raises his eyebrows.

"I don't know. I don't go on dates," I say. I'm being tragically uncool. It's kind of amazing how uncool I'm being, considering I'm actually pretty fucking cool. "I don't do this. Dates. Not then. Not now. Not ever, really."

He looks at me. There's no judgment. I don't think. He might be curious. Or maybe concerned?

"It's not weird," I say.

"I didn't say it was. I don't think it is."

"It's not something I'm interested in," I say. "Sitting across from a stranger and having to make small talk. 'What do you do?' 'Oh, what do *you* do?' Mortifying. Not how I want to spend my time."

"What do you do again?"

I roll my eyes.

"I'm not a stranger," he says.

"I know. I know you're not."

"I don't have any expectations," he says, taking a Tupperware container full of meatballs out of the fridge. "It's cool that you're in town and we get to hang out again."

He scoops some meatballs into another pot, then adds a fistful of spaghetti to the boiling water.

"Bullshit you don't have expectations," I say. "You're trying to *Lady and the Tramp* some spaghetti with me."

He shakes his head. "Would never."

He's true to his word. We eat on opposite sides of the table, off different plates. I choke down some spaghetti even though all I really want are the meatballs.

He tells me about his house, about how it was built in 1898, that it used to be a bank, but eventually the bank closed, and it sat vacant for years. They were going to knock it down, so he bought it, and then he and his dad fixed it up. He tells me there're a vault and some old lockboxes in the basement. He offers to show me later.

"I'm actually more interested in what's upstairs," I say, my true self cutting through my nerves for the first time all evening.

He doesn't blink. He's unflappable. "Okay."

After we finish eating, I offer to help him with the dishes.

"No," he says, leaving them in the sink and pouring us each a bourbon. We clink glasses, but then he puts his down.

"You don't want it?" I ask him.

"I shouldn't. Have to drive you home."

I snort. "Yeah, I'm not going home."

He lets me finish my sip before taking my glass and setting it down on the counter. Then he holds my face and kisses me.

It's like the swing-set kiss, only better.

I reach up to him, and he glides his hands down to my waist and lifts me up. The contact with my side, his grip on where I was bitten, doesn't hurt, exactly. It's vivid in its intensity but ambiguous in its pleasure. I wrap my legs around him, and he presses my back into the wall.

This want has me feral. I paw at him. His hair, his shoulders. He's got one hand on my waist, still pressed to the bite, and the other under my ass, holding me up off the floor.

I think it'll happen right here, and I'm fine with that, but then he lets me go.

He pulls back from me, gently lets me down.

"What is it?" I ask.

"I lied before," he says, out of breath. "I do have expectations."

"All right," I say. "What are they?"

"Not expectations," he says. "I don't expect anything. But I don't want this to be *this* and nothing else. It'll fuck me up. If you're back, if you're in my house and we hook up and then you leave and it's nothing, that'll fuck me up. I'm not asking you to know what you want. I'm just telling you what I want."

"It's unclear," I say. I'm also out of breath. "What do you want?"

"If you know for sure you're not looking for anything else out of this, then let's just stay friends."

"I don't know that," I say, feeling the smile creep up my cheeks. I still do have the power here. Some of it anyway.

"Okay. Then let's go upstairs."

After, we lie in the wreckage of torn sheets and obliterated pillows. There are lamps knocked over, broken glass, books once stacked neatly on the nightstand splayed out on their spines. We're on our backs, and my head rests on his chest. He strokes my tangled hair.

"You're strong," he says. "I think I have bruises."

"Apologies. I'll be gentle next time."

"Next time, huh?"

"Unless I'm too rough for you."

He tugs my hair, pulling my chin up toward him. "Not too rough."

He releases my hair and kisses the top of my head. "Though rumor has it you took out a bear a few weeks ago."

"Mm." Sure. A bear. "To clarify, that was a very different interaction."

"Good to know."

There's a moment of quiet, and I worry he's going to persist with some follow-ups re the "bear" attack.

He doesn't, but it doesn't matter. Because now I'm thinking about it. Thinking about those red eyes stalking me in the dark, the sensation of being chased. Of being caught. Of lying there, a helpless witness to the destruction of my body.

I could close my eyes and summon that feeling easily. The feeling of being so totally aware, awake for my own desecration, distraught by my powerlessness to stop it.

I didn't stop it. I couldn't stop it. So that's on me, isn't it?

You're strong, he said just a minute ago.

I should have told him. Tried to explain.

I am strong, just not strong enough.

I reach up to feel for the silver burn around my neck, but it's gone. It's healed.

I'm changing. My body is changing.

What happens in a week? What happens when the moon is full?

I press my ear to Ian's chest, listening to the steady thump of his heart. He rests an arm over my back. I never do this. I never stay after. But I want to. I want to stay. I don't ever want to get out of this bed.

Right now I could give a fuck about a full moon.

I open a single sleepy eye to watch Ian get out of bed. Sunlight's coming in from somewhere. A skylight? I hate it.

"Go back to sleep," he tells me.

No objection.

I sleep for a while longer, and when I finally wake up again, there's no more sun. It's gray and raining. The room around me has been tidied. The books restacked, lamps now standing. The sheets are still a mess. We ripped them. And at least one pillow. Pillow guts are everywhere.

I step cautiously out of bed in case there's still glass on the floor. I tiptoe into the bathroom.

It's very clean, this bathroom. Either he knew I was coming or he's the rare gem of a man who keeps a clean bathroom.

I pee, then wash my hands. Briefly check my reflection. My

hair is a nest. I think I smell. That goddamn wet-dog smell. I have a perfume roller in my bag downstairs that I desperately need. I take some of his toothpaste on my finger and swish it around my mouth.

I head downstairs and find it's empty. No Ian.

I grab my bag off the kitchen table and check my phone. He texted to tell me he was going out to get breakfast seven minutes ago. Which means . . .

I have some time alone in his apartment.

I commence snooping.

His books are first. There's a decent variety. Classic literature. Some Stephen Hawking, which . . . sure. A lot of music books. Rock biographies. Autobiographies.

I spot something tucked between two books and carefully untuck it.

It's a photograph. A Polaroid of Ian and a girl. His arm is around her and she's pulled close to him. To my horror, she's a stunner. I squint and bring the photo closer. Yep. Gorgeous.

Is this jealousy? It's like heartburn, only a thousand times worse. No, thanks.

I hear keys jiggling. I stuff the picture back in and plop myself on the couch, pretend to be preoccupied with my phone.

"Morning," he says.

He holds up a paper bag full of something. I smell bacon. And sausage. Across the room I can smell it like it's right under my nose.

"Morning," I say.

He smiles at me, and I wonder if he ever looked at the girl in the photo this way. I was never jealous of Kelly Iwanowski, but that girl in the Polaroid, the thought of him with someone else now, it makes me want to climb the walls.

He scoops coffee beans into a grinder. He gets out a French press. He would have a French press.

"You talk in your sleep," he says.

"I doubt it," I say, digging a bagel sandwich out of the bag.

"One's bacon, one's sausage. Whatever you want," he says. "Did you have bad dreams?"

"Bacon. Always bacon," I say. "I don't remember. Why?"

"You were breathing heavy. You kept saying no and tossing around. I tried to wake you, but I couldn't."

I deconstruct my sandwich to get to the bacon. "Can't recall."

He nods, plugging in an electric kettle.

It occurs to me that just because I don't remember having a nightmare, it doesn't necessarily mean I haven't had one. I always sleep alone, so how would I know?

It's a frightening thought.

"Sorry if I woke you," I say.

He looks back at me. He's got this expression, this singular look that is infuriatingly mysterious. There's no grin, no frown, no arch of the eyebrow, no hint of emotion. But I know there's something there, behind the steady mouth, the still brows. I can sense his thoughts, but I don't know what they are.

The need is what scares me.

I need to know.

The only reason it's gotten this far is because I've been 100 percent confident in his feelings for me, but it's possible for things to change. He said himself he had expectations. What if I didn't live up to them?

Not the sex. I know the sex was next level. But how he feels now. What if he doesn't feel the way he thought he would now that it's happened?

"What are you thinking?" I ask him. The question comes out mean. Accusatory.

He's not thrown by my tone. "I'm thinking a lot of different things."

"Care to enlighten me?" I ask. Cooler this time.

He pours the hot water over the coffee grounds. He waits until he's done to speak so he can look at me.

"I'm thinking about how much I liked you when we were kids," he says. "I'm thinking about how fucking amazing last night was. I'm thinking about how unreal it is to wake up next to you. You look the same. You are the same. And it's messing with my head, because I go between feeling like I'm fourteen again and knowing I'm not. Knowing I'm not the same. And also, I'm thinking about how impossibly cool you are."

"I'm cool?"

"Yeah," he says. "You know that."

"No, I know," I say.

"I liked you back in middle school, high school, but I also wanted to be you. You and Scarlett were so cool. You knew exactly who you were. You had so much confidence. I wondered what it must be like. I aspired to be like that."

I don't know what to say. He just says these things. These disarmingly honest things that I don't know what to do with. I take a deep breath and pick at my bagel.

"That's how you felt then," I say, unable to meet his eyes. "How do you feel now?"

I can't believe I just asked that question. This is the worst.

"No," he says. "Nuh-uh. It's your turn."

"What do you mean?"

"You tell me."

"Tell you what?"

"You tell me how you feel."

Absolutely not.

"I feel . . . like . . ." I say, "we should fuck on the kitchen floor."

He laughs. "That's cheating."

"What?" I ask, approaching him. "You asked me how I feel."

"You know that's not what I meant."

I put my arms around him, tilt my head back to look up at him with my eyes big. He lifts me up and puts me on the counter. I start to kiss his neck. I take his earlobe between my teeth.

"You're an animal," he tells me.

My heart stops. I stop.

I can smell his sweat. Briny and delicious.

"Yeah, maybe I am," I tell him, and I can only hope he's listening.

I'm there for three days. He drops me off Sunday night, and I stumble into the house on tired legs. Reaper barks at me, but I don't match his hostility. I ignore him, walk straight over to the couch, and collapse there beside Scarlett.

"Sorry. Do you still live here?" she asks.

I steal some of her blanket. "Mm."

"I'd ask you how it went, but . . ."

I giggle.

"Good for you," she says. "You reek."

I grab one of her legs and cuddle it. She doesn't kick me away. "I'm sorry I was gone for so long. I missed you."

"Yeah, sure," she says. "Sure."

"I did!"

She sits up. "I had a doctor's appointment Friday."

"What? How come you didn't tell me? I would have gone with you."

"I'd rather go alone." She clears her throat. "Anyway. There are pictures upstairs. On my nightstand. She looks like a Xenomorph."

"Aw!"

"Oh, Mom gets in Saturday at eleven forty-five. Can you pick her up? I'll be at work."

"Sure." I'm in such a good mood, I'd agree to just about anything right now.

"Thanks," she says, stretching. "The kid is kicking. It feels intensely weird."

"If she is a baby Xenomorph, you're totally fucked."

She glares at me.

I smile big and goofy. I'm trying to ignore the steady simmer of my rage. The idea of Scarlett going to all her appointments alone because Matty is an asshole is too much. He was never my favorite, but I liked him fine. He had his moments. He made Scarlett laugh, genuinely laugh, which is hard to do. He could match our sarcasm. But I could never quite figure him out. Mom always adored him because he looks like a movie star. He might be the most beautiful man on the planet. But he knows it. He's aware.

"I'm excited to see what she looks like," I say. "When she's born."

There's a long pause. Then Scarlett says, "Me, too."

Later that night, after a shower and a power nap, I open my laptop and there it is. I thought I cleared my browser, my search history, but somehow one of the forums is up. Once again, I'm reminded that I'm running out of time to figure this werewolf shit out.

The full moon is on Friday.

VI

I find a crate in the basement that once belonged to Cloud, Scarlett's dog before Reaper, a sweet but smelly German shepherd mix with a penchant for crotch sniffing.

I stare at it.

I decided it's best to prepare for the worst, as ridiculous as it feels. The alternative is to do nothing but cross my fingers, and that seems pretty high-risk.

Luckily, I was able to pick up my car from the shop yesterday, so now the plan is to tell Scarlett that I'm going to Ian's, then drive somewhere and lock myself inside this crate in case I turn into a werewolf.

Yeah. Fine. Cool. Totally normal.

If nothing happens, then I'm just a relieved idiot in a dog crate somewhere. If it does, well, fuck me, I guess.

I crawl inside the crate. No smaller than your average NYC apartment.

It's easy enough to open the latch from the inside with my human fingers. From what I remember, the werewolf's claws were long, dexterous. But they looked broken. They bent weird.

They looked painful.

I remember ripped skin, glimpses of bone.

I get out of the crate.

I start disassembling it the best I can with trembling hands. When I'm done, I carry it piece by piece out to the trunk of my car. I get my handcuffs, too, for good measure. The only reason I brought them here is because I didn't want Laura happening upon my sex accessories. It's truly unfortunate that I'm repurposing them for this.

After I'm done packing the car, I make stir-fry and wait for Scarlett to get home.

When she does, she's quiet.

"How was your day?" I ask her.

"Oh, fine," she says.

I fix her a plate and she accepts it but doesn't eat, just prods at it with her fork. I make my own plate, mostly beef, avoiding the rice and vegetables.

"I'm going to Ian's tomorrow night," I lie.

"Okay. Just remember you're picking Mom up from the airport Saturday."

"Yep. Got it."

"And remember I'm working tomorrow," she says.

"The shop or studio?"

When she's not tattooing, Scarlett works as a freelance illustrator and has a studio space she shares with a few other local artists.

"Studio," she says. "I've got a headache. I'm gonna go lie down."

"Okay," I say. "You need anything?"

"No. Thanks, though."

She goes upstairs, leaving me alone with Reaper, who grunts in my general direction. I finish the beef on Scarlett's plate, and whatever's left in the wok. After, I go out back and hit my vape. The sky is clear, and the moon gleams above me, resurrecting the pain in my side. My bones undulate, and when I exhale, the thick cloud of my breath unfurls from my nostrils down across the lawn, rolling like a fog.

I put my vape away and go back inside.

I struggle to sleep, anxiously anticipating tomorrow night. My phone lights the dark.

It's a message from Ian. It says, Thinking about you.

What else is new? I text back.

Not a thing.

I close my eyes and fall asleep smiling.

We used to go to the distillery to party as teenagers. It's been abandoned for years, a big stone shell overgrown with moss, filled with beer cans and tasteless graffiti. It's in the middle of the woods, the middle of nowhere. We never got caught, so I figure it's as good a place as any to set up shop.

It's a frigid November dusk. Doesn't matter. I can barely feel the cold. The sun has almost set. I'm scrambling through the woods with a dog crate and sex handcuffs, praying for that pinkish twilight to hang on a just little longer. The day went by too fast. I slept in too late. Kept doing stupid internet searches in hope of answers, all in vain.

The distillery comes into view. It's deteriorated significantly since I was last here. The roof has partially collapsed, and I doubt it's safe for me to go inside, but it's even less safe for me not to.

I enter through the gaping hole of a door. It's as I remember. Dank. Pipes jutting out from all angles. Smashed beer cans and bottles. A rat skitters along the edge of my view.

I don't have any time to waste. I start setting up the crate. I make quick work of it, ignoring the rats scuffling through piles of dead leaves and rotting wood.

I set my mind to this. This is the plan. I can't question myself.

My heartbeat keeps skipping, but I won't stop.

I can't stop. There is no second-guessing.

I made the mistake of doubting myself before. Such a big mistake.

Shadows pool around me.

I get into the crate. I reach through and close the latch. I go to handcuff myself. I hesitate.

I hesitate like I did in the car, with Dave. I don't know why tonight feels like that. It feels just like that afternoon. That sick in my gut. My heart in my throat.

I'm stuck. Trapped in this crate, this body, this moment. There is no out. No distraction. No escape.

The light fades. The shadows sneak toward me. Like his fingers. Like his hands in the car.

When she first brought Dave around, I knew right away. She let him come to our eleventh birthday party. That's when we first met him. I saw him there, through the orange glow of my birthday candles, in blue jeans and a white T-shirt. His hands were deep in his pockets, and he kept licking his lips. His eyes were big and unblinking, focused on me. He smiled with his entire face. His eyes, his eyebrows, his cheeks, his mouth. Everything except his teeth. Those he kept hidden.

It was a blaring alarm, a physical reaction. A visceral disgust.

I don't like him.

I remember the sugar smell of the frosting, the burning wax.

I don't like him.

"I don't like him," I told Mom the next morning over oatmeal after he'd left for work.

"You don't know him," she said. "Scarlett?"

"He seems nice."

The night before, as we fell asleep, I told Scarlett. I warned her.

"He's the worst one so far."

"You say that about all of them," she said. "At least he's not Jesse."

Jesse would get drunk and call Mom a bitch, a slut. He hit her once. After, he cried on our front porch, apologizing and begging Mom to take him back. She did, of course. I wanted to tell him that he didn't need to beg. She would have taken him back no matter what.

"Jesse acted nice at first," I said to Scarlett.

She ignored me, pretended to be asleep. She didn't mind Mom's boyfriends as much as I did. Scarlett was the sweet one, easygoing, liked to get along with everyone. Didn't care for confrontation. I was the problem child.

"Can you please try to give him a chance?" Mom asked, pouring some chocolate chips into my oatmeal.

"He's weird," I said. "Skeeves me out."

"Rory. For me? Please? Don't you want me to be happy?"

It's dark. I'm waiting for something to happen. I look up through the hole in the roof.

No moon yet.

What's taking it so long?

I don't want to think. I don't want to feel. I want to run, but I can't. I'm stuck. Trapped.

"I hear you're not my biggest fan," he said, sitting next to me at the kitchen table as I did my homework.

"No," I said without looking up.

He laughed. "I like you, kid. You speak your mind. I like that. And I like a challenge."

He opened his palm to reveal a small hot pink pencil sharpener. He set it on the table. "Stay sharp, kid."

I was using a pencil, and it needed to be sharpened. I don't know how he knew what I needed, but he knew. He was good at knowing things. He was always paying attention to me. I thought maybe I was wrong about him.

Because there were more little gifts like the pencil sharpener. Like a new rainbow notebook and purple highlighters. Like raspberry-flavored dark chocolate bars.

"Don't tell your sister," he'd say, and I thought it was nice to be treated like my own person. Scarlett and I, we'd always been a unit. Until Dave.

Dave saw me as a separate entity. I appreciated that.

He started taking me to the library. Or to the video store to pick out a rental. Trips with just us. Mom was grateful for the extra effort he was putting in with me.

"Your opinion is important to him. He knows how much you and your sister mean to me."

I didn't mind these trips. I liked the experience of getting to go places, of getting to select books and videos. It felt very adult. It felt special.

There's a prickling at the back of my neck. My hands and feet go numb. It's so cold. It's so cold tonight, and I can't feel it. It's there but it isn't. And I can no longer hear my heart. Is it even beating anymore?

I can hear the crate as it rattles around me, an incessant reminder of my confinement. Of my isolation.

I was alone in my room. I had a cold, and I'd gone up to bed early.

"How you feelin'?" he asked me, sitting on my bed. This was the first time I remember him touching me, though I know he touched me before then, because at first this touch didn't feel strange to me. Because there had been a hand on the shoulder, a ruffling of the hair. High-fives and fist bumps.

He put his hand on my forehead, like he was trying to take my temperature.

Then his hand moved. It was on my stomach. On my chest.

I coughed, and then he kissed me. A peck on the corner of my mouth.

"Feel better," he whispered in my ear. "Because you know I like you best."

Everyone had always liked Scarlett best, because she was easier. More polite. She never talked back. Never asked questions. I was always asking questions. I asked so many questions.

That night, I had fever dreams. I sweat through my sheets.

I'm sweating now. Sweltering. There's no cold, no trace of it at all.

There's nothing except these memories. They're unyielding.

"Dave was really worried about you," Mom said the next morning.

It was just the two of us. I was too sick to go to school, so she had to call out of work. We sat side by side on the couch, eating plain overdone toast.

"It's so sweet, your bond."

"He kissed me," I said. "Here."

I pointed. She clicked her tongue and shooed the crumbs from her lap.

"It's paternal affection. That's how it's supposed to be. I know you're not used to it, but trust me, it's good to have a man in your life who can set an example of how you should be treated. You and Scarlett."

"He's different with Scarlett."

"He's not."

"Yes, he is."

"Well, he cares about you. You should be grateful."

I didn't know what to say to that, so I said nothing, just choked down my toast.

I can taste it now. Burned and bitter. It's heavy on my tongue. It's in my nose, my throat, my lungs.

I don't want these memories. I don't want these thoughts. I don't want to go back there.

But there's nowhere else for me to go.

I'm stuck. Trapped.

I take off my winter coat. It's too warm. I'm soaked. Dripping.

My shoes now. I take off my shoes. My socks. The rats are watching. I feel their eyes on me. I'm exposed. Vulnerable.

The heat was on. In his car, the heat was always on. I took off my jacket.

"You're a beautiful girl," he said, his eyes on me. "Your mother. Your sister, but especially you."

"Scarlett and I look the same," I said.

"You're prettier."

No one had ever said that to me before.

We'd been in the car alone together many times. Many, many times. But this was the time. A rainy Tuesday, on the way to pick up a pizza. He let me sit in the front seat of his truck. He always did that.

He pulled off the road and parked in a random driveway in front of an empty lot. There were trees on all sides. The leaves were green. It was spring.

"Rory, I have to tell you a secret," he said.

I didn't want to know it.

"I really like you a lot," he said. "I think you're really special. And I

want to do something special with you. I want to show you something special."

There's a sound. A faint tearing somewhere.

I'm rocking back and forth now. It's involuntary. My lips are glued together. My eyes are closed.

I'm afraid. I'm losing control. And it's bringing me back, keeps bringing me back. There's no escape.

I shake my head. It's a violent shaking. Something has a hold on me. It's blazing.

He started to do something I didn't understand. He touched himself. He made this horrible groaning noise. He kept looking at me. With those eyes. Those big hollow eyes.

I didn't know what to do. I wanted to reach for the door, to unlock it, but I couldn't. There was panic and there was fear and confusion and I wanted it to stop but it kept happening and I wanted to close my eyes but I was too scared, and I wanted to scream but I couldn't find one, and I wanted help but there was none. I wanted to escape but I didn't know how. I was stuck. Trapped.

I had never felt so young, but I knew I would never be young again.

When he finished, he said, "Our secret?"

I nodded. I was silent through dinner, and that night when Scarlett asked me why, I told her. I told her everything.

"What should I do?" I asked her.

She shook her head. At first, I thought she was upset, confused like I was. But then I realized. Then I saw it. Doubt.

"What?" I asked her.

"I don't know," she said. "Maybe he had an itch."

I snuck downstairs to the kitchen. I found my mother there alone, standing at the counter, smoking a cigarette over a tall stack of bills.

"I need to talk to you," I whispered. "About Dave."

"Not now, Rory," she snapped. "I've got a million other things. I don't want to hear it. I really don't."

I was too tired. I couldn't bring myself to plead, to beg just to be heard. I retreated upstairs. I crawled under my bed, held my knees, and cried myself to sleep.

The next day, I went straight to Mrs. Meyer, the guidance counselor, and told her what had happened. She said I did the right thing, coming to her. She told me that everything would be okay, and that it wasn't my fault.

She listened to me, believed me. No one else had listened. If they'd listened . . .

Dave was already a registered sex offender when my mother met him. When she brought him into our house to sleep under our roof.

And he's somewhere out there. Out of prison by now. Under this same . . .

Moon.

The screaming isn't just of my throat. It's every fiber of me. Every bone, every muscle, cartilage, organs. My insides are seizing.

The moon pecks out my eyes. It roves down my throat, twists through my ears, up my nostrils. It's underneath my fingernails, my toenails, peeling them up and off slowly. It's in me. It's in me now.

I fall over onto my back, thrashing. My clothes rip. My skin splits at my side, the bite reopening. I watch as it stretches thin, as I expand, and it bursts apart. It's loud. I can hear it over my screaming. The fur spreads from the bite, from wherever the skin is broken. There's no blood. Only fur. Horrible, matted grayish fur.

The piercing shrieks of bones breaking come in quick succession like fireworks. It's my ribs rapidly broadening, the wrench of my spine, my neck snapping so my head falls dead to one side, only for it to re-form. Agony rakes my legs. I watch as they grow. I don't want it. I don't want it.

My kneecaps emerge like tiny skulls, staggeringly white domes. My shins swell. My feet. The skin explodes open, the bones splintering as they lengthen. I can feel the calluses form. I can feel it like someone's holding a lighter to the pads of my feet, like someone's stroking the burns with sandpaper.

I flip over onto my stomach, as my arms reach out in front of me. Reach, and reach, and reach. I'm not screaming for the pain alone anymore. I'm screaming at the absolute loss of control. I'm trapped in this deranged body. I'd rather die.

I'm screaming because I want to die.

The screeching ceases because there's something happening to my throat. It's the moonlight. It's scraping me out from the inside. It's taking things. It's taking me.

I'm choking on it.

My jaw comes unhinged. I feel it hit the cold metal of the crate. And my teeth. Each tooth falls like hail onto the ground. The new ones grow in slow. It's the slowest part; they stab through my gums. Now I'm spitting out blood. Silver blood. There's so much of it, my hands slip, only they aren't my hands anymore.

New nails stick through my fingers and toes.

"No!" I scream, though no one's listening.

I can't say it again. I don't have a voice anymore. Nothing comes out but roaring.

It's done now.

I know because I feel good. I'm here but I'm not.

I have so much energy. So much hunger.

I sniff. I claw.

I smell blood. Where's blood?

The crate doesn't make any sense anymore.

I break it easily.

I'm so strong. I snap it like twigs. I crush it.

There's movement. I've got a rat in my jaws. I clamp down. It ruptures. I swallow it mostly whole.

It makes me only hungrier.

I scale the walls of the distillery until I'm standing on what's left of the roof. The moon is so close to me, I feel like I can touch it. I feel . . .

I feel fucking incredible.

I let my head fall back and howl.

Then the night goes black.

I come to, shivering in a ditch.

I'm naked, and my head is pounding so badly, it's unreal.

I climb barefoot out of the ditch, still in a daze. I see the distillery through the trees and am able to orient myself and get back to it. I put on my coat, my shoes. Find my keys. I follow the path to my car. I blast the heat and sit for a moment before opening the car door and vomiting out of it. It's a brutal puke. I blink when it's over. My vomit is red. I see fur. And teeth.

I vomit more.

I find an old water bottle in the backseat and drink from it. Then I vomit that up, too.

I wonder if I'll ever stop vomiting.

I search for Advil in my bag and swallow three. I wait another few minutes to make sure I don't puke those up. I pull down the sun visor and check my reflection in the mirror. I look like myself. A little dirty, but otherwise fine. I curl my lips back. My teeth look like my teeth, though my gums are red. I prod them with my tongue. They hurt.

I speed home. It's seven o'clock in the morning. I sneak into the house. Luckily Scarlett's in her bathroom showering, so she can't see the state I'm in.

Reaper, on the other hand, lunges at me. He gets me. Latches onto my ankle. Weirdly, I can't feel it. He seems disappointed by my indifference and lets go.

I start the shower and take off my coat. I drink some water from the faucet, then turn around to vomit it up. I spy a few tiny teeth in the bottom of the toilet bowl before I flush.

I'm so nauseous, I don't want to exist.

I smell so bad. So bad.

I scrub myself in the shower, trying not to pass out as the night comes back to me in flashes.

I remember seeing myself transform. I remember it was painful. I remember the horror of my screaming, of writhing there in the crate, hearing myself scream like I've never screamed, but I can't summon any of the sensations. They're elusive.

My body carries no trace of the gruesome transformation. My skin is smooth. No fresh cuts. No bruises. Nothing except the faint array of marks at my side, the tomb of the bite that devoured my body, my life.

When I get out of the shower, I wait for the steam to dissipate and take a quick, cautious look at my reflection.

Despite feeling like absolute garbage, I look good. I have no dark circles under my eyes. No blemishes. My hair is thick and dries almost instantaneously in perfect loose curls.

I dart into my room, hoping to avoid any interaction with Scarlett, or Reaper, though his bite from less than an hour ago has already healed.

I stand naked, running my hands over my skin.

"I'm okay," I say to myself, but my voice is so hoarse, I sound possessed.

I cough, and the fit becomes so violent that it knocks me off-balance and suddenly I'm on the floor, retching on all fours.

Something slithers up from my esophagus and out onto the carpet.

It's a rat tail.

I run back to the bathroom and hover over the toilet for the next hour so exhausted, I can barely form thoughts.

When I'm done, I pick up the rat tail with a wad of toilet paper and flush it. Then I get into bed and close my eyes, hoping that when I open them, I won't remember any of the things that came out of me this morning.

I wake up sometime later, my head still hammering. I stumble out of bed and put on a pair of sweatpants, a bra, and some thick socks. I zip up a hoodie over my bra, and even that feels like too much effort. I slide down the stairs on my ass, too dizzy to keep upright.

I'm spent but starving. I yawn on my way into the kitchen.

"Hello."

I gasp.

It's my mother. She sits at the kitchen counter, drinking coffee from a to-go up, her suitcase beside her.

"You scared me," I say. "Oh, shit."

"That's all right," she says, jumping up to hug me. "My baby."

She wraps her arms tight around me. She smells like Chanel No. 5 and French vanilla coffee and Virginia Slims and airplane. A hint of airplane bathroom. My sense of smell has become too keen.

"I'm sorry. I have a migraine," I say. "I was supposed to pick you up. I slept in. I didn't mean to."

"I know, I know," she says. "I figured. I took a cab."

"I really am sorry," I say.

She's still hugging me. "No worries, baby." She finally pulls away from me. "Look at you. I did something right with you girls, didn't I? Gave you all my good genes. All your daddy's good genes. None of the bad, none of the bad."

My mother is beautiful. She takes great pride in her appearance. Her favorite thing now is to be asked if she's our sister. I'm surprised she's let her hair go gray, but it suits her. Highlights the green of her eyes.

She wears an elegant black trench coat, a gray turtleneck sweater dress, and ivory knee-high boots with a significant heel.

"You want Advil?" she asks me.

"I took some."

"Water?"

"Had some."

"Cigarette?"

"Sure. Why not?"

We sit on the front steps sharing a cigarette. It's overcast, not as cold today as it was last night.

Last night.

"So," Mom says, "how is she?"

"Where's Guy?" I ask.

Guy is my stepdad. Only took a few dozen losers to find him. He's smart, kind, successful. A little milquetoast. They live in Charleston.

"He had a work thing," she says. "He'll come when the baby is born. Besides, I thought maybe if it was just me, Scarlett might feel more comfortable opening up about the situation."

"The situation," I say, scoffing.

"Well . . ."

"Don't bring it up. She doesn't want to talk about him. And she's not into baby stuff, so please don't bring that up either."

She hands the cigarette back to me. "It's just because of Matty. If he were here, everything would be different. Trust me."

"It's not just Matty. She doesn't like being pregnant."

"It's because she's alone," she says.

I pass the cigarette back.

"I don't think so," I say. "I don't know. I don't blame her. Seems pretty sucky to me. Not to be in control of your own body."

I blink and see the spread of my rib cage. The deficiency of my skin. I hear it splitting.

"It's a beautiful experience," Mom says. "You'll see. Someday."

I scoff again. "Sure."

Despite my best attempt to resist the thought, Ian is there. Does he want kids? Is there a life possible with him, a future?

I doubt it. Because I'm a fucking werewolf.

"Can I have my own cigarette?" I ask.

She offers me the pack, then reaches over and tucks some stray hair behind my ear. "My girl."

"Proud of me?" I ask sarcastically as I light my cigarette.

"So proud. My smart Ivy League girl. My big-city girl. It's so good to see you. I miss you, you know? I miss you all the time. Every second of every day."

"Every second?"

"Yes," she says. "We never get to spend time together like this. I've been really looking forward to this week. And I'm grateful that you came here to be with your sister when she needed you."

Another flash of memory, this time of shoving a wiggling rat into my gullet.

I close my eyes and rub my temples.

The moon appears, a bright perfect circle in the dark behind my eyelids.

I shudder.

"You okay, baby? You want to go lie down?"

"Yeah," I say. "Once I finish this cigarette."

I lie on my back, staring at the ceiling.

I was attacked. I was bitten by a werewolf. Now I'm a werewolf. Now, according to lore, once a month, every full moon, I will transform into a monster. It will hurt. Every time, it will hurt. And while I'm this monster, under the influence of the moon, I will have no control over what I do. I will lose myself.

And the next day, I will wake up and have to go on. I'll have to accept the suffering. The regular, involuntary surrender of my body. I have no other choice than to deal with it. What can I do?

There's no telling anyone. No sharing this burden. It's mine. It's my body.

I clutch the pillow and cry.

I come down around dinnertime, after about an hour of listening to Mom's and Scarlett's laughter and the clanks of cookery echoing through the house.

They look chummy as usual. Mom drinks a glass of red wine, Scarlett drinks a Diet Dr Pepper through a curly straw, and they huddle over a magazine. It's a scene I'm familiar with. The two of them, thick as thieves, not caring about the things I care about.

"Hello, sleepyhead," Mom says, spotting me in the dark of the living room. "You want a glass of wine?"

My head is still misery, and I know I can't get buzzed from it, but I say yes anyway.

Scarlett refuses to meet my eye, and it doesn't take long to figure out why.

"Your sister tells me you have a boyfriend," Mom says, pouring my glass to the brim. "I always liked Ian. Good manners. Calm. He had positive energy. Lovely light blue aura. You know, I ran into him last time I was here. I told you, they never stay that skinny. I like a man like that. Burly. Like a big bear."

I put my head down on the counter, feel its coolness against my forehead.

"I can't believe you just said that," Scarlett says.

"Oh!" Mom says. "I didn't . . . Oh, I'm sorry. Not like a bear."

I hear her set my wineglass down. I pick my head up so I can chug it.

"I'm sorry, baby. I forgot about that," she says. "You know, I only heard about it from your sister. I did call. And text. Many times. I wish you'd called me back. After something like that."

I finish the wine and set the glass back down.

"More, please."

"Anyway, I'm glad you're seeing someone," Mom says, honoring my request for more wine. "Life isn't meant to be lived alone."

"It is," I say. "By design."

She makes a disapproving smacking noise with her mouth.

"And let me just say," I start, continuing despite Scarlett's eye roll. "One, I'm not really alone. I have Scarlett. I have a twin. I came in a set. Two, I don't have a boyfriend. Ian Pedretti is not my boyfriend. It's not happening."

I lean back and pour the wine straight down my throat.

I should not have gotten out of bed.

"Why not?" Mom asks.

"Because," I say, "I'm going back to the city in five months."

"And what will you do there? What are you doing there?"

"My job. My career. Making damn good money. Experiencing everything the greatest city in the world has to offer. Going to museums. Seeing friends. Having casual fun with strangers I never have to see or think about ever again. I'm living the dream."

"Going to museums," Scarlett mutters under her breath.

"I always thought you'd make a great teacher," Mom says, sipping her wine. "You're generous but no-nonsense. And so smart."

"I'm the youngest VP at my firm."

"You could have a nice life here. With your sister. With Ian."

I look at Scarlett for help, but she appears to be distracted by whatever's in the large pot on the stove. She's happy leaving me out to dry so long as Mom isn't picking on her.

"I can't have a life with Ian," I say, throwing my hands up. "I can't. It's not happening. So why don't we change the subject to something more pleasant, like—I don't know—the death penalty? Where do we land on that?"

"Or an actress," Mom says. "You could have been an actress. You're pretty enough. You've always had that dramatic flair."

"A woman dares present an opinion about anything and suddenly she's dramatic."

"It's a shame you aren't tall enough to model," she says. "You're too beautiful to be single. Both of you."

I press my fingers into my eyes. "You know, if you really want to talk about my love life, I'm happy to discuss the time I gave a certain New York Yankee a hand job under the table at Soho House."

"No, thank you," Mom says.

"I've already heard that one," Scarlett says.

"Moving on, then," I say, raising my glass. "What are we eating?"

After a dinner of baked salmon and mashed potatoes and asparagus—which of course I don't eat—I wash dishes while Mom dries. Scarlett works on an illustration in the living room.

"She seems fine," Mom whispers. "Happy."

"She's in a good mood tonight," I say.

As much as I'd rather not acknowledge it, the truth is, it is kind of nice to be together. The three of us. Just us. No Guy. No Matty. It's been a long time. It's the nostalgia factor, I suspect.

"I was thinking about a shower," she says.

"Okay, I can finish up."

"No, for Scarlett. A baby shower."

"Oh," I say. "Absolutely not. She'd hate it."

"She needs things. She doesn't have a crib. A stroller. A changing table. She needs these things. I already spoke to Ashley. She put together a registry."

"You talked to Ash?"

"*Shh!* She'll hear you."

"This is a bad idea," I say, aggressively scrubbing a plate.

"She hasn't had the opportunity to be excited," she says. "This is the perfect occasion for her to celebrate with her friends and family."

"She doesn't like attention," I say. "I like attention, and even to me a shower sounds harrowing."

"See? So dramatic," she says, literally throwing in the towel. "It's Friday. I hope you'll consider helping me."

"Yeah," I say. "I'll consider it."

She squeezes my arm and joins Scarlett over on the couch.

I finish the dishes by myself, then take the bottle of wine and Mom's cigarettes out onto the back patio. It's cloudy. There's no moon, so I'm at peace. As much peace as possible after what happened last night. What was confirmed.

Not so much peace as just not agony.

I drink the wine and chain-smoke the cigarettes, lighting them with matches. I let the flame burn down to my fingers. It doesn't hurt when it reaches my skin. It leaves a mark, but it fades fast.

These things, they won't go unnoticed forever.

I realize I actually can't go back to the city. I can't be like this there.

It'd be a logistical nightmare. I couldn't transform in my apartment; it's not exactly a discreet process. It's violent and loud; my neighbors would most definitely call the cops out of concern or to complain. Also, I don't trust that a door or window would stop me from attacking one or more of the millions of people wandering around. So I'd need to leave, to go somewhere else. But I can't take off multiple days from work every month for the full moon. Having a car in Manhattan is both insanely expensive and inconvenient, though I doubt I could take the train with the necessary equipment. And what about traffic, delays? And where would I even go? It'd take hours to get somewhere remote enough, and I'd need to somehow acquire, store, and transport a sturdier cage. . . .

Yeah. My life as I know it is over.

I down the rest of the bottle, hoping that maybe if I drink it quickly, I'll feel something. A relaxing buzz. But all I feel is nauseous. I burp, and out comes . . . something. I feel a kernel traveling up my throat, across my tongue. I spit it into my palm.

It's a small yellowy mystery tooth.

I shake it from my hand.

It would sure be nice if I could get a break for a fucking second. My body won't allow it. I feel like a dog wearing a retractable leash.

I heave again, and it's followed by a small acidic burp, my body asserting itself, always asserting itself with blood and sweat and aches and pain and gas and bile. A reluctance to process dairy.

"I get it," I whisper into my skin. "You win. I'm at your mercy."

My body answers with another heave, because I belong to it more than it belongs to me.

VII

The next few days tangle together, a mess of sleeping in too late, going to bed too early. Waking sweat drenched and breathless from nightmares I can't quite remember. Avoiding my reflection because I know the wolf will be there waiting in the mirror. Going out to the gas station to replace my mother's cigarettes and getting some for myself. I stop at the liquor store and buy a fifth of Fireball, not that it has any effect. I keep hoping.

I'm desperate for anything that will numb me to this endless string of shitty realizations.

Realizations like I'm now going to have to plan my entire life around when there's a full moon. I'm going to have to find somewhere new to live. Maybe a new job. Realizations like I can't keep seeing Ian.

If he knew the truth, he'd want nothing to do with me. I could lie, try to keep this part of me a secret, but for how long?

It seems excessively cruel. My entire life I've reveled in my independence, and the second I open myself up to the possibility of a relationship, it's snatched out of my hands.

He's texted me twice. Once to send me an article about a band he told me about, and another time to ask me if I'm free next weekend after my mom leaves.

I haven't been able to bring myself to respond.

I have managed to send some strong words to Ash about the ill-advised baby shower.

Your mom reached out! I couldn't say no! she said.

Fair. It's hard to say no to my mother.

It's happening Friday afternoon.

None of those horrible games, I told Ash.

I'm doing my best!! she said.

I don't know how I'm getting through this week without anesthetic.

"I'm worried about you," Mom says.

It's Thursday. We're out running errands for Scarlett's shower, and she insisted we stop for a mother-daughter lunch. Scarlett had sent me a stern text about spending time with Mom, so here I am.

We sit inside at the Bedford Inn, the oldest restaurant in town. I can smell mildew. There's rotten food hiding somewhere. There are also some good cuts of meat in the fridge.

They're serving brunch. I order steak and eggs and a Bloody Mary. Mom orders an arugula salad and a mimosa.

"What are you worried about?" I ask, sipping my Bloody Mary. "Scarlett's the one knocked up."

"She'll be okay," she says. "I know she will. And once the baby's born, I think Matty will be back."

"Ew. Fuck him," I say.

The surge of anger surprises me. For a moment, I see nothing but red. My fingers curl in, nails digging into my palms. I huff and puff until I can regain control of myself. I take a deep breath and another sip of my Bloody Mary.

She gives me a look.

"What?"

"You know, I held it against your father for a long time, him leaving. But it ended up being for the best."

Best for whom? I wonder.

"It's not for you to be angry with Matty," she says. "It's not good to be so angry. With Matty. With me. For the past."

For Dave is what she's trying to but can't say.

"I'm not having any serious discussions over brunch," I say, gnawing on my celery just to have something to break between my teeth. "We can talk about this baby shower, or how things are in Charleston, or I can talk to you about my job, or preferred brands of powdered collagen, or gossip from my rich-person gym. Those are the approved topics."

"Fine," she says, unfolding her napkin across her lap. "But you know I love you, and your sister loves you, and now we're going to have a new family member, and I know it weighs heavy on all of us. There are a lot of feelings that have resurfaced over the past few years. I wish you'd talk to me. It's not healthy to leave these things unresolved."

"It's been unresolved," I say. "It can wait until after brunch."

Our food comes, truly perfect timing. She lets it go. We talk about the things we need to get for the shower.

She pays the check, then drives us to the grocery store and then to Target to pick up some supplies to drop off at Ash's.

Ash is hosting so it can be a surprise, because the only thing better than a baby shower is a *surprise* baby shower. Ash left the door unlocked for us, and we find her in the kitchen, hovering over her stand mixer, wearing a frilly apron.

"Your hair," she says, sweeping it out of the folds of my hoodie. "It's so shiny! I feel like it's grown inches since I last saw you! What are you using?"

"Nothing," I answer. "Honest."

"You Morris women and your good genes," she says. "Cyndi! Hi!"

She hugs my mother.

Luca comes scooting into the room atop a tiny fire truck. He presses a button and a musical alarm sounds.

"Beep beep!" he screams. "Beep! Beeeeeep!"

He runs over my toe, looking me right in the eye as he does it. Frankly, I admire his fortitude.

"Oh, he's gotten so big!" Mom says. "Those curls! Those dimples!"

"He's a little terror," Ash says, smiling proudly. "He makes such a mess. Come, sit. There's coffee and shortbread."

"So what's the plan for tomorrow?" I ask.

I smell pee somewhere. I suspect Luca's potty training is not going well.

This new sense of smell is distracting, and I miss something Mom says.

"Sorry. Can you repeat that?"

She lays out the plan. I'm meant to get to Ash's early, help set up. Mom's bringing Scarlett over around one o'clock. Scarlett thinks we're having lunch with just Ashley. Surprise.

I'm still uneasy about the whole thing, but I haven't really had the energy to dedicate to worrying about it. I've been too busy sleeping eighteen hours a day and sweating through my sheets and chain-smoking and trying to navigate the minefield that is my relationship with my mother and, occasionally, Googling "werewolf cure" before getting discouraged and crying and/or laughing at the absurdity of my circumstance.

Putting a stop to this baby shower hasn't been as high on my priority list as it probably should be.

Too late now.

Mom gets up and goes to the bathroom, leaving me alone with Ash. Luca's once again been given the iPad in exchange for silence.

"How's it been having Cyndi around?" she asks.

Ash is one of the few people who knows about what happened with Dave. She was over at our house all the time; there was no way for her not to know, not to sense something was amiss. She didn't pry; Scarlett asked for my permission to tell her, and I gave it, not wanting to deprive my sister of someone to confide in. I knew Ash was trustworthy. She's always been considerate, respectful, nonjudgmental. She never asked me why I didn't get out of the car or any of the other unfair questions that I always asked myself.

"Fine, I guess. She picks on me, and I know it's coming from a good place, but it doesn't matter. We've talked about this. I made excuses for her for so long. Once the spell's broken, it's hard to see anything else. The manipulation, the selfishness, the immaturity."

"I hear you," she says. "I understand."

"I know you do, angel face. Anyway . . ."

"I'm sorry about the shower," she says. "I do think it's a good idea. I think it'll be fun. I think she'll like it."

I shrug. "Maybe."

"How's Ian?" she asks, grinning.

"Wouldn't know."

She frowns. "What do you mean? Did something happen?"

"It's not serious," I say. The words come to me, and I can't help but laugh. "I'm a lone wolf."

"I just think you'd be so good together."

Luca interrupts by stripping naked and flailing around on the floor. Mom and I take it as our cue to go.

On the drive home, Mom tries to bring up Dave again.

"I love her," she says of Ash. "She's always been such a good friend to you girls. When everything happened, she was there for you and your sister. She's done a lot for us."

"Yep."

"I know you have a lot of resentment toward me," she says. "I can feel it."

"Mom. I don't." The lie is so big, it barely fits through my lips.

"You've been avoiding me," she says. "Up in your room. I was hoping we could finally talk."

"This is the first break I've had," I say. "Undergrad, MBA, work . . . I'm enjoying being lazy, that's all."

"I don't know what happened," she says. "It never used to be like this. Even when you were a teenager, it was never like this. You always talked to me. Now you don't talk to me. I rarely get any time with you."

"Well, let's not ruin it by bringing up the past," I say. "Let's do something else. Let's go to the mall."

This gets her. She can't resist a mall. Honestly, neither can I.

We drive an hour away to the ritzy mall. We browse designer bags, waltz around Fendi and Chanel and Nordstrom, pretending to be rich but not actually buying anything. Not for ourselves anyway. We get Scarlett an assortment of fancy lotions.

We find a baby boutique nearby and go nuts. We buy onesies and little outfits and blankets and bags full of organic baby products.

It's the best time I've had with Mom since I can remember. Nothing like throwing money at a problem.

I'm in a fine mood until on the drive home when she says, "Tomorrow morning I'm going to need you to get the balloons."

"Okay. Where?"

"Party City."

Maybe the wolf did kill me and I'm in hell.

It's late. I'm smoking a cigarette out of my bedroom window like a teen delinquent when my phone rings.

It's Ian.

When we were kids, sometimes we'd talk on the phone for hours. We traded numbers so we could text each other complaints about Rich and Scarlett's excessive PDA, but our conversations quickly evolved beyond that. We'd talk about music and movies. I'd speculate wildly about the private lives of our teachers, and he'd occasionally chime in with something ridiculously specific, like how he suspected our history teacher Ms. Bleeker would whisper-sing ballads to her houseplants, and our gym teacher Mr. Shandy would cry whenever he lost at board games.

"Like, openly weep?" I remember asking.

"No, in private," he'd said. "He'd go to the bathroom. Lock the door. Muffle the sound with a towel."

"I can see it," I'd said. "When you're right, you're right."

At the time, I viewed these fun, easy conversations as standard, unextraordinary. When you're young, you're oblivious to what is rare because you don't have enough experience to identify it.

A diamond is just a rock until you hold it up to the light.

I know now how rare it is to have these fun and easy conversations. To understand someone and be understood.

But understanding someone and accepting them are two different things. One doesn't guarantee the other.

I clear the missed call from my screen and put my cigarette out on the back of my hand.

It's the middle of the night, and I'm descending the stairs. The house is dark and quiet. Quiet enough I can hear someone breathing.

Their inhale/exhale is interrupted by something. A slopping. A crude, wet noise so unnerving, I lose my balance and slip down the final step, alerting the breather to my presence.

They snarl.

If I could, I'd run back upstairs, hide in my room, lock the door.

But I can't. I'm dragged forward, towed into the kitchen like a hooked fish.

"Scarlett?" I ask.

The lights flick on, and I'm staring at myself. A version of me partially transformed. My mouth isn't my mouth. It's a wolf mouth, and it's saturated in blood. Red tendons dangle from my fangs. I'm feeding on something. There's carnage on the counter, and I hunch over it, feasting. Devouring. Fervently lapping up pools of blood, grinding bones between my teeth.

I look up, and my eyes burn red.

"Rory?"

I turn around, and behind me, it's Ian. He looks past me, through me. He can only see the monster.

It's the day of Scarlett's shower, and I am overwhelmed with dread. Also, I'm supremely pissed off. I'm mad that this is happening. That Scarlett has to suffer through this. That *I* have to suffer through it. That once again no one listened to me. My mood is foul.

I'm up early to make myself look presentable, to change out of this grimy sweat suit, which has become my uniform. I peel it off and toss it into the laundry, then go into the bathroom for a long-overdue shower.

I take a deep breath and face myself in the mirror.

It's there, lurking behind me. A smear of knotted fur and red eyes and cavernous jaws. I know if I just close my eyes, it will be gone when I open them, but I can't look away. I can't blink.

I smell it. I can smell the creature's breath. The fresh death lingering inside its open mouth.

I can almost feel the coil of its hand around my side. The sinking of its nails into the place where it bit me. Where it took me. Where it turned me.

"Fuck," I shout, throwing my hands up over my eyes. I leave them there, breathing into my wrists.

I allow my left hand to come down, let it slowly drop.

The wolf is still there. There, with one eye covered. Like me.

I step away from the mirror, and it does, too.

Its lips curl. My lips curl. It growls.

I growl.

I watch myself growl. Teeth bared. Face desiccated. Hateful.

I'm transfixed. Horrified.

And I'm alone now. Just me. Growling. Alone.

"This is bullshit," I snap.

I get it. I understand. The wolf will always be there in the mirror. The wolf is me. My second face.

I turn away from my reflection and step into the shower. I turn the water all the way hot, then all the way cold. I wait for my fists to unclench, for my spine to unwind. I wait to calm down.

I don't think it's going to happen for me. It's one of those days. My mood has been ordained. I'm a wretch.

I towel off and blow-dry my hair. It doesn't take long. It's thick and shiny and perfect. My lashes dark and curled, no mascara required. Lycanthropy is good for something, I guess.

I clip my nails, which has now become a daily requirement; otherwise it's like I've got on stiletto acrylics. There have been several unfortunate incidents including accidental scratches and a severe eye poke. Also makes it challenging to masturbate.

After carefully considering everything in my closet, I select a fitted navy dress with a cowl neck and long sleeves. I put my white satin blazer on over it and pair it with my rose gold heels.

I feel like myself again, like the person I was before I left the city. The person who woke up at four thirty a.m. for prework Pilates and wore high heels and jewelry and perfume, who drank green juice. A person who didn't sleep all day and hoard bags of beef jerky in their nightstand drawer.

I find some gold jewelry in my case. A pair of chunky hoops and a delicate necklace with, ironically, a moon charm. Fuck it. Why not?

I put it on.

All dressed up for . . . Party City.

I sneak out of the house before Scarlett can see me and ask me why I look nice. It's sad that my looking nice is now cause for suspicion, but I suppose I've earned it, since lately I've been couch fuzz incarnate.

It's too early to pick up the balloons, so I drive around for a while, listening to the band that Ian recommended. I've been doing my best not to think about him, but my best isn't good enough. I want to hate this band, but I don't. I really love them. Upbeat indie rock, a raspy-voiced singer, solid lyrics.

Ian knows my taste. We used to make each other playlists back in high school. I still listen to some of them.

I sit in the parking lot of Party City with my head on the steering wheel, stewing in my bad mood. I decide this is all Matty's fault. If he'd never left, I wouldn't have had to come here, and I wouldn't have been bitten. I hope he never comes back around. If I ever see him again, I might kill him.

I could.

It's an astonishing thought. It should scare me, but it doesn't. I catch myself smiling in the side-view mirror.

A feeling floods me like smoke through a burning building. My grip around a living thing, the easy squeeze, the swift crack of its neck. The red glaze of blood on my fur, shimmering in the moonlight. My rough tongue sweeping across the jagged edges of my teeth. So sharp. And my nails. So sharp. Lethal.

My eyes close, and it's here. The transcendent knowledge that nothing can touch me. That I'm not in danger, because I am danger.

I take a deep, gasping breath and accidentally graze the horn. It gives a short, startling beep that snaps me out of it. Brings me back into reality.

I throw myself out of the car and into the soberingly cold morning. I go get the fucking balloons.

I don't so much help Ashley decorate as I watch her decorate while eating breakfast sausages like they're potato chips. Luca is with her in-laws, and though I do find him exceptionally entertaining, it's nice to have a reprieve from his tyranny.

Ash made multiple quiches and a fruit tart, and set up an impressive mimosa bar. She also bought a cake shaped like a rattle, which I think looks vaguely phallic, an observation I choose to keep to myself.

"You think she'll like it?" Ash asks. "I incorporated as much black as possible."

She went for a bumblebee theme, pale yellow and black. There are adorable little bumblebees all around. The balloons I picked up are yellow and black, with some helium bees mixed in.

"It's different," I say. "I think she'll like it."

I do not think she will like it.

A few of Scarlett's friends arrive shy of one o'clock. Some I've met before, people she's known since college and coworkers. The people I haven't met marvel at how alike we look.

I get the sense that everyone is nervous. There's tension in the room. Usually, I'm impervious to tension. I've been known to enjoy watching people squirm. But this is different.

I get a whiff of something, and it clicks.

I can smell it. I can smell their sweat. Their uneasiness. Their dread.

I sniff.

Yep. It's so pungent, I can almost taste it.

These people all know Scarlett, and they know. This isn't her kind of thing.

"Kill me now," whispers a voice at my ear.

It takes me a second to identify the voice as something outside of myself, to distinguish it from my own cynical inner monologue.

It's Mia. She wears a zebra-print miniskirt and a low-cut white blouse that ties up the front. Her hair is pulled back in a high ponytail that falls straight down her back, sways as she moves, a swish of bright blond. She looks both stunning and stunningly out of place.

Bet Scarlett will be thrilled.

"Hey," I say. "What are you doing here?"

I don't mean it the way it sounds. She takes it in stride.

"Ashley is such a doll," she says, adjusting the clasp of her necklace, a black leather choker. She sports a fresh manicure that matches her zebra skirt. "She was probably just being nice, inviting me. Then I felt obligated."

She shrugs and looks around. "Regretting my decision now. I'm bored already. Mimosa?"

"Please."

"She's pulling up!" Ash says. "Hide in the dining room."

Mia and I lock eyes. I watch her take a bottle of champagne and slip it behind her back.

"I don't know if jumping out and shouting 'Surprise!' at someone seven months pregnant is a great idea," I say.

"We won't shout," Ash says.

Is it too late for me to leave and, if confronted, claim ignorance?

The front door opens.

"Surprise!" Ash shouts.

The friends come filtering out of the dining room.

Scarlett's face drains of color.

"Welcome to your baby shower!" Mom says, throwing her arms around Scarlett's shoulders in a chaotic hug.

"What?" Scarlett asks. Her eyes find me, and I mouth, *Sorry*.

"Come in, come in," Ash says, leading Scarlett into the kitchen.

"What's happening?" she asks, still looking at me.

"We wanted to celebrate," Mom says. "Celebrate you and the baby."

"Oh . . ." Scarlett says.

She pulls out a chair and sits down. I can sense her anxiety. It's palpable.

I get her a plate and a glass of sparkling cider. I sit next to her, and she squeezes my kneecap.

"I couldn't stop it," I whisper. "It's gonna be fine. None of that corny shit."

I expect some well-concealed anger, something only I'd be able to pick up on, but get none. All I get is a reserved "Thank you."

Mia strolls over and kneels in front of Scarlett.

"You look beautiful," she says, slipping Scarlett an envelope. "Maybe it's tacky to give cash, but I've heard babies are expensive. And I've never had a problem being tacky."

"Really? Never noticed," Scarlett says. "Thanks for coming. It's good to see you, Mia."

Overall, their reunion is surprisingly cordial.

People compliment the food, and from there the conversation starts. There's no fussing over Scarlett, no measuring her circumference like she's a science project. None of that. Just talking. It's surprisingly chill.

Time passes, and as it does, the unease dissipates. People are enjoying themselves. Scarlett is enjoying herself. I hear her laugh. Her friends are all cool, laid-back, similar in temperament to my sister.

Just when I start to relax, the front door opens, and in walks Matty's mother, Joann.

All my orifices cinch simultaneously.

"Sorry I'm late," she says. She walks straight up to my sister and kisses her on the cheek.

"Hi, Joann," Scarlett says.

I'm horrified, but Scarlett doesn't seem to be. They've always had a good relationship, but I would think that the current situation would have some effect.

"Thanks for coming," Mom says, giving Joann a hug.

I don't bother to hide my disgust. Ash pinches my arm, trying to get me to change my face. She can pinch me all she wants because I can't feel it. I'm undeterred.

I watch Scarlett closely, searching for some hint of something, a sign of how she's feeling, but she goes on smiling like she's fine.

Maybe I was wrong. Maybe this shower was a good idea. Maybe she's grateful for it.

She opts in to opening presents in front of everyone, so maybe she's been body-snatched, because the Scarlett I know would never. Her coworkers chipped in and bought her a stroller. Joann bought her a crib. Ash got her some diaper device.

I dig holes in my palms with my fingernails. They heal as fast as I can make them. I feel the skin break. I feel it come back together. It doesn't hurt. It just is.

After presents, we get cake. Scarlett is made to cut it for some superstitious reason.

"Didn't it kind of look like a dick?" I whisper in her ear as she passes a plate.

"Everything looks like a dick to you," she whispers back.

"Stop whispering about dicks," Mom says. She hands me a piece.

I give the plate to Ash.

"You don't want any?" she asks me. "It's good cake! Have some."

"I'm keto," I say.

"It's your sister's shower," Mom says. "For fuck's sake, have a piece of cake."

I can smell it. Sugary. Lemony. Gross. I want steak. Or a burger. Rare. Juicy. The thought alone has me drooling.

"No, thank you," I say, wiping saliva from my bottom lip and ignoring my mother's death stare. I forget Scarlett isn't the originator of that stare. Mom is.

At around four o'clock, people start trickling out, until it's only me, Mom, Scarlett, Ash and Joann.

"Did you invite her?" I ask Ash when the two of us are alone at the mimosa bar, which is now just an array of empty bottles.

"No," she says. "Cyndi."

"I'm so mad, I can't see straight."

"I understand," Ash says, patting my hand. "But it turned out fine. Scarlett had a good time, right?"

I can't tell if the anger is for Scarlett, on her behalf, or if it's for me. It's just there, hovering like a radioactive cloud.

"I should load the car," Mom says.

"We'll help," Ash says, volunteering me.

I lift the crib box with one arm.

"Careful. That's heavy," Joann says.

"Not for me." I take the stroller with my free hand.

"Damn," Ash says.

I load as much as I can into Scarlett's Prius and the rest into my car.

"Why doesn't Mom go with you?" Scarlett says, putting her bag down in the passenger seat. "I don't really have room."

"All right," I say. "Cyndi, you're with me."

"I was going to hang back and help Ashley clean up," Mom says.

"Oh, no worries," Ash says. "I like to clean. It's my me time."

"Ash, I love you, but that's the saddest thing I've ever heard," I say.

"Aurora!" Mom squeals.

"I'm taking you out drinking. A proper night out," I tell Ash. I give her a hug. "Thank you for everything."

"Of course," she says.

I get in the car without acknowledging Joann. I wait for Mom to say her goodbyes, though I am tempted to drive away without her.

She starts in as soon as she gets in the car.

"See? She had a lovely time."

I turn the music up loud.

She turns it down.

"You were rude to Joann."

"She shouldn't have been invited," I say. "And she definitely shouldn't have come."

"It's her grandchild."

"Yeah, well, she did a bang-up job with her son," I say. "She shouldn't be allowed anywhere near the kid."

"That's not how it works," she says, adjusting the heat. "Would it kill you to be nice?"

"No," I say. "Pretty sure only a silver bullet can do that."

"I appreciate that you feel protective of your sister," Mom says. "But as I've said, it's not your place to be angry at Joann. Or Matty."

"Right," I say. "I shouldn't be protective. You're right. Absolutely right. Why try to protect my family? What could possibly happen?"

"Aurora."

"Never mind," I say. "I don't want to get into it."

"You hold such resentment," she says, suddenly on the verge of tears. "And you won't talk about it. How can we put it behind us if you won't talk to me? I don't understand. It was like a switch. Out of the blue, you hate me. It wasn't always like this."

She's not wrong. Right after, I wasn't angry. I was mostly confused. Confused and tired. I just wanted to pretend like it never happened.

She picked me up from school, and the first thing she said to me when I got in the car was "Why didn't you tell me last night?"

"I tried." Even if I had, would she have believed me?

"You should have told me. You should have said."

She didn't say that she was sorry. She didn't comfort me. She started to cry. I wondered if it was because she was sad about what happened to me, what I'd been through, what I'd seen, or if she was sad about losing Dave. He'd been arrested. He was still on probation for his first offense, which was—surprise, surprise—also for exposing himself to a minor.

I was so desperate for it to be over, so desperate not to have to think about it anymore. The more I acted like I was fine, the more I believed it. They believed it. Mom and Scarlett were just as desperate to forget. Better for everyone to just sweep it under the rug.

For years I never told anyone, the exception being Mia. We were drunk at one of Tommy Haskins' bonfires, the two of us off sitting on the hood of someone's car, passing a bottle of 99 Bananas back and forth. She listed every guy at the party, figuring out whom she wanted to go home with.

"I can't go back to my dad's tonight," she said.

She told me, through casual laughter, that he had called her a whore and kicked her out. Then she showed me. The marks. Bruises. Scars from cigarette burns.

"He's sweet when he's sober," she said.

Not quite knowing how to respond, I told her about Dave.

When I was a sophomore in college, I was hanging out in my friend's dorm. There were seven of us, and we were all talking, smoking a bowl, and I forget how it came up, but suddenly there were stories. I was horrified by the stories, by how we all had them, every one of us. Compared to what some of them had endured, to what Mia had endured, what I'd gone through wasn't even that bad.

That's what I told myself. It wasn't that bad.

It was another excuse to not give myself permission to be upset. To dismiss it.

"Therapy helps," one of my friends said.

It took me another few years to see a therapist. I was too busy with school and side jobs and internships and then working full-time. When I finally got around to going, I was twenty-four and more motivated by the fact that everyone I knew had a therapist than thinking I actually needed the help. I thought I'd vent about office politics and subway manspreading.

I liked my therapist. Her name was Stella; she was soft-spoken and compassionate and she wore wooden jewelry. Before I knew it, I was telling her about my past, about my mother, about how I had been raised. When I started saying these things out loud, that's when I realized how fucked-up it all was.

She recommended books. Books about being the child of immature parents, about healing from trauma. It gave me all this perspective I didn't know what to do with.

And it hatched this anger. There was suddenly so much of it. Too much.

I didn't know how to experience it. I didn't know how to hold it, where to put it.

When you're sad, you cry. When you're happy, you smile, you laugh. But what do you do when you're angry? Not just mad, but filled with this ugly, consuming rage?

And the thing is, women aren't allowed to be angry. Nobody likes a mad woman. They're crazy, irrational, obnoxious, shrill.

I did what I could to control it. After about six months, I stopped going to therapy and stopped answering my mother's phone calls, her texts. I've done my best to avoid her the past two years, because she sets me off.

"Will you talk to me?" she asks. "Please?"

What kills me is this isn't for me. The conversation she's begging me for isn't for my benefit; it's for hers. She wants to be absolved of all guilt without admitting any wrongdoing. What I want is for her to apologize and take responsibility. I'm not going to get what I want. I know this. So any conversation would only exacerbate my anger.

"No," I say. "I'm not going to talk to you about it, Mom. It's not a conversation I want to have. We're not having it."

The rest of the drive is just her sobbing into the passenger-side window.

Maybe she is genuinely sad, but I'm willing to bet this is just a tactic to get me to relent and give her what she wants.

When we get to Scarlett's, I unpack the trunk as she continues to cry in the car. I take all the presents inside and wait for her. Ten minutes pass. I put the kettle on.

I go out to the car and knock on the window, because another thing that women aren't allowed to be is heartless.

"Come in," I say. "I made tea."

"I need a minute," she says.

I go back inside and pour two cups of Earl Grey.

I fully expect a continuation of the car unpleasantries, but when Mom comes in, she's got a weird look on her face.

"Scarlett left the same time as us?" she asks.

"Yeah," I say. "Why?"

"She should be home by now."

"Maybe she stopped somewhere."

"I texted her. She hasn't replied."

"She's probably driving."

She doesn't look convinced. Now she has me worried. We sip our tea in silence.

Half an hour goes by. No Scarlett.

"I'm calling Ashley," Mom says.

Ash confirms that Scarlett left when we did.

I call Scarlett. I text her.

Nothing.

Another half hour.

"I can't take this," Mom says. "Let's go."

She grabs my keys off the counter. I follow her out to the car.

"What are you doing?" I ask, climbing into the passenger seat.

"Going to look for her."

"Maybe she doesn't want us to find her," I say. "Maybe she's pissed about the shower."

"Don't say that."

"Wouldn't that be the best-case scenario?"

"Aurora."

"Fine."

We drive around in silence for about forty-five minutes, just circling through town.

"Where could she have gone? Has she responded to you?"

"Nope," I say.

"What if she was abducted?"

"What if she's running errands?"

I wish my mother had shown even a fraction of this concern for me when I was an eleven-year-old child being sent out for fucking pizza pickup with Dave.

She's crying again.

"What?" I ask.

"You hate me!"

"Pull over. You can't drive like this."

She pulls into the parking lot of a strip mall. We're between a nail salon and a Dunkin' Donuts.

"You hate me," she repeats. "I tried so hard. I did my best. You have to believe me. I tried my best."

"I don't doubt it," I say, playing with my gold chain, with my moon charm.

"What will it take? What can I do? I couldn't have done anything differently. I didn't know, Aurora. He fooled me, too."

"He didn't fool me," I say. "You asked me to give him a chance."

"A year. He was in our lives for almost a year. I didn't once see anything that gave me any reason to doubt him, to suspect."

"How about me saying that I didn't like him? That I didn't want him around."

"You were eleven. You didn't like anyone."

"That's not the point! You're missing the point. You badger me to talk about it, and then when I do, you don't listen to anything I say. You don't want to hear what I'm saying."

"I am listening," she says, gripping the steering wheel tight with both hands. "I am. I can't change what happened. I wish I could."

"Why can't you just say you're sorry? Why can't you apologize?"

This is the question. It carries with it the most rage. The most savage anger.

"You blame me," she says. "You blame me."

"You refuse to take any responsibility. Do you understand what that's like for me?" I ask. My skin is too small. It can't contain the anger. "Why can't you just admit your part?"

"Because I can't!" she screams. "I can't!"

I'm too mad to stay in the car. I don't trust myself.

Because I'm imagining what it would feel like to make her stop. To make her stop talking. Stop crying. Stop moving. To just stop.

I could. Easily. The violence is there, always there, waiting for me.

"All right," I say.

I get out.

It's raining, but I don't care.

I walk back to Scarlett's, cutting through the woods. The same woods where I was bitten.

Try me now.

By the time I get home, both my car and Scarlett's are in the driveway. I'm soaking wet, my blazer ruined, but I don't really give a shit.

No one's around except Reaper, who is, naturally, not happy to see me. I bare my teeth at him. He whimpers and backs off.

I change into a pair of leggings and a sweatshirt that smells like teriyaki beef jerky and wet dog. Like me.

I take shelter under a mountain of covers and attempt to sleep, but I'm not tired. I'm not calm enough. The anger is still there. It's receded; the walk helped. But it's not gone. It's like I can hear it murmuring under my skin.

I walk into Scarlett's room. The door is open, but she's not there. That's when I hear the whirring. A drill.

It's coming from the baby's room.

I open the door, and there she is, assembling the crib.

"Hey," she says. "Close the door behind you. Mom's sleeping."

I do as I'm told.

"She was hysterical," she says. "She relayed what happened."

"Where were you?"

"I needed some time alone. Listen, she can't take responsibility because she couldn't live with herself if she did," Scarlett says. "Here, can you help me with this? Or would you prefer to watch?"

"I'll help—geez," I say, holding up a side of the crib.

"You do understand that, right?" she asks, a screw between her teeth. "It's too hard for her. She couldn't live with it."

"I have to live with it," I say.

"I know," she says. "I know it isn't fair. I know, and I'm sorry."

"You don't need to be sorry. You have nothing to be sorry for. You were eleven, too."

She takes the screw out of her mouth. "Still . . ."

She puts the screw on the drill bit. It whirs for a few seconds. She looks up at me. "I think about it. What I could have done. Should have done. Why it wasn't me."

She and I have had a few conversations about it, and they're all like this. Short. Because they never feel how I want them to feel. There's no relief in them. Just hurt.

She can't heal me, and I can't heal her. No matter how badly we want to heal each other, we can heal only ourselves.

There's wet on my cheek. I wipe it away before she sees.

"All right, this side," she says. "Can you hold over here?"

"I never knew you were so handy," I tell her. "We should have our own HGTV show."

"Yeah? Assembling cribs?"

"Assembling all types of furniture. Possibilities are endless," I say. "We'll call it 'Banging and Screwing'!"

She laughs. "Yeah, okay."

"I think they'll go for it. They love the twin thing," I say. "Everybody loves the twin thing."

"Are you all right?" she asks me.

"Yeah," I say. "I'm fine."

"You seemed weird today. At the shower."

"I thought you'd hate it. I was nervous."

"It wasn't my favorite," she says, setting the drill down. "I don't like surprises."

"I know. I'm sorry," I say, going in for a hug. "You still love me?"

"Yes, but you smell terrible." She dodges me. "What is going on?"

"Hey. I do have feelings, you know."

"You smell incredible. Amazing. Like roses."

I pick up another side of the crib. "All right. This baby cage isn't going to assemble itself."

She gets the drill, and we resume construction.

"I really am sorry about the shower," I say. "My objections were overruled."

"It wasn't that bad. I just . . . I keep feeling like I don't feel the way I'm supposed to. I don't know how to articulate it. There's all this pressure. So many things I'm supposed to be doing, to be reading, to be learning. It's overwhelming. And it's like nothing is mine anymore. Not my body. Not my mind. Not my emotions. And there's nothing I can do about it. And—"

I snort.

"What?"

"Nothing. I just . . . I think that makes perfect sense," I say. "Another few weeks."

"Yeah, but then what? My whole life will be different. And I'm not going to look the same. I know that's shallow. But it's like I'm not allowed to grieve my body. I'm meant to be, like, 'This is magical. I'm a mother now, so nothing about me matters anymore.' I don't know. Maybe that's terrible and selfish. Maybe I'm a monster."

"You're not," I say. "Take it from me. An actual monster."

She ignores me, not understanding. "Can I have the instructions?"

"I could put this together on my own if you're tired."

"I should at least be able to do this," she says. "I need to do something. I've been meaning to paint in here. I wanted to do a mural. Was thinking something cosmic."

"Cosmic?" I ask, passing her the instructions.

"For the room. Stars. A big moon."

"A moon?"

"Maybe all the phases of the moon."

"All right, fuck it," I hear myself say. "I have to tell you something."

"I have something to tell you, too. But you first."

"I'm a werewolf."

"Sorry?"

"I'm a werewolf," I say. I've committed to it now, for better or worse.

She laughs. "If this is a sex thing, I'm not sure I want to know."

"It's not a sex thing. It's a monster thing. I'm serious. I'm a werewolf. A legit werewolf. I know that's a wild thing to say, but trust me, it's an even wilder thing to be!"

She leans back against the wall.

"I wasn't attacked by a bear. I was chased and bitten by a werewolf. And I wasn't at Ian's last Friday. It was a full moon, so I took Cloud's old crate out to the distillery. I locked myself inside it and waited. It was more a precaution because I still wasn't a hundred percent sure. But then I turned into a werewolf. And I broke out of the crate and ate a bunch of rats. And maybe other things, too. I don't really remember it that well. But yeah. That's also why I smell like a wet dog sometimes, like right now, and why my hair has been looking so amazing."

She's expressionless.

"Yep. Werewolf," I say. "A real thing apparently. Who knew?"

She starts to laugh. It's a weird, breathy laugh. Or maybe she's sighing? It's a very strange noise that she's making.

It goes on for a while.

"I don't get this joke," she says, still doing her breathy laugh-sigh thing.

"Scarlett, I'm not joking. I'm telling you the truth."

"I'm not sure how to react," she says. "I don't know how to react. I don't know how to react. I . . . I don't know . . . how to react."

"All right, let me show you something," I say, waving her toward me.

I roll up my sleeve. I take a screw and drag it across my forearm. The skin opens, and out oozes the silver goo, and a few sprigs of fur.

She gives a silent scream, clasping her hand over her mouth as she staggers backward. I catch her before she falls.

"Look," I tell her. "Keep watching."

The skin curls into itself and becomes seamless once again.

She stares at me, her eyes wide, both hands now over her face.

"My sense of smell is crazy now, too. I can smell that you recently had McDonald's," I tell her. "McChicken with fries and barbecue sauce. Guessing you went through the drive-through post-shower. Uncool you didn't bring any back for your beloved sister. Also, I'm not keto. I just only want to eat meat, because, as I said, I'm now a werewolf."

Her hands slowly slide from her face. Her mouth is open. No sound comes out.

"I'm sorry," I say. "I don't want it to be true. Trust me."

"What the fuck?" she yells. "What the fucking fuck? What? What? What the fuck? Are you, what? Fuck!"

I nod. "Tell me about it."

"What the fuck? What the fuck?" She's backing away from me, backing into the corner, sliding down the wall.

I'm beginning to regret my decision to share this information. "Perhaps I should have kept this to myself."

"You just . . . I saw . . . How are you calm about this?"

"I don't really have a choice, do I?" I sit beside her on the floor. "It happened. I got bit. There's not a ton of reliable information out there on what to do about it. If there *is* anything to do about it."

"I don't . . . I don't understand," she says. "I feel like I'm dreaming."

"Look, I know I really just laid it on you, but can we please skip to the part where you believe me and we can talk about it without it being as big of a deal as it actually is?"

It takes another hour for her to calm down. After that, I explain everything the best I can. She listens, then takes my hand and leads me downstairs, where she feeds me deli meat as we sit in silence. I watch her processing.

"Who was the werewolf?" she asks after a while.

"What do you mean?"

"Who bit you?"

"Wish I knew," I say. "Would quite like to have a word."

"Be serious. You don't have any idea?"

"How would I? I only ever saw them as the wolf and just the one time. They were MIA during the last full moon. I don't know how to go about finding them or if I even want to. Not sure it would accomplish anything. Doubt I could sue in monster court."

She stares into space.

"What?" I ask.

"I believe you. I just can't believe it. Do you know what I mean?" she asks, chewing on her bottom lip.

"Yeah," I say. "Don't stress out about it, please."

"Sure, no problem."

"Yeah, like, just be chill about it."

"Yeah, super chill," she says.

"I feel like I shouldn't have told you. Maybe that was a mistake," I say, rolling up a piece of ham. "I guess I just couldn't be alone with it anymore."

She nods.

"It doesn't change anything," I tell her.

I feel compelled to reassure her. If I can convince her that everything's fine, maybe I can believe it, too.

Even though I know.

Everything is not fine.

I sleep next to Scarlett in her bed, though I'm not sure how much sleep either of us really gets. We haven't shared a bed since we were kids, and we're both active sleepers. She's constantly adjusting her five thousand pillows, and I retaliate by stealing all the blankets.

At some point, she whispers, "Are you awake?"

"Yeah."

"I know a really good therapist," she says. "I think you should go see her."

I know what this means. I know her doubt. I'm painfully familiar.

"I think it'll help. She'll help you. And I can help you."

"I'm supposed to be helping you."

"You've been under a lot of stress," she says, "coming back here."

"Did you not see me bleed silver?" I ask her. "Did you not see it? Did you not see my skin heal?"

She takes a long time to answer.

"I saw."

I wonder how many more times I'll have to cut myself open for her to truly believe it.

She's next to me. I feel her warmth, the tide of her breath. I smell her shampoo. But she's never been further from me.

VIII

We roam around the house like the undead, communicating in grunts, making minimal eye contact. Mom is on a flight out tonight, and Scarlett offered to drop her off at the airport. I catch the two of them whispering to each other around lunch.

"We're going to Starbucks," Scarlett says.

"All right."

I wait for an invitation that doesn't come. Not that I'd want to go anyway.

As soon as they're gone, I cook myself some ground beef and eat it with a spoon straight from the pan.

I'm starving. I'm frustrated. There's something gnawing at me.

Literally.

I look down, and Reaper is there, once again having attached himself to my ankle.

I try to shoo him away, but he clamps down harder, growling.

I growl back.

This only makes him more aggressive. He digs his heels in and tears out a chunk of my leg. I watch him give it a few hearty chews before swallowing.

He retains his attack posture.

There's a smear in my peripheral vision. It stirs something in me, a defensive reflex. My arm goes up. I catch him midair, hold him up by the scruff of his neck.

"You," I tell him, "are in desperate need of an attitude adjustment."

He huffs.

I carry him into the laundry room and attach his leash. "Think we could both use a walk."

I'm relieved to be out of the house and away from the tension lingering inside it. I don't know how I thought Scarlett would react, what I was hoping for. This isn't exactly inspiring optimism for ever sharing this information with anyone else. And by "anyone else," I mean Ian.

When we get back, Reaper continues to pester me. I give up and allow him to chomp on my arm, which he seems to appreciate. I voluntarily watch about half an hour of local news. That's how I know I'm depressed.

Mom and Scarlett have been gone awhile. It's clear they're avoiding me, each for different but perhaps equally valid reasons. If I could avoid me, I would.

I can only hope that Scarlett hasn't decided to ruin a twenty-seven-year streak of twin loyalty by betraying my werewolf secret to our mother.

I turn off the news, trudge upstairs, and take a scalding-hot shower. I don't have the energy to stand, so I sit.

Local news and sitting in the shower. I feel like I'm playing depression bingo.

Two months ago, I was probably having cocktails with friends at the Standard, or seeing a film at the Angelika, or having dinner with coworkers at some buzzy new restaurant in the Village, or hooking up with an aspiring filmmaker in a Bushwick dive, or role-playing with a divorced Park Slope dad in his sparse studio apartment, reveling in his gratitude.

Oh, how the mighty have fallen.

I let the water flow over me and breathe in the steam. I examine the faint scars on my side, the traces of the bite.

I've always been good at barreling ahead. I always worked hard in school, no matter what was going on at home. I played lacrosse, joined debate. I became head cheerleader, ran for president of the student council, and won. I took all AP classes. Got a scholarship to Columbia. Undergrad. MBA. Internships. Job. Apartment. Promotion. Better apartment. Always somewhere to go, something to do, someone to fuck. Something on the horizon to go after, to run toward.

There's nothing now. No light anymore. No horizon.

I could stay in this shower forever. What does it matter?

I dig a nail into the blemished skin beneath my ribs. Apply pressure. Sink another nail in. Another. More pressure. I want to tear it away, this damaged skin. This evidence. I don't want it on me anymore. I want it off. I want it gone. I want to rip it out. All of it, like a rotted root.

There's a gumminess at my knuckles, and I know I've gone too far. Too deep.

When I pull my fingers back, I'm met with resistance, like I'm stuck in tar or cement. It's the bite being greedy, trying to swallow other parts of me. It takes a hard yank to free my hand. Silver ooze spatters. There's some fur caught under my nails.

What have I done?

I press down on the flaps of torn skin. I hold them there, waiting for restoration. But this wound is different. This wound refuses to heal.

I turn off the faucet with my foot and flop over the side of the tub onto the bathroom floor. I want to stay here until I'm numb to the tile underneath me, but I'm oozing everywhere. Making a mess.

I crawl on all fours into my bedroom and find some of my bandages. I dress the wound, then change into some clean clothes. A pair of joggers and an oversized Led Zeppelin T-shirt that once belonged to my mother.

When I get downstairs, Mom and Scarlett are at the kitchen counter.

"We got you a cappuccino," Scarlett says.

"Oh, thanks!" I say, mustering as much enthusiasm as possible, smiling big and pretty. I want to come across like someone who isn't in the midst of an existential werewolf crisis. That's what I'm striving for.

"I should get my things," Mom says. "Need to leave for the airport! Don't want to miss my flight. Guy will be waiting for me."

She hurries past me. I sip my cappuccino. It's cold.

"So what did you guys talk about?"

Scarlett gives me a look. "I didn't tell her what you told me last night, if that's what you're asking."

"It was a general inquiry, but good to know."

"I would never tell Mom anything you shared with me in confidence," she says. "But I'm concerned, Rory. I'm worried about you. I'm allowed to share that. And she and I have our own stuff to talk about, between us. She's my mom, too."

"Fine," I say. If I bite my tongue any harder, I won't have one anymore.

I help Mom carry her suitcase out to Scarlett's car, toss it carelessly in the trunk.

"Well," Mom says, still unable to meet my eye.

I hug her.

She puts her arms around me and pulls me in close. "Love you."

"Love you, too."

I hold her. I've wanted her to leave ever since she got here, but now that she's leaving, I want her to stay. I don't understand it. Our relationship is a hydra. It has too many heads.

"I'll be back soon," she says, kissing my cheek.

Scarlett walks around to the driver's side. She's got a funny gait, and she wears a sour face. She doesn't acknowledge me.

They're in the car, and then they're gone again. I'm alone. The most alone.

My phone vibrates, and for a second I allow myself to want it to be Ian. Sure, I haven't responded to him all week, but maybe he can sense it's because I'm really going through it, and he'll tell me not to worry, everything's cool, and maybe also reveal he has a fur kink. I don't know. Something, anything, to absolve me of doubt so I can continue to pursue this relationship. Because I wish he were here right now. I miss him. I really fucking miss him.

But it isn't Ian.

It's Mia. I pick up.

"You want to get into some trouble?"

"Stop apologizing," she says.

I sit on the passenger side of her van. It's one of those glam travel vans. She decked out the inside with a bed and a kitchenette, colorful wallpaper, excessive succulents. A Pinterest wet dream. It smells strongly of gardenia, an obscenely powerful floral scent that burns my nostrils.

"You know I don't give a shit."

"Yeah, but still," I say.

I didn't have it in me to get changed, to put on real clothes. I threw on my camel coat over my sweats and Zeppelin tee, rolled on some perfume, brushed my hair, but there's no disguising that I'm a mess.

"I doubt this is what you had in mind."

She blows a raspberry. "Please. It's not like there are any hot clubs we could hit up. I'm good doing what we used to do. Driving around and making our own mischief."

"Remember the senior prank?"

"Our best, I think."

I watch her as she drives. There's something different about her. More subdued. Maybe it's her makeup? The lack of false lashes and contour? It somehow makes her look both younger and older. Innocent and exhausted. She wears a pair of painted-on jeans and a fuzzy sweater.

She takes us to our old spot, a decommissioned train station at the edge of town. It's not a romantic place. A squat utilitarian building chained up to prevent break-ins, and behind it a platform, neglected, left to the slow creep of nature. Mia and I used to come out here and smoke cigarettes and drink beer and smash our bottles on the tracks, a small act of defiance, of destruction, a slice of heaven for two teenage girls who found power in rebellion.

"I've got a pack of cigarettes and a pack of beer," she says. "We're about to time travel."

We wade through weeds to get around the building and out to the platform, which is pretty much as we left it. Mia takes out two beers, opens them, then hands me one.

"To us," she says.

"Cheers."

We clink our bottles.

"Now," she says, "tell me everything about your life."

I laugh.

"For real! I want to know. All of it."

I give her the CliffsNotes of the last decade. College. MBA. Life in the city. My friends. My job. I give her the highlight reel of all my hookups. I don't tell her about the werewolf stuff, obviously. And for some reason I don't tell her about Ian.

"Good for you, girl," she says, raising her bottle. "Always seemed like things were going well, but you never know off social. And you rarely post."

"I'm not an Instagram star like you."

She revels in the compliment.

"What about you? How you've been?" I ask her. "I'd say I'm sorry to hear about your dad, but I know that was . . . complicated."

"Thanks," she says, flicking something off her jeans with a neon acrylic. She shakes her head, takes a swig of beer. "I was so ready to get out of here, the second I turned eighteen. Thought I'd never come back. Never see him again. But turns out, he's everywhere. He's every guy I ever dated. Can't seem to get away from him. He's gone now. He's dead. But everything he did, everything he was, I still have to carry that. I tried to outrun it. Trust me. Not that I have to explain it to you. You know. You know how it is."

She pulls out a cigarette and carries it to my lips. Slips it between. Lights it for me.

"Thanks," I say.

She lights her own, takes a drag. "I've missed you, Rory."

She's not often serious. Even now, though I know she's being sincere, the corners of her lips flirt with a grin.

"I've missed you, too."

Whatever whispers of daylight remained suddenly go dead. It's dark. Foggy.

"We understand each other. With our pasts. Everything we've been through. Everyone else, they want to judge girls like us. Hate us. Keep us. Either call us sluts or call us brave. Blame daddy issues for the choices we make. Blame us for the choices made for us." She pauses to laugh, to ash her cigarette. "They don't know anything, do they? They'll never know."

Girls like us. I take another drag, another sip of my beer. I wonder if she's buzzed. With her it's hard to tell.

"You're the only person I ever told," she says, letting her head back so her long hair scrapes the ground.

"Really?"

"I did tell one of my exes," she says, whipping her hair in front of her face. "But he basically took it as permission to treat me like shit, too. That was the end of that. Once you tell them, once they know, they never look at you the same."

The night goes cold around me. Cold and bitter. I shiver.

She shrugs. "Funny how being back here brings it all to the surface."

"Hilarious."

She shakes her head, then raises her bottle to me. "All right. You ready to do this?"

"I'm ready."

We chug our beers, then step to the edge of the platform. We count down. *Five, four, three, two, one.* We hurl our bottles onto the tracks. We listen to the sound of shattering glass, to the music of something breaking outside ourselves.

Then we yell. We whoop and holler and laugh and stomp and spin.

I wait to welcome the freedom I felt doing this at seventeen, but it isn't coming. Because it's not enough. This petty destruction. It's just not enough. I look at Mia, searching for some hint that maybe she's come to the same understanding, but her back is to me.

"Pretty sky tonight," she says. "Pretty moon. Don't you think?"

"Sure. Another round?"

We each have another beer, share another cigarette. Reminisce. But it's hard for me to be present, to focus on the conversation instead of how eager I am to smash something else. It's got me on edge. I lie and tell Mia I'm tired, even though it's only eight thirty. She doesn't tease me about it; she puts her arm around me and offers to take me home.

When she drops me off, she says, "Let's do this again soon."

"Yeah. I'll call you."

"Pinkie swear?"

I reach over and we link pinkies.

"This is legally binding," she says.

"Oh, I know."

I hop out of the car, and we blow each other kisses. It's only after she drives away that I realize Scarlett's car isn't in the driveway.

She's not back yet.

She should be back.

I take my phone out and call her.

No answer.

I call again.

Still nothing.

Mom should be in the air by now, but I try her anyway.

"Rory, hi."

"Hi. Did your flight get delayed or something? Scarlett's not back yet and I was—"

"Scarlett was having some pains on the way to the airport, so I took her to the hospital."

There's a sharp, concerning sound, and I realize that, reckless in my distress, I've cracked my phone screen with my razor of a thumbnail, my grip too tight.

"Actually, baby, could you come and bring a change of clothes for her? Sorry. I have to go. Please come."

She hangs up.

I run inside, up the stairs to Scarlett's room, the sound of my footsteps echoing through the quiet house. I open Scarlett's drawers and pull out a black tunic and a pair of maternity leggings, some underwear, a bra. I grab my bag and shove the clothes inside. I'm scrambling, not paying attention, and I trip on my way down the steps.

I land on my feet at the bottom, but the impact makes the house cry out. Frames fall from the walls. One of Scarlett's taxidermy birds hangs loose off its mount, and I nearly lunge for it, an ugly instinct taking over, eclipsing me for a moment. I force myself out the door and to my car. I force myself to forget how close I just was to devouring a stuffed dead bird. I force myself to ignore the bloom of hunger. I wipe the saliva from my chin and go.

The drive to the hospital is torture. There are so many things that could be wrong, that could go wrong. And no one even bothered to call me.

When I walk into the emergency room, my memory flares. I get snippets of the last time I was here, when they discovered what they thought was minimal damage.

Looking at me, you'd never know what prowls beneath my skin.

I can smell blood. There's so much blood here. It blurs my vision. Makes me weak.

I call my mother, keeping the phone away from my ear to spare my cartilage from the shattered screen. She picks up right away.

"I'm here," I say. "Where are you?"

"Miss." A nurse behind reception calls to me. "Miss?"

"We're in the maternity ward. She's okay."

"She's okay?"

"It's the . . . I actually don't know where we are," she says. "I'm sure if you ask someone—"

"She's okay?"

"Yes. Her and baby, both fine."

The relief is euphoric. I release my shoulders from under my ears.

"I'll find you."

I hang up and wander the halls. Good to know security is tight. I follow signs for maternity. It's not a big hospital, but it's a labyrinth. I get in the elevator and go up to the third floor. When the doors open, the first person I see is Matty.

He paces the hall. He's on his phone. He wears a leather jacket and black jeans and combat boots. His dark hair is up in a half bun. He plays with his necklace, a long chain with a pendant etched with the letter S. He's worn it for years, ever since they first got together. He also has a tattoo of my sister's name on his right pec.

I was always certain that he loved her. Had I ever thought there was a chance he'd fuck her over so royally, I would have never let him near her. I would have . . .

He sees me. He hangs up the phone.

"Hey, Rory," he says, reaching out to me for a hug.

"Do not fucking touch me, you piece of shit." I take one hand and shove him back.

He screams.

He hits the wall behind him. Hard. He grabs his shoulder. His arm hangs limp from it, and I can tell even through his jacket that I've done real damage. I think I dislocated his shoulder.

Good.

"How dare you show up here?"

I'm in his face. He's been drinking. He smells like liquor and fear. His heartbeat is out of control. His pulse is fast, his blood churning. He turns his face away from me. There's dark stubble on his chin, a small cut at his jawbone. I wonder what it's from. I wonder if I were to reach out and hook my nail in, how much of his skin I could peel away, how much of his face. I wonder what it would sound like. Smell like. Taste like.

The rage wraps itself around me like vines, like moss swallowing a rock. It's a natural state. It's good. It's symbiotic.

He hurt my sister. I hurt him.

I could kill him.

I would like that. It would be so much *fun*.

"Back up," he says, trying to get away from me by stepping to the side. He holds his limp arm. "You fucked up my shoulder."

"Lucky that's all I've done." Think how easily I could remove his genitalia. A single tug.

"Jesus," he says. "Why are you mad at me?"

"Why am I mad at you?" I think my head might explode.

"You're making a scene," he says. He nods his head and turns the corner into a side hallway. I follow him. "Why do you always need to make a scene?"

"Why are you still talking? Stop talking."

"Hey, she broke up with me, okay?" he says. "She threw me out, so I don't know what your problem is. This wasn't my call."

The hospital comes back, the scene around me materializing as the rage wanes, giving way to confusion.

"What?"

"Convenient," he says, rolling his eyes. "She told me she didn't want me around. She didn't want me at the house. She asked me to move out. What should I have done? She asked me to leave, so I left."

I'm stunned into silence.

"I don't know what she told you," he says. "But I'm just doing what she asked. She said she needed space, so I gave her space. Your mom called me tonight and I came. Ow, Jesus, my shoulder."

"You must have done something," I say.

Scarlett isn't the type to be unhappy in a relationship. She's like my mother. She'll do whatever it takes to make it work. She had her first boyfriend in the second grade and hasn't been single since. She was with Rich from seventh grade through when they left for college, and even then, even with him at school hours away, they still tried to make it work. The slow dissolve of their relationship was aided only by Jake, her interim boyfriend, whom she dated for a year before meeting Matty. If she'd never met Matty, I would undoubtedly be standing next to Jake right now or some other handsome yawn.

I love my sister, but she doesn't exactly have standards. She doesn't like being single. She doesn't like the chase, doesn't like flirting. She likes intimacy. She likes to love someone, to give her energy to them, to know someone and be known by them. She likes to share her life. To hold hands and cook and plan picnic dates and go apple picking. She followed our mother's model, and I rejected it wholeheartedly. That's how it's always been.

I would think getting pregnant would make her more inclined to fight for her relationship, not less. And I sort of assumed her lack of excitement about the baby was a direct result of Matty having fucked off, but if that's not it, I'm not sure I understand what's going on with my sister.

"What did you do?" I ask him. "She wouldn't just kick you out for no reason."

"You'd have to ask her," he says.

"Where is she?"

He tilts his chin back toward the main hallway.

"Does she know you're here?"

He nods, then winces as he looks down at his shoulder. "Good thing we're in a hospital."

"Better if we were in a funeral home," I say, walking away.

I peer into a few rooms before finding her. She looks tired, her ever-perfect eyeliner smudged. Mom sits in a chair near the door.

"I'm here," I say. "I brought clothes."

"They're keeping me overnight," Scarlett says in a voice not her own. Her eyes are glazed over, and she stares at the ceiling.

"Everything okay?"

"Yes," Mom says. "False alarm. Just some cramping. Hard to know what's what."

"I knew it was probably fine," Scarlett says. "Mom panicked."

"Better to be cautious," Mom says. "Is it not?"

I suspect that either Scarlett is playing it off not to acknowledge any vulnerability, or Mom manipulated the situation as an excuse not to get on the plane. Perhaps a little of both.

There's only one chair in the room. I don't really know what to do with myself. "Do you want anything? I can get food or . . ."

"You can go home," Scarlett says. "You don't need to stay."

"Of course I'll stay."

"Mom's here," she says. "Matty's here."

"Yeah, I saw."

"Yeah," Scarlett says. "Rory, please go home."

"You asked me to be here," I say. "You asked me to drop everything and come here to be with you, and I came. You said he left."

"Aurora!" Mom grabs my hand. "Your sister is lying in a hospital bed. Can you please relax?"

I can't. The anger is teeming, untamable.

"You lied to me," I tell Scarlett.

She won't look at me. She's still just staring at the ceiling.

"You lied to me and now my life is over."

"Aurora," Mom says. "Please."

"Fine," I say. "I'm leaving."

I pass Matty on my way out. He's talking to Seth, who sees me but doesn't wave. His eyes are dark, his brow furrowed. I listen. I don't need to be close to hear what they're saying.

"She's crazy, man," Matty says. Me. He's talking about me.

"She can be aggressive," Seth says. "She can be intense sometimes."

I force myself out to the parking lot before I really lose it.

I drive around for a while. I don't want to go back to Scarlett's. I don't really want to be anywhere. I pass the high school and see that the field lights are on. There's a track there that I used to run on weekends. I pull in and get out of the car. I slide out of my leather mules and walk barefoot across the cold, cracked pavement. I start running the track, my legs alive beneath me, moving in a new way. The wind whips my hair back. I cut through the night like a knife.

I can see everything. My peripheral vision has expanded. My hearing. Smell, taste. It's all intensified. Someone smoked weed here earlier today. They had on brand-new sneakers. Axe body spray. There are leaves decaying. Dog shit. Dead birds. There's a collection of expired milk cartons in the fridge in the cafeteria. Someone left a turkey sandwich in their locker. It's got Dijon mustard and tomatoes.

In the houses nearby, everyone's getting ready for bed. I hear running water, the foaming of toothpaste, the swish of brushes. Heartbeats slowing. Bedtime stories.

I see lights going out in first-story windows. I see the wind journeying through the trees, leaves abandoning their branches. Stars burning. Airplanes blinking.

I run and run. It doesn't matter how fast I'm going, which I know is fast, animal fast, my senses are not dulled by the speed. My pace amplifies everything. There's no outrunning any of it. Not my senses. Not my feelings. Not myself.

The werewolf thing only enhances all the parts of me that

were already broken and wrong. It's trapped me with the worst of myself. It's my reckoning.

I crave destruction, desire consequence. I want to rip the world apart, limb from limb, and now I can. Before, it was an urge, one I could quiet and conceal. One I could hide behind a slick facade. It's not an urge anymore. It's a need.

I drop down on all fours and go.

When I get home, I wash my hands and feet in the tub. I cut my dagger nails. Then I open my laptop and Google "werewolf cure." I scroll through weird subreddits and random blogs, read about plasma therapy, about wolfsbane. I oscillate between moments of hope and devastation, between grim acceptance and righteous fury. I breathe through the moments of wanting to smash my laptop and scream at the top of my lungs. I breathe.

It's eleven twenty-eight p.m. and I'm starving. I go downstairs and find the fridge empty of meat.

I decide to venture out to the 7-Eleven in hope they have hot dogs.

They do.

"Hi," I say to the clerk. "Can I have all the hot dogs?"

There's a long pause.

"I'm sorry. Did you say you wanted all of the hot dogs?"

"Yes," I say.

"You want *all* of the hot dogs?"

"Yes. Please."

Another pause.

"Okay," they say, shrugging.

I eat them sitting on the trunk of my car while watching traffic whiz past. I can swallow them whole. A whole hot dog easily. Without ketchup or mustard or any lubricant. It's pretty incredible. I'm in six deep when I hear, "Rory?"

I look over.

It's Ian.

Shit shit shit.

"Hi," I say, the seventh hot dog traveling down my gullet.

"Hi," he says.

He wears a winter coat, scarf, beanie. I'm still in my joggers and the Led Zeppelin T-shirt. No coat. Sitting on my car next to a box full of hot dogs.

I'll admit, not my finest look.

He raises an eyebrow at me, and I shrug. He laughs.

I missed the sound of his laugh.

"What are you doing here?" I ask him.

"Getting cigarettes," he says. "Aren't you cold? Do you want my jacket?"

"I'm not cold," I say.

I'm aware that it's cold out, that I should be cold. I'm not. In fact, I'm a little warm. There's some sweat happening, a shallow puddle forming in the small of my back.

He stuffs his hands into his pockets. "I'll leave you to it."

"Oh," I say. "Okay."

He nods and walks past me. I hear the door open, then close behind him.

I shove another hot dog into my mouth.

I haven't responded to any of his calls or texts since the full moon last week, so it's been eight days of radio silence on my end. I know I should have said something, but what, exactly? *Sorry.*

BRB, trying to figure out if I can still date you as a bloodthirsty supernatural monster?

I guess it's for the best if he's mad. If he's not interested in me anymore. It's not like we could ever be together. I'm stuck in this body. A body that's volatile, that's vicious, that I can't trust. I wake up with this truth and fall asleep with this truth. A truth he can never know.

It's too risky to try to pull him close. Too dangerous. For both of us. He could get hurt. I could get hurt.

I know this. I know it and yet . . .

I want him.

Seeing him just now, I can't ignore it. My feelings won't just disappear. I want him like I've never wanted anything.

The door opens and I hear the clink of his Zippo, the crinkle of plastic.

He comes around the back of my car, a lit cigarette hanging from his lips. He takes it between his fingers and exhales.

"G'night, Rory."

He's walking away from me. He's vanishing into the dark. All of a sudden, the hot dogs rebel inside me. I'm nauseous. I'm panicked.

"Ian!" I call out.

He turns around. "Yeah?"

"Where are you going?"

"I'm going home," he says. "Why?"

Fuck it. "You weren't going to invite me?"

"Didn't think you'd want to come," he says. "Also, you look pretty busy."

I wipe my hands on a napkin, instead of my pants like I've been doing. I look up at him.

"I'm sorry I've been MIA. I had a bad week, okay? Like, epically bad."

"I wasn't sure what was going on," he says. "You weren't responding. If you don't want this, that's fine. I'm not going to hold it against you—I never have. But I think I made it clear where I stand and would hope you'd respect me enough to not just ignore me."

"I'm sorry." Why did I eat all of those fucking hot dogs? "I wasn't ignoring you. It's . . . I've had a rough couple of days. That's really all it is."

He pushes his glasses up his nose and takes another drag of his cigarette.

"Do you want to come home with me?"

"So forward. I'm a lady, you know."

"Rory."

Then I say what I know I shouldn't.

I say yes.

We make it inside but not up the stairs. His hands are in my hair; mine are unbuttoning his jeans. His lips are on my neck, and I'm not thinking about anything but how good it feels to be with him.

When it's over, we lie on the rug, listening to each other breathe. He takes my hands in his. I like when his hands swallow up my hands. I like everything about him.

"You want water?" he asks me.

"Mm," I say. "Thank you."

He gets up and goes to the kitchen. I put my pants back on and sit on the couch. I pull one of the blankets around my shoulders like a cape.

He comes back and hands me a glass.

"You want to talk about your bad week?" he asks.

Do I?

"Actually, yeah," I say. "I kind of do. Is that all right?"

"No, I just asked to be polite. I don't really give a shit," he says, grinning.

I throw a pillow at him.

"I want to hear," he says. "I'm relieved you weren't avoiding me."

I was avoiding him, but he doesn't need to know that.

"Well, my mom's here and our relationship is not great at the moment. I don't think it was ever great. I just didn't know better when I was a kid. It's that thing like when you're in a cult and you don't realize you're in a cult until you're out of the cult," I say, stretching my legs over his lap.

He rubs my feet. "Right," he says. "Are you comparing your mother to Charles Manson?"

"No, I would never," I say. "Her vibe is way more Heaven's Gate."

"I've met your mother, and I could see it," he says, wiggling my toes. "Sorry. I don't mean to make light of it."

"No, I know," I say. "It's just complicated. Scarlett didn't have the same experience as I did growing up, so it's different for her. Their relationship is good. And it just feels like it's on me, like I'm the problem child."

"Yeah, I get that."

I tell him about the baby shower, about Joann showing up, how the whole thing was tense and weird. I tell him I got into arguments with my mom and Scarlett but don't specify about what. I tell him how no one called me when Scarlett went to the hospital.

He goes rigid. "Wait. What? Is she okay?"

"Everything's fine. She was taking my mom to the airport, and she had pains or something, so they went to the hospital. And when I show up, the first person I see is Matty."

"Fuck that guy."

"That's what I thought," I say. "But turns out, so Scarlett told me he left, right? So I've been thinking for weeks that this guy bailed on my sister."

"Right."

I decide to tell him the truth. Test the waters.

"I'm fairly certain I dislocated his shoulder," I say. "Not on purpose. I pushed him, and it happened. I think."

He nods. He doesn't appear to be alarmed by this information.

"Then he tells me he only left because Scarlett kicked him out. Something she just failed to mention. And either she has a valid reason that she isn't sharing with me, the closest person to her, or it was a strategic omission to make herself more sympathetic."

"Why would she do that?" he asks, running the back of his hand across my cheek.

"I guess she knows how much I hate being back here. Maybe she thought if she was honest with me, I wouldn't come? I don't know. Doesn't really make sense. Nothing makes sense."

"Is it really that bad?" he asks.

"What?"

"Coming back here?"

I look away from him.

"Things happened here," I tell him. "Things I don't care to revisit."

"I'm sorry," he says. "I'm sorry about that."

It's too serious. Too real a moment.

"Now do you understand the hot dogs?" I ask him. "I feel like I smell like hot dogs. Do I smell like hot dogs?"

"Oh, yeah," he says. "Definitely. A lot."

He's telling me the truth. I thought he might lie to spare my feelings.

Honestly, I'm glad that he didn't.

"I'm sorry," I say, nestling into his shoulder. Smelling him. His smell is the best smell.

"That's okay," he says. "I don't mind. Obviously."

"Obviously."

"I'm sorry you had such a shitty week," he says. He does this thing where he massages my scalp with his fingertips. It's the greatest. "And you shouldn't feel bad about Matty. You didn't know. There's also just something really punchable about that dude. I don't want to condone violence, but at the same time, kind of wish I'd been there."

"There is something punchable about him, isn't there?"

"He's smug."

"I'm smug."

"Yeah, but it works on you."

"I know," I say, sliding down and using his thigh as a pillow. He plays with my hair.

Maybe there is hope. Maybe there is a horizon.

"I was so mad," I tell him. "I've been mad a lot lately."

"At Matty or just in general?"

"Well, my mom's a factor, for sure. But beyond that, I don't really know."

It's not a lie. Not exactly. I'm being as honest as I can, telling him as much as possible without getting into the furry specifics.

"It's kind of worrying me, my anger," I say.

I watch. I wait for some hint of disgust at this confession.

"I think having some anger is probably healthy, to a certain extent. There's plenty to be mad about."

"Do you ever get angry?"

"Yeah," he says. "Everyone gets angry."

"I don't think I've ever seen you mad before."

"I'm usually pretty quick to skip to sad," he says. "If something's bothering me, I just shut down. Get quiet. I don't yell. It can be frustrating for people close to me."

"That you're quiet?"

"Yeah," he says. "That when I'm feeling some type of way, I disconnect. Sometimes I wish I could yell. Have that external release. Get out whatever's going on in my head."

"What's in it?" I ask, reaching up to tug gently on his ear. "Your head."

"A lot," he says. "A lot of shit."

"Will you tell me?" I ask.

"What's in my head?"

"Mm."

"This is what you do," he says, grinning. "You want me to put all my cards out on the table and you get to remain a mystery. You know how I feel about you."

"We're not thirteen anymore," I say, sitting up.

"I know that."

"You said I was the same. The morning after bowling. But what if that's not true? What if I'm not who you think I am? What if you don't really know me?"

"I don't assume that I do," he says. "What I meant the other day wasn't that you're exactly how you were in high school. You're as funny and smart and witty and cool as I remember. But I know you've lived a lot of life since then. So have I."

"Yeah," I say, pulling the blanket over my head so I look like a Jedi.

"I don't just like you because I had a crush on you in high school," he says.

"I also don't like you because I had a crush on you in high school."

"Cute."

"Because I didn't have a crush on you in high school."

"Gathered that, thanks."

"Sorry." I pull the blanket down over my face.

"I'm not playing relationship chicken," he says. "I want to be with you. I want to see where this goes."

"You say that now."

"What are you alluding to?"

"Nothing," I say from inside my safety blanket. "I don't know what I'm doing."

"Come out of there," he says.

I peek a single eyeball out through the folds of the blanket.

"I've got hot dogs out here."

"Stop trying to tempt me out of my blanket cave."

"That's my blanket," he says. "Technically it's my blanket cave."

"Doesn't sound right to me."

He scoops me up inside the blanket and carries me upstairs to bed. He unwraps me carefully, like an anticipated gift.

I wait for him to ask me about my bandages, but he doesn't. His eyes don't stray from mine.

I want him to promise me that he'll keep looking at me the

way he does, the way he always has. I want him to promise me that his feelings won't change no matter what.

"You're so beautiful," he says as he kisses along my clavicle, one hand loose around my neck and the other moving up my thigh. "You're so beautiful."

But I need him to love me ugly.

IX

"Morning," he whispers. "I have a lesson."

I squint into vibrant sunlight. He stands over me, already dressed.

"You can stay in bed if you want," he says. "I'll be downstairs with a student."

"Mm. I should probably go to the hospital to check on Scarlett."

I roll out of bed, and he walks me out. We kiss in the doorway for too long.

"Don't ghost me again," he says.

"I'm not a ghost," I tell him as I leave. I add to myself, "I'm much scarier."

I swallow my guilt. I don't know if it's for shutting him out last week or for allowing myself to get close to him again, knowing what I am, how easily it could all fall apart, and how badly it will hurt if it does.

The walk to the 7-Eleven parking lot is short but unpleasant. I'm too tired to use my legs.

I drive to the hospital, head up to the third floor. Matty sits in the waiting room, wearing a sling, looking exhausted.

I find the vending machines and get him some shitty coffee, pretty much my only olive-branch option in the vicinity. When I sit next to him, he flinches.

"Relax," I tell him. "I brought you coffee."

"Is it poisoned?"

"No. I'm not that resourceful."

He takes a sip. "Thanks."

"I'm sorry about your shoulder," I say. It's a reluctant apology. It tastes like sulfur.

He sighs. He's adopted Scarlett's sigh. That's hers.

"I hate this," he says.

"Have you seen her? Is she doing okay?"

"Doctor said everything's normal," he says. "But mentally, I don't know where she's at. She won't really talk to me."

"I don't have any answers for you," I say. I take a sip of the coffee, but it's so bad, I spit it back into the Styrofoam cup. "Clearly."

"My mom said once the baby comes, it'll all blow over," he says. "But I don't know, man. I'm worried."

I can't tell if I should be on his side or not. I find it hard to believe that Scarlett would kick him out of their shared home while carrying their child without good reason. But he looks like a fucking mess. It's hard not to feel sorry for the guy.

The sling is a significant factor, especially since I'm the one who put him in it.

"You still love her?" I ask him.

He reacts with a look that I truly do not appreciate.

"Yes," he says. His tone I care for even less. "Of course."

"All right," I say. "I can try talking to her."

"I bought a ring," he says.

"Does she know?"

"Yeah, she knows. I told her."

He takes a nip of Jack Daniel's out of his inner jacket pocket and offers it up to me. I open the lid of my coffee and he pours some inside.

I replace the lid. "I'm going in."

"She should be released soon. Just waiting for the doctor to see her again."

I go to pat him on the shoulder but figure I should probably avoid touching him for the foreseeable future. I keep my hands to myself.

Scarlett's asleep in the room. Mom sits in a chair at her bedside.

"I can get you coffee," I whisper to her.

"I'm okay," she says, standing. She hugs me. "I moved my flight back another week."

"That's good," I say. I can't resist adding, "For Scarlett."

"We can have Thanksgiving together," she says.

"Great." I actually mean it, because she'll happily cook a turkey and I'll happily eat a turkey.

"You smell like whiskey," she says.

I lift my coffee cup. "A gift from Romeo out there in the waiting room."

"He's so devastated," Mom says. "I don't know what Scarlett's thinking."

I lower my voice. "Has she said anything to you?"

She shakes her head. "It was horrible last night. She started having pains. She had to pull over. She threw up. The doctor said she was dehydrated. Her blood pressure is a little high. I imagine it's the stress of it all."

I sure hope it's a coincidence that the day after I tell Scarlett I'm a werewolf, she ends up in the hospital.

I wish I could be that naive.

"It's all right," Mom says, giving me another hug. "I know you're worried, but the doctor said everything was fine."

I look over Mom's shoulder and see that Scarlett's awake, watching us.

"My gorgeous sister," I say.

She starts to cry.

I freeze.

"Oh, honey," Mom runs over.

"Can't you respect my privacy?" Scarlett asks. "I could hear you. I just want some privacy. Please? Can I be left alone for a minute?"

"Honey," Mom says, pushing Scarlett's hair back out of her face, "you don't mean that."

"I do," she says, looking over at me. "Please."

She closes her eyes. I hate seeing my sister cry.

"I will be leaving, then. It's been a pleasure," I say, giving a regal wave. "Until we meet again. Auf Wiedersehen, goodbye."

I down the rest of my Irish coffee and toss the cup into the trash on my way out. I hear Mom calling my name, but I ignore her. I'm not going to get her out of that room; there's no point in trying. What I can do is listen to Scarlett and give her the space she's requested.

I make myself useful by stopping at the grocery store on the way home. I buy all the things Scarlett likes and, for myself, enough meat to feed a football team.

I unpack the groceries, then channel my guilt into cleaning. I vacuum. I open the rest of the gifts from the shower. The diaper thing. Some clothes. I remove the tags and put them in the washing machine with organic detergent. I scrub toilets and refill soap dispensers.

I finish construction of the crib. I assemble a mobile. I get the clothes out of the dryer and fold them.

I hold up a pale yellow onesie and try to picture a baby inside it. I wonder what it will be like to have this new little person in our lives. I wonder how her weight will feel in my arms.

I take my phone out of my back pocket. There's a single shard of screen left. Still works, though.

The next full moon is in twenty days.

I can't undo what's been done, but I can try to figure out a way to live with it. To harness it. Find some control.

I run the soft fabric of the onesie between my fingers.

If I can hold on to myself, every second of every day and through the transformation, if I can stay awake, stay "me" even as the monster, then maybe my situation isn't so hopeless after all.

I tuck the onesie neatly inside a drawer. There's a stack of children's books on top of the dresser. I flip through thick cardboard pages. Bright pictures of animals, smiley faces. The book at the bottom of the stack isn't cardboard. Its pages are thin, edges gilded. It's a book of fairy tales. On the cover is a girl in a red hooded cloak wandering into the forest.

In all the fairy tales, the wolf is big and bad and dangerous. A predator. Devious and evil. Something to be feared. But fairy tales are bullshit. Maybe wolves just get a bad edit.

There are worse things to be. I know because I've faced those monsters.

"Are we there yet?" I ask Ian as soon as we pull out of the driveway. He's taking me somewhere, but he won't tell me where.

"Do you have your passport?"

"What?"

He grins.

I'm grateful to get out of the house. Scarlett has been put on something called "activity restriction." Her mood has not improved since the hospital. She's been pretty much nonverbal, so Mom decided to talk enough for the both of them. We had an insufferably awkward Thanksgiving. Scarlett silent, me gracelessly devouring turkey, Mom chattering incessantly.

I keep trying to summon the emotion I had that moment in the driveway when I didn't want her to leave. But nah, it's long gone now. Her flight out is tomorrow night, and I'll be whistling my way to the airport to drop her off.

Ian's got one hand on the steering wheel and the other on my thigh.

"We could just go back to yours," I say.

We haven't seen each other in a few days, not since the 7-Eleven night. I missed him. He's sitting right next to me and I miss him.

He's been good motivation for me to stop spiraling and get my shit together. I've been going for long runs. Staying hydrated. Practicing breathing exercises. I slept well the past few nights, for the first time in weeks. I feel calmer. More in control.

Well, I did. Until I got in this car. Now I just want to pull over somewhere and rip our clothes off.

But that's probably not wolf related. That's just me.

"You're really not gonna tell me where we're going?"

"No," he says. "I'm not."

"Okay," I say. "Really rolling the dice here, but suit yourself."

Twenty minutes later we arrive at a big unmarked warehouse.

"You're murdering me, aren't you?" I ask as he opens the passenger-side door for me.

"Yes. That's exactly right."

We walk up and enter a small office. There's a front desk topped with stacks of clipboards and paperwork and a container of pens. I look around and see jumpsuits and heavy-duty goggles. I step toward the window near the desk. On the other side of the glass is a massive space filled with junk. Old cars, furniture, electronics. A huge Christmas tree with ornaments and presents underneath. Freestanding drywall.

"What is this?" I ask him.

"It's a rage room," he says. "We get to go in there and smash all of that shit."

"Are you serious?"

"Yeah," he says. "You said you were mad lately. I thought . . . Was this a bad idea?"

It takes me a few seconds to speak, to untie my tongue and form the words.

"No, this is great," I say. "This is really great."

A tear stings the corner of my eye. Maybe it's stupid to be so moved by this, but I told him I was angry, and he didn't judge me for it. He wasn't turned off by it. He accepts it, is giving me space for it.

A man appears behind the counter. He has us read and sign the forms, gives us a little speech about how it works, then hands us the jumpsuits and goggles to put on. We finish off our looks with plastic face shields. Ian selects the baseball bat, leaving me to choose between a golf club and sledgehammer. I go sledgehammer.

"Those are heavy," the man says. "Women have a better time with the golf club."

I don't bother to respond, just can't help but laugh.

"She's good," Ian says.

"Okay, then," the man says, opening the door to the warehouse. "Have fun."

I wander out through the rubble. I climb on top of one of the cars, a rusty decades-old Toyota. I lift my sledgehammer up high over my head, and in a swift, efficient movement, I smash it through the windshield. The hair on the back of my neck pricks up. I take off the side mirror with a lazy swing.

I hop down and open the driver's-side door. I kick it once to get it loose, then again to take it clean off. It slides across the floor to Ian's feet.

I feel him watching me. His attention doesn't deter me. I tighten my grip on the handle of the sledgehammer. I hold it in both hands and listen to the sing of my blood. Then I spin around and obliterate the headlights.

I won't stop until it's nothing. I want it to be nothing. I want to destroy it. Pick it up and throw it across the room.

I could.

I could crush it with my bare hands. I'm strong enough.

The violence has me salivating. When given the opportunity to rage, I will rage.

"Rory?"

Ian crosses behind me, baseball bat over his shoulder.

I come back to myself. "Sorry. I got carried away."

He shrugs. "That's why we're here. You want help? Or you want to finish this off yourself?"

"Oh, I don't know," I say.

"I think I'm gonna go for the Christmas tree," he says, pointing toward the tree behind a mountain of VCRs.

"Go for it."

I can't picture him destroying anything. He's six five; he's a big guy. He could do some damage if he wanted to. But there's no belligerence in him, no trace of aggression in how he carries himself.

I watch him bat at one of the ornaments, sending it into the wall with a satisfying crunch. He does it again. He's methodical in his demolition of the ornaments. The way he goes about it, it's almost merciful.

It's endearing.

"Yeah, fuck Christmas," I shout.

"I actually like Christmas," he says.

"I can tell."

His laugh echoes through the space.

I feel my pulse slow as I approach him, the rage swell subsiding. I take a few deep breaths to calm down, to ease myself out of it.

These rabid spells, like just now and with Matty, these moments that escape me, where I get hostile and power drunk, I need to find a way to curb them. I need an anchor, something to tether me to myself. Right now it's him.

It's watching him bat these tacky Christmas ornaments into the wall.

"You want a go?" he asks, offering up the tree.

"I like watching," I say. "I like watching you."

"Now I'm self-conscious," he says.

"Come here."

He lets the bat drop and steps toward me. I put my visor up. I step on an old TV to get closer to his face. I push his visor up and kiss him.

Next thing I know, we're tripping over the VCR mountain, and he's got me on the hood of the car I smashed to shit.

"You guys can't be doing that," the man says over the loudspeaker. "You can't do that in here."

"We're not allowed to make out in here?" I ask.

"No, ma'am."

"Uh!" I say to Ian, sliding off the hood. "He called me 'ma'am.'"

Ian puts his hands up in surrender. "Rules are rules."

I pull my visor down. "Fine."

We find a pile of creepy porcelain dolls in the corner and bash their faces in. We stomp on some VHS tapes, throw bottles at the wall. If I feel the rage swell, I take a deep breath and look at him, and it goes away.

Not a problem. I like looking at him.

I don't know why I tell Mom about my date with Ian. She's the last person I should be talking to about a potential relationship, but it's an hour to the airport and we don't exactly have a wealth of palatable topics to choose from.

"After the rage room, he took me back to his place and made me chicken parmigiana," I say. "It was nice."

"What a story it would be," she says. "Childhood sweethearts coming back together."

"We weren't childhood sweethearts. We never dated."

"Wouldn't it be something if you two got together, and then Scarlett got back together with Rich."

"I think Rich is married."

Mom waves her hand like she's clearing smoke. "Marriages don't last."

"You're married."

"Guy and I are soul mates," she says.

"Ah, right," I say. "Of course."

"Maybe you and Ian are soul mates."

"Definitely."

I did look up our zodiac compatibility earlier, a true low point for me. The match seemed promising, but I bailed when it got into moon signs. All set there.

"I know you're a skeptic," Mom says, cracking the window even though the heat is on. "But if you open yourself up to the possibility of love, I think you'll be pleasantly surprised."

"Do soul mates make each other cum a lot? Like, multiple times in a row? Because then, for sure, we're soul mates."

"You're vulgar," she says. "But yes, they do."

I start chuckling. She tries to resist, but eventually joins in.

"You surprise me," she says. "You're my daughter. You're of me. I raised you. But I don't know where you came from."

"It's a mystery."

"I'm very proud of you," she says. "I just want to see you happy. If that's with Ian or in Manhattan with your job. Whatever life you choose."

"Thanks, Mom. I appreciate that."

"You'll be successful no matter what you do. You're very driven. Smart. Strong," she says. She pauses long enough for me to get nervous about what she's going to say next. "Everything that happened, everything you've been through, it's made you the strong woman you are today."

I think I understand what's happening here. I think she's insinuating that the incident with Dave was actually for the best because it made me a "strong woman." I think she's trying to tell me that I should be grateful for my trauma because it's somehow positively contributed to my personal development.

There's no winning. The trauma is either your fault or it's a gift. It's either *You should have done this to stop it* or *Look what good has come of it!* If you don't get over it, why can't you get over it? Why can't you get past it or learn how to cope? Or if you do find some way to move on with your life in a socially acceptable manner, then you're so brave and so strong, and aren't you amazing? Let's applaud you for moving forward while there's a knife at your back.

The wind shrieks through the crack in the window.

"You're a survivor."

It's like Scarlett said. Mom can't accept any responsibility. She can't accept responsibility for letting him into our house, for not listening to me, for not paying attention, for not being more supportive in the aftermath. She couldn't live with herself. She can barely live with herself now. Why else would she say something like that? Why else would she keep trying to rationalize, to justify what happened?

I know I'm not getting an apology. I know that it's never going to come, that I'm never going to get what I want from her. She doesn't have it to give. And still, I'm waiting. I'm hoping.

That's the problem. I know, but I can't truly accept it because I'm holding on to this hope.

"Rory?"

I grip the steering wheel. My pulse quickens. The gallop of my heart is earsplitting.

I inhale. Through the open window, I smell roadkill. Meat. Whatever it is, it hasn't been dead for long.

Saliva pools under my tongue.

There was a rabbit. The night of my transformation. I remember now. It was fast, but I was faster. It was easy to skin with my teeth, sleek underneath the fluff of its fur. Very pink without its coat.

I can taste it. Metallic. Sweet.

I'm so hungry.

"Rory?"

My vision tints red.

"You should have told me," she'd said back then. Should have, should have, should have.

"I loved him," I heard her say. She was crying at the kitchen table the week after Dave had been arrested, crying to a friend on the phone. "I really loved him."

"I'm sorry," I whispered.

And I was. I was very sorry.

"Rory, are you all right?"

The taillights ahead of me blur. The highway blurs. They're lost in the swell.

There's no more roadkill. That scent is gone. There's only Chanel No. 5.

And my heartbeat. That's gone, too. I listen for it, but it's lost to me. I can hear hers, though. I can hear hers so clearly.

Knock, knock, knocking inside her chest, among fluttering lungs, arteries, a tangle of veins. And blood. Her blood. Warm, warm blood.

Her neck. Her throat.

She wears a silver chain. From it hangs a Tiffany locket. Inside there's a picture of Scarlett and a picture of me.

The picture of Scarlett is from when we were little. She wears a black turtleneck. She's missing her front teeth.

The picture of me is from my college graduation. I wear a cap and gown and a funny face.

She says these are her favorite photos of us. But I wonder if it's not a coincidence that I'm older in my picture. That I'm not a child.

I blink. In the fleeting dark, I see myself. I see my goofy face in that graduation picture.

"I don't hate you," I say. "I love you. And I forgive you."

She rolls up her window.

"You don't need to say anything. But you should know that I forgive you."

I'm not sure if it's true. It feels true. It also feels transient. Like I want to add the caveat that I reserve the right to change my mind.

"Thanks, baby," she says. Her reaction is mild, like I just offered her a mint.

But I guess the forgiveness isn't for her. It's for me. Because it's either that or taking her head off with my teeth. There's no more in-between.

"You have to get over," she says. "It's the next exit."

"Put that away," Scarlett says.

I'm vaping on the front steps and she's in the doorway, wearing a long black robe. Honestly, it doesn't look so different from her Halloween costume.

"It's away," I tell her.

She steps out and slowly lowers herself to sit next to me. I present the chocolate-covered gummy bears I got for her on the drive home from the airport.

"Thank you," she says. "My favorite."

"I don't know how you eat those."

"You're missing out."

This is the most she's spoken to me since the hospital. I rest my head on her shoulder as she opens the bag and pops one of the bears into her mouth.

"You still love me?" I ask her.

"Yes, but much less than I used to."

"Hey, I got you candy. Doesn't that count for something?"

"You told me I ruined your life."

"No, I didn't," I say, lifting my head. "I never said that."

"You said you came here and now your life is over." She doesn't seem upset. She's being very matter-of-fact.

"I'm sorry. I was angry," I say. "I'm working on it. My anger."

"That's good."

"But you lied to me."

"I didn't lie."

"You weren't truthful."

"It's complicated."

"Try me."

She sighs. "Not now, okay? I'm not ready."

"That's even more cryptic. I don't get it. I was honest with you about . . . you know, my whole deal. Why can't you just tell me?"

She twists the bag closed. "Let's go inside. It's freezing."

I help her up.

"I know you're the one who fucked up Matty's shoulder."

I consider denying it.

"He didn't tell me. He's suddenly wearing a sling and wouldn't say what happened. Seth told me."

Have to say, newfound respect for Matty for not ratting me out.

"It was an accident," I say. "I swear."

"Okay."

She drops onto the couch, puts her feet up on a pillow. I sit on the floor between the couch and the coffee table.

"You're really not going to tell me why you kicked him out?"

"Just . . . take it easy on him," she says. "Please?"

"Seriously?"

"Let's watch TV. Take this candy away or I'll eat it all."

I do as she asks.

"You want something to drink?" I call from the kitchen.

"No, I'm okay," she says. "I've got water."

I spot a note on the counter. It's in Scarlett's neat handwriting. My name is at the top. Then an address. A date. A time. Another name.

A doctor.

"Hey, what's this note?" I ask.

"I made an appointment for you with the therapist I mentioned."

"Why do you think I need to see a therapist?"

"Why do you think you're a werewolf?"

"I am a werewolf."

"Well," she says, "that's why you need to see a therapist."

"Scarlett," I say, stepping in front of the TV, "I showed you."

"Listen, Rory, I don't know what to think. I don't know what's going on with you. But you need to talk to someone. I wish I could be that person, but I've kind of got my uterus full."

"*I* need to talk to someone? What about you?"

"I have a therapist," she says.

"Oh."

"Actually, can I have the gummies?"

I give her the candy back. I move her legs so I can sit beside her on the couch.

She flips around for fifty years before selecting *Beetlejuice* on some obscure streaming service.

We fall asleep watching it.

Mom's absence simplifies our dynamic. The next day, with nothing to do and nowhere to go, we spend 99 percent of our time on the couch, reading and working and watching TV, getting up only for food and bathroom breaks.

I'm not sure if this is what the doctors meant when they restricted Scarlett's activity, but I'm too afraid to ask and rock the boat. I let days pass like this before suggesting we leave the house and go for a walk.

There's a chill in the air. It's going to snow soon. I can taste it.

"A year ago," Scarlett says, pausing to zip up her jacket. "A year ago, everything was so simple. How did things get so fucked so fast?"

"I'm guessing a lack or failure of birth control."

She grumbles.

"For me it was really just the werewolf attack," I say. "That's when things started to get weird."

Another grumble.

"It's not that I don't believe you," she says.

"Doubt, disbelief. Tomato, to-mah-to."

"What do you want from me? How would you react if I came to you and said I was a unicorn?"

"You are a unicorn," I say, petting her head.

We cross the street and pass a house with rotting pumpkins on the doorstop, pass another with a giant turkey inflatable, another with Christmas lights.

It's a confusing time for everyone.

"There is such a thing as clinical lycanthropy," she says.

"All in my head," I say. "I'm imagining it."

"It's possible," she says. "The physical symptoms could be manifestations of a strong mental belief."

"If I could will things of my body, I would have much bigger tits and never get my period."

"Did you know Mom's going through menopause?" she asks. It's an unexpected shift in subject.

"No, that's not information I received or cared to receive, but thanks."

"I never see her as getting older," she says. "She kept referring to herself as a grandma and it made me—"

She shudders.

I watch her walk down this street where she's lived for the past five years, in the town where she's lived her whole life, and I realize maybe it's not that she's content to be where she's always been. Maybe she's just terrified of change.

"Matty told me he bought a ring," I say, tripping over some uneven sidewalk.

"Mm," she says.

"No comment on that?"

"No comment." She's suddenly out of breath. "Let's turn around here."

The sky has gone gray and gloomy, the wind bitter.

"I'm dealing with it, you know?" I tell her. "The werewolf stuff, I'm handling it. I don't need your help. I just want to be able to talk about it with you. I want you to believe me."

She doesn't look at me. Doesn't speak for a few minutes.

"I wouldn't say anything about this to anyone," she says finally. "I know you've seen Ian. I wouldn't say anything about this to him. Not until you talk to the therapist, at least."

It's a hurt that makes me yearn for a transformation. For physical pain. Something obvious. The piercing of a sharp tooth through tender gums. The shattering of a bone. The give of skin. That hurt is easy to identify. It's simple.

This hurt, it's enigmatic. The sting of my sister's doubt and how it makes me doubt myself.

When we get back, she goes upstairs to nap, and I cancel the appointment with the therapist.

The full moon will be here soon enough. If she needs more proof, I'll get her more proof.

X

I order a new pair of handcuffs, since I left my old ones at the distillery, and luckily, they arrive just in time. It's the morning of the full moon.

I don't have the crate anymore, but it wasn't particularly effective, so I'm not sure it matters. Besides, I'm trying to control myself through the transformation.

I read that exhaustion is a possible remedy, which seems like a stretch, but I figured it couldn't hurt. I got up early and drove to the bike trail, ran until my legs felt like noodles. After, I went grocery shopping and bought a family-sized portion of pulled pork, roast beef, and multiple rotisserie chickens. Werewolf snacks. If I have meat in front of me, maybe I won't hunt. Then maybe tomorrow I won't have to vomit up rat teeth. Wouldn't that be nice?

I put the groceries away and take a quick shower. I dress in one of Ian's shirts. I wore it home earlier this week after he "accidentally" ripped the buttons off my blouse. It fits like a tent and smells like him.

I'm hoping it stays on when it happens.

Handcuffs plus exhaustion plus meat plus the comfort of Ian's smell. And I've been going through breathing exercises, practicing mental tricks. The 3-3-3 rule. Also, if I could restrain myself from biting my mother's head off, I think I've generally leveled up in the self-control department.

I'm optimistic that I'm not going to be quite such a terror this time around. I've done it once before. I have the advantage of experience. I know what to expect. I'm prepared.

Though, even if I can control myself as the wolf, I still have no choice in becoming the wolf. I've been successful at staving off the dread of the transformation until today. I keep getting phantom sensations, little hints of what it was like last time, what it will be like tonight. Almost like growing pains. Like if electric shocks and growing pains and stabbing and burning all joined forces.

Fun times.

"You're going out tonight?" Scarlett asks me over a late lunch of ham-and-cheese sandwiches.

"Yep."

"I'm worried about you," she says. "I think you should stay home."

"Ah, no."

She peels the crust off her bread. "You didn't go to your appointment."

"If you still want me to go after tomorrow, I promise I'll go," I say, crossing my heart.

"What's tomorrow?"

"The day you start believing in unicorns."

She gives me a look.

The sun sets so early this time of year. I leave at four just to be safe. I drive out to the distillery with my handcuffs, the meat, and my fully charged brand-new phone.

When I get there, I find the ruins of the crate inside, along with some scratch marks and faded bloodstains on the concrete.

I use what's left of the crate to prop up my phone at the right angle; then I set the meat out in front of me. Then I handcuff myself to a loop of exposed pipe.

Then I wait, watching the sky.

I'd wondered if it was possible to just stay out of the moonlight, but there's too much conflicting lore. And it's not like I could test it at Scarlett's. I'd need to find somewhere remote. A cabin in the woods. Sit in a closet all night or something. An underground bunker.

I look up in anticipation, scan the looming mist.

How long do I have left?

"Three-three-three," I say to myself.

When you're anxious, if you name three things you see, three sounds you hear, and then move three parts of your body, it's supposed to help calm you down. The 3-3-3 rule.

"I see the sky. I see the distillery. I see . . . meat."

The saliva leaks from my mouth before I can swallow it down.

"I hear . . ." I hear my heart beating itself up. It's the only sound.

"My, my . . . head . . ." I shake it back and forth, back and forth. Only now I can't stop. I can't stop.

"My . . . tongue . . ." I run it over my teeth.

"My . . ."

Fuck. I need to focus. I need to breathe.

I burrow my face into my shoulder and inhale the scent of Ian's shirt. It's a sanctuary, his smell. A brief, happy peace. A peace invaded by another smell. The meat.

I'm hungry.

I reach for the chicken. I knock it over. It goes tumbling out of the plastic container onto the ground.

I want, very badly, for this to bother me. I want to be disgusted by it, by this chicken now coated in dirt and dust and animal waste. I want not to want it anymore.

But I'm so hungry, it's all I can think about.

It's a maddening ache.

I'm the hungriest I've ever been.

My stomach is eating itself. It hurts.

I need it. I need that chicken. I need to feel its veins between my teeth, the slime of its skin on my tongue.

I reach for it. I reach and reach.

And I watch as the moonlight takes the tips of my fingers.

It's slow. The split of my nails. Slow as the others come in underneath, black and sharp and heavy. My knuckles bloat. Joints fizz as they reassemble. My skin bubbles in the moonlight, fat blisters that erupt into gray fur.

There's an inferno of screaming. The sound of my suffering permeates the woods, charges the mist with an electric danger. All other creatures, anything else alive out there, holds still, arrested by the violence.

My eyes burn. There's a pressure inside them, coming from the reshaping of my head. I reach up and press my leathery palms into them so they don't seep from me.

I'm on my knees, but then they give out and I fall forward. The fur spreads like fire, like I'm being flayed with hot irons. It's un-bearable.

I'm dying.

The force of my screams sends my teeth from me. The new ones descend, and with them comes the howling.

And the rapture.

I snap the handcuffs off easily.

The chicken is gone. I crunch the bones between my teeth, taste their delicious marrow.

The rest of the meat. It's gone so fast. I blink and I'm gnawing on my own fingers.

The squirrel. Hanging over my jaws as I hold it by its long, soft tail.

It's not dead when I swallow it.

I can hear its heartbeat for a few seconds after. Feel it writhing there in my gut.

Until.

There's a loud heartbeat. The loud heartbeat of a big heart.

I claw up the side of the distillery and jump down into the clearing.

There's a flash of fur. It's fleeing. It knows.

I'm after it.

I've got it by its back leg, by its sweet doe foot. I rip it off. The mess of the tear splashes in my face. I shake it from my fur.

Without its leg it won't get very far.

I'm on it again, my fingers in its eyes. In a fury, I twist, and it stops moving.

The moonlight is heavy on the back of my head, forcing me down, deeper inside the deer as I feed. I lap up its blood, let my hungry tongue soak in it.

The awareness is both sudden and slow.

There's the squish of insides against my snout. The red film over my eyes, like I'm looking through tinted warped glass.

It's like I'm chained to the frenzy, but a second ago I was nothing but the frenzy. I'm a whisper. But I'm here now.

A hostage in my own body.

I try to pull away from the deer. To spit it from my jaws. But this body won't listen. It keeps eating and eating and eating.

There are things beyond our control.

My body.

My body is beyond my control.

This is the truth. The truth of me.

What if I can't control myself in this form because this is what I really am? What if this is what I really want?

Power and violence and freedom and oblivion.

I let my eyes roll back and the monster win.

I wake up naked in the distillery. Ian's shirt is crumpled up beside me, ripped and stained. I put it on backward. My ass is out, but what can I do?

I gather up my phone and keys and stagger down the path to my car.

When I get to Scarlett's, there's another car in the driveway. A guest.

"Great," I say.

As soon as I speak, the scratch of my throat calls up the vomit. I hold it in until I'm inside. I barely get into the downstairs bathroom before it happens. What is truly the most revolting and exhausting experience of my life.

I fall asleep with my head on the toilet seat. When I come to, I hear hushed voices in the kitchen.

Scarlett's. And Matty's.

I crawl over and press my ear to the door to listen.

I can't make out anything they're saying. My head throbs. I'm too queasy to move, so I don't. I close my eyes and fall asleep again.

When I come to the second time, I don't hear any voices. I reach up and twist the knob, opening the door a crack so I can peek out to see if the coast is clear.

It is.

I stumble upstairs and take a shower, vomit some more, then nap. I remember to plug my phone in before I pass out.

It's charged when I get up however many hours later. I slept all day. It's dark out.

I take a palmful of Advil and venture downstairs, where I find Scarlett alone on the couch.

"Sleeping Beauty," she says.

"Wrong fairy tale. Move over," I say, squeezing next to her.

"I was worried about you."

"Sure," I say, pulling up the video on my phone.

"What's this?"

"I haven't watched it yet."

I probably should have, just to confirm that I got it. But I don't want to see it. I don't need to.

She does.

I hand her the phone and hit PLAY.

I watch her watch.

"What is this?" she asks, looking up at me. She's horrified.

"I think there's probably a while where I'm just standing there. Here, let me fast-forward."

I take the phone and drag to the point where I fumble the chicken.

"This is so fucked, Rory. I don't want to watch this."

"Please."

She returns her eyes to the screen at the sound.

The hideous sound of my new nails coming in.

She squints.

The screaming starts.

Her eyes go wide. She inhales sharply.

There's the ripping, gasping, gurgling, fizzing. Bones snapping. The teeth. I can hear the teeth coming in.

Then the howling. Clear and sad and eerily beautiful.

She drops the phone. It bounces off the coffee table onto the floor.

"Oh, good. That's my new phone."

A few minutes pass with nothing but Scarlett's quivering breath.

"Did you see it?" I ask.

She nods.

"Me in all my wolf-ness?"

"I can't breathe," she says. She tilts her head back. "I can't breathe."

"For real? Hey," I say, taking her hands. "Hey. It's okay."

"No," she says. "No!"

She scrambles forward and grabs my phone.

"Unlock it," she says, throwing it at me.

"I don't know if it's a good idea for you to watch it again."

"Rory!"

I unlock it and pull up the video.

She watches it over and over and over. Every time it ends, I watch her doubt reset. Then she rewinds, and I watch it vanish over my screams.

"How is this real?" she asks me.

I shrug. "It's easy to get stuck on how. Doesn't really matter, though."

She has tears in her eyes. "It looks so painful."

"I'm not trying to upset you, Scarlett. I just needed you to believe me."

"I am upset," she says, wiping her nose on her sleeve. "How could I not be upset? This is deeply upsetting!"

"It's not your problem. It's mine."

"You're my sister. How is it not my problem?"

"Because it doesn't happen to you," I say. It comes out meaner than I intend it to.

"I don't know what to do now," she says.

"Me either."

I let her cry on the other side of the couch. I don't comfort her because I shouldn't have to comfort her. It's my bad thing. My rotten thing. My burden.

"Scarlett?"

"I have a headache," she says, standing. "I'm going to bed."

"What?" I ask, calling after her as she hurries up the stairs. "Scarlett? Scarlett, wait."

I hear her door shut. I hear it lock.

I thought if she knew, I would feel less alone. But I feel even more alone now. Because I am alone. I'm alone in this.

I pick up my phone.

I watch the video.

I watch myself waiting at twilight in a dirty, abandoned building. I handcuff myself to a pipe.

I wonder if when Scarlett watched the video, she saw me or if she saw herself. Maybe we don't ever really see each other, just a confused reflection.

The chicken spills, and I lunge after it. The handcuff breaks my wrist. My hand goes limp. I don't even notice.

I'm salivating, spitting, foaming at the mouth.

The scene grows dim, and soon I'm screaming.

It's all worse than I could have imagined. The cruel expansion of my shoulders, the broadening of my back. My skin disappearing, replaced by coarse gray fur. The rising knolls of spine.

I stop the video.

I failed. I couldn't control myself. It might not even be possible.

What the hell do I do now?

The woods are dark. There's a second set of footsteps. There's someone behind me. Following me.

I'm wearing the same clothes I was the night of the attack, but I'm little. I'm young again.

I move faster.

"I like a challenge," he says.

It's Dave.

"I like you, kid," he says.

His breath grazes my ear.

I'm fifteen now, in the front seat of Jay Coker's car. I know what he wants because I know that look. Only this time I want it, too.

It feels wrong to want it, but it won't always. Soon, the confusion will fade, and only the want will remain. Soon, I'll know my want is mine. All mine. It belongs to me. It's under my control.

"I like you, kid," he says, even though he's not much older, even though I know he's not much more experienced than I am.

I climb across the console to straddle him. He puts the seat back as I unzip his jeans.

"You want to?" he asks me.

"Yes," I whisper in his ear. I take the lobe between my teeth. He plays baseball and was voted Class Flirt. He's not that good at flirting, but he is a good kisser.

Senior year, I'll get voted Class Flirt, but that's not what they call me in the halls.

I'm at my locker, but I'm not fifteen. I'm the wolf.

The lights are bright, those terrible school fluorescents.

"Hey."

It's Ian. High school Ian. Lanky. Wearing a band T-shirt and beat-up Chuck Taylor's, his hair long.

I need to tell him to run, to get as far away from me as possible, but I can't speak. I can only growl and snap my jaws.

He's not scared of me. Why isn't he scared of me?

He should be scared. He should be running as fast as he can in the opposite direction.

But he's coming closer, a stack of books tucked under his arm.

"Why?" Scarlett says. She's behind me, clutching a naked baby to her chest. She sets the baby down on the floor. "Why won't you let me help you? Why can't you help me?"

The baby's crying.

Why would she leave it here for me?

"I think you're really special," he says. Dave. We're standing in the distillery. I'm still the wolf.

"I want to show you something special," I tell him.

And it's like the deer. The head comes off easily. Like nothing. Like opening a jar.

I wake up late the next morning. I listen for Scarlett before leaving my room. When I hear nothing, I poke my head out into the hall. Her bedroom door is shut, and I assume she's still locked in there, avoiding me.

Reaper, an early adopter of the anti-Rory stance, turns his back when I step into the kitchen, pushing his food bowl into the laundry room and away from me.

I sit at the counter, gnawing on a pepperoni stick, trying to think about anything besides my last transformation. Trying to ignore the violence that keeps replaying behind my eyelids, a violence that makes my heartbeat something uncomfortable.

My phone chimes. It's Ian.

Listening to a song that reminds me of you.

I instantly relax into sweet happy wooziness. Yeah? What is it?

"Mad World."

There was this moment at our junior prom. He took Kelly and I went with Jay Coker or Tommy Haskins. I forget. I was hot from dancing, so I went outside, and Ian was there. I remember being really excited to see him. I had this sudden, overwhelming urge to run to him. I dismissed it as lingering dance floor adrenaline.

"Look who it is," I said. "Mr. Too Cool to Dance. Where's Kelly?"

"Bathroom. If they played good music, maybe I'd dance."

"Maybe. What would you want them to play? Ska?"

"Yeah, actually," he'd said. "That would be great."

"What do you think would be the worst song to play at prom?"

"Uh, 'Tears in Heaven'? Or maybe 'Mad World'?"

"Should I go put in the request? I'm chummy with the DJ."

"Don't doubt it."

"Would you dance with me?" I'd asked. "If they played one of our songs?"

"No. You know that would cause trouble," he said.

I knew what he meant. Kelly would get mad. Jealous. And she would have had good reason. She knew. Everyone knew that Ian Pedretti had always had a thing for Rory Morris, and that Rory Morris was a man-eater. Future Class Flirt.

"Me? Cause trouble?" I gave a wry smile and turned to go back inside.

I set my pepperoni stick down on the counter and stare at my phone, stare at his last message. I don't want to cause any more trouble.

But I am trouble. And this is trouble. Big trouble.

Will you dance with me? Next time I see you? I ask him.

Maybe.

☹

Yes, of course I will dance with you to our depressing prom song. When can I see you next?

I lean into myself and take a whiff of my animal reek. I slip my fingers underneath my shirt and find the trace of the bite, the subtle scarring. To unknowing hands, it'd be nothing. The rise and fall of skin so slight, barely a whisper.

It's a miracle and it's a curse, the secrets our bodies keep. The ability to carry the invisible burden of these secrets.

I'll let you know, I tell him, dread like a shadow sewn to my heel.

I take my pepperoni stick upstairs and spend the rest of the afternoon glued to my computer. I can't be the only one dealing with this. I know I'm not. Someone bit me. And someone probably bit them. There are others out there. Somebody must have answers, and I'm committed to finding them. Committed to hope.

After hours of frantic research, I find an occult shop about an hour away that specializes in "supernatural phenomena." I'm not too keen on revealing my werewolf status to a complete stranger, especially one who will likely just try to sell me crystals, but if I want my life back, I don't really have any other choice.

It does have good reviews on Yelp. And where do I get off being skeptical? I'm a fucking werewolf.

I plug the address into my phone, get in the car, and drive before I have a chance to talk myself out of it.

The shop stands alone on the side of the road. It's . . . very sketchy. I pull into the parking lot. I want to leave, to turn around and go home, but I close my eyes and see Ian. I see Scarlett. I see my niece. I have to try this.

There's no indication the shop is open except for the fact the door is unlocked. Inside, it smells intensely of incense. There are barrels of crystals, packets of herbs. Bookshelves. Candles and jars and jewelry and small statues.

"Hello?" I ask.

A figure appears. A bearded man with big eyes and long hair wearing jeans and a thick wool sweater. He's not what I was anticipating.

"Welcome," he says, giving me a warm smile as he steps behind the counter. "May I help you?"

That is the question.

"Uhh . . ." I probably should have come up with a plan of action here. "Just looking, thanks."

He nods.

I wander around the store. I check the bookshelves for anything werewolf related but most of the books are about witchcraft. Not sure a spell would be of any use.

The man's eyes follow me as I browse, like a constant tapping at my shoulder.

"How did you find us?" he asks.

"Internet."

"And there's nothing specific you're looking for?"

"Um . . ."

"I'm a practicing psychic. I have thirty-three years of experience. I know it can be difficult for people to talk about the paranormal. This is a space where you will not be judged. Whatever it is that you are dealing with, I assure you, I've seen it all."

"How psychic are you?" I ask. "Do I need to tell you . . . ?"

He gives me another warm smile. "You are quite blocked. Not open."

"Right."

He steps out from behind the counter and waves me over to the crystals. "Black tourmaline. Black tourmaline and pyrite. For protection. To combat negativity."

"Oh. Cool. Yeah, thanks. Um, do you have any werewolf stuff?"

He turns to me, the smile vanishing from his face.

"Like werewolf information. Or treatments? Possible cures? I'm doing research. On werewolves. For a, um, podcast."

"Werewolves?" he asks. He seems offended.

Have to admit, not the reaction I was hoping for.

"Yeah."

He leans back, presses his fingertips together. He clicks his tongue and shakes his head.

"I'm afraid we do not carry any fantasy literature. We specialize in true phenomena, the spiritual realm. Monsters are for the movies."

Part of me is flustered, dismayed. And part of me isn't the least bit surprised. Of course. Of course this guy doesn't believe in werewolves, doesn't think they exist. What I am, what happened to me, in his eyes is fiction. He can't fathom. He'd need proof. And even if I gave it to him, if I showed him the video, would that be enough?

And if it was, if I were to convince this stranger, if I were to expose my darkest secret in hopes of getting help, who's to say he could help me? Who's to say he'd be willing?

"Right. Of course," I say. "Sorry to bother you. Thanks for your time."

"I believe we do have dried Aconitum petals. Also referred to as monkshood, wolfsbane. If you're interested. The petals are meant to be kept in a satchel underneath one's bed for those who are wary of adversaries, who may want to keep their enemies close or have their foes reveal themselves."

"Sure." At this point, what do I have to lose? "Throw the crystals in, too."

I stand at the register, embarrassed and defeated, as he rings me up for a plastic baggie full of dead flowers and a bunch of shiny rocks. There's a tickle in my throat, and I realize I'm dangerously close to tears.

Am I really about to cry in public? In here? In front of this guy?

He's watching me. I pretend I'm admiring the jewelry in the display case.

"Are you interested in seeing anything? All real silver," he says. "It boasts a wealth of mystical properties."

"I'm allergic," I say, handing over my credit card.

"Silver is featured prominently in werewolf lore, yes?" he asks. "I have found, in my years of experience, there is always truth at the heart of lore, though it's never quite what it seems."

He smiles at me. I'm mortified.

I squeak out a thanks and leave the shop, laid bare.

I'm about to get in my car when I hear the man calling out to me.

"Miss! Miss! I must specify, the monkshood is under no circumstance to be ingested. It is highly toxic."

I give him the thumbs-up, get in my car, and drive home.

I'm anxious to talk to someone about my misadventure, but the only person I can talk to is Scarlett, and when I get home, she's gone. I wait, pacing around, turning the packet of wolfsbane over in my hands.

I kind of do want to eat it, just to spite that guy.

I contemplate opening the plastic to touch and smell the petals but change my mind and slip it under my bed.

Where are you? I text Scarlett.

Out, she responds. With Matty.

Her absence puts me in a fragile state. I'm clinging to this hope that I can salvage my life, that I can figure out a way to exist, and yet my own sister can't stand to be around me. I went against my nature to seek outside help only to be met with more disbelief.

No one can help me. I'm on my own.

I change into scrub clothes, raid the kitchen to discover I've eaten almost all the meat in the house. I'll have to go out soon to get more.

Until then, it's this bag of frozen chicken nuggets. I'm too impatient to let them thaw.

I'm sitting on the couch with the sack of cold, pale nuggets in my lap, wearing a bralette and plaid pajama bottoms, when the doorbell rings.

Reaper comes running, barking.

I cautiously approach the peephole.

It's Ash.

I open the door, and Reaper leaps into her arms, sweetly licking her face.

"Hello, hello, friend," she says.

"Are you talking to me or the dog?"

"Both!"

"What are you doing here?"

"Scarlett thought you could use some company."

"She said that? When?"

"Let's go out tonight," Ash says, ignoring my question. "I got a babysitter. And you promised you'd take me out drinking."

I groan. Going out is the last thing I want to do right now. I didn't anticipate being a werewolf would turn me into such a drag.

"I brought a change of clothes and all my makeup. Let's get ready and go out. I think we could both use it."

"I'm good," I say, eating a nugget. "Clearly."

"Clearly," she says. "Then for me."

Tricky little minx. Ash knows I'd do anything for her. She's a selfless angel who asks for nothing. Her only character flaws are being too nice and encouraging certain vulnerable parties to get bangs.

"Remember when you told me I should get baby bangs and then I did and looked fucking ridiculous?"

"You did not! They were adorable on you."

Oh, Ash. "Okay. Let's go out."

"Yay! Girls' night!"

"Should we invite Mia?"

"More the merrier," she says. "I'm surprised she's still around. I guess she probably has to settle her dad's affairs or whatever. God, I can't even imagine. My heart goes out to her."

"Mm."

It's not my place to tell anyone what Mia's been through, about her dad, but I do feel a little weird that she hasn't shared with anyone besides me and some terrible ex. It's a heavy secret.

I clear my throat. "So what are you wearing? What should I wear?"

Ash insists I take a shower, which, fair, considering my stench. She also insists on picking my outfit. She chooses a little black dress, black stockings, my red stilettos, and a black faux-leather jacket that she steals from Scarlett's closet. She wears a hot pink long-sleeved jumpsuit.

She plays bad pop music as we do our hair and makeup.

"I *need* your hair secrets," she says.

She really doesn't.

"Where should we go?" I ask her.

"Corner Pub?"

"Corner Pub is full of townies."

"I'm a townie," she says. "Scarlett's a townie."

"Scarlett's something, that's for sure. Matty's been to the house. Did she tell you?"

She mimes zipping her lips.

"Really?"

She's had a strict policy since we were kids. She does not play monkey in the middle.

"Does Ian count as a townie?" she says, changing the subject. "He left for a while, but now he's back. For good, I assume. He owns that place on East."

"Has he dated anyone recently? I found a picture of him and some blonde in his apartment."

"Found it where?"

"Just casually happened upon it while perusing his bookshelves."

"Oh, my God," she says, laughing. "You really like him! Going through his stuff, you cute little psycho."

"Don't insult me."

"I think you like him more than you want to admit."

"I'm not denying that I like him," I say, borrowing her blush. "I don't know where it's going yet. I don't want to get ahead of myself."

"Rory, I know you. I know what you're doing," she says, making eye contact with me in the mirror. She can't see what I see. She can't see the wolf.

I'm getting used to it, to seeing it. My other face, my second self.

"I'm not doing anything, Ash."

"Why can't you let yourself be happy?"

I feel my cheeks getting hot. I put the blush down.

"So should I tell Mia Corner Pub?"

"Yeah," she says, blotting her lips. "Ready?"

"One sec," I say, spinning like Wonder Woman until I'm so dizzy, I can't remember my problems. "Ready! Let's go."

The Corner Pub isn't so bad. They've got up holiday decorations. Tinsel and snowflakes and stars and pinecones. Colored lights strung everywhere. There's clunky furniture, wood paneling, neon signs, a jukebox. Peanut shells on the floor. There are billiard tables in the back, Skee-Ball and darts downstairs. The drinks are cheap and come with a ticket for a free personal pizza. Only a dollar if you want to add pepperoni, which I will.

"How come we don't come here more often?" I ask.

"Because you're too snobby!" Ash says.

She orders us whiskey sours. Ash loves a whiskey sour. Any drink that comes with a cherry, really.

Mia arrives shortly after us. She's got on a full face of makeup, nails done, her long blond hair blown out in perfect beach waves. Her dress is essentially sheer. She's a walking anatomy lesson, and everyone in the bar wants to study.

"You want shots?" she asks. She gives us no time to answer. "Yeah, let's do shots."

She orders us tequila shots.

If I could get drunk, I'd say this was a recipe for disaster. But I can't, so . . .

We lick salt off the back of our hands and take the shots. We suck the lime wedges and wince.

"I needed this," Ash says. "I haven't been *out* out in forever. Not since before Luca, I think."

"What?" I ask, the tequila burn lingering in my throat. "Really?"

Mia shoots me a horrified look.

"It's crazy. Time goes by so fast. Just gets away from you. Your whole life changes like that." She punctuates with a snap. "Don't get me wrong. I love being a mom. I love Luca. He's a lot of work, but it's worth it."

I shrug. "I'm not one of those mom shamers. You can be honest. If you wanted to lock yourself in a closet or scream into a pillow, I'm not clutching my pearls."

"No judgment here," Mia says, though her face says different.

"I do have my moments. But I wouldn't trade it. I'm always laughing. With Seth, with Luca. Even if they're driving me up the wall, making a mess. They're also making me laugh."

I down my whiskey and signal the bartender for another.

"I know you guys like your freedom," Ash says. "I think Scarlett does, too. She's just not as outspoken about it. But I don't see being a wife and mother as, like, sacrificing freedom. Yes, I make sacrifices, but I'm also getting things in return. From my partnership with Seth. From my relationship with my son. I know you're looking at me, thinking, 'Oh, my God, she hasn't been out to a bar in years, and she likes to stay home and clean,' and you think it's sad and scary—"

"No, I—"

"It's okay Rory. It's okay. I don't mind. I'm happy," she says. "I'm really happy."

I think she's already tipsy.

"I'm happy for you."

"You could be happy here," she says. She's just talking to me now, her back to Mia. "I miss you. I wish you would move closer. I know you're big-city now. You've always been big-city. But we could do this all the time!"

"We could," I say, lifting the cherry out of my drink by the stem and dropping it into her glass.

I'm a little off-kilter. It's distracting, being around this many people, having them so close to me. All these strangers. I can hear their hearts beating, the air as it enters and exits their lungs. I can smell their sweat. It's sensory overload. The colors in the room are too much. The lights glow aggressively. My peripheral vision is extensive, and there's this primal, uncanny awareness of the space around me. This terrifying ability to razor-focus on the humidity of that guy's breath, the notes of that woman's perfume, on hands moving and feet moving and mouths moving. Tongues. Saliva. Teeth and the remnants of dinner wedged between them. Distant conversations, words across the bar that reach me as if they're being spoken directly into my ears.

My skin crawls. The hair on the back of my neck stiffens. I don't want to pay attention, but there's a need I can't ignore. A base need to know everything that's going on around me.

This is just a reminder that I'm not normal, that my body is functioning at a different level, and there's no on-off switch. I can't opt out of this supernatural surveillance.

"Are you having fun?" Ash asks me. Her voice cuts through the noise, wonderfully familiar.

"Yeah," I lie.

"Cheers to that!" Mia says, and we clink our glasses.

"We should dance," Ash says, pulling at my hips. "Let's dance!"

"We need to put on some good music," Mia says, shuffling over to the jukebox. She selects "Girls Just Want to Have Fun." "Remember that time we went to Planned Parenthood to get condoms and they were playing this?"

"Yeah," I say. "We were, like, this is either very appropriate or very inappropriate."

She laughs. "Little of both."

The three of us sing along loudly and dance like lunatics. When a Spice Girls song comes on after, Ash screams.

Our antics get the attention of a group of four men. They look older than us, but not by much.

"They're staring," Mia says, grabbing my arm. "Let's go talk to them!"

"Nah," I say, trying to remember some *Spice World*–era choreography.

"Rory's got a boyfriend!" Ash giggles.

"Really?" Mia asks. I'm a little offended she seems so surprised.

"Ian Pedretti!" Ash yells.

"Shh!" I tell her.

"Huh, that's weird," Mia says, her face bittering.

"Why is it weird?" I ask.

"Because I went out with him a few weeks ago."

All sound in the room dies, and suddenly the only heartbeat I can hear is my own.

"What?" Ash asks.

"He took me out for a drink. We haven't hung out again, but he's definitely texted me since. Like, 'Hey, how are you?' That kind of thing. Not super flirty but not *not* flirty. I'm sorry. I had no idea you two were together."

Their eyes are on me. There's a sensation in my chest, like a harsh wind, like a cold front, like a light being snuffed out. A freezing. A calcification. Then nothing at all.

"I think those guys are coming over," I say. I turn to Mia. "How's my hair?"

"Please," she says. "You're the hottest bitch I've ever seen."

Ash slips her hand around my waist. "Rory. Are you okay?"

"Why wouldn't I be?" I ask, unleashing a cool grin.

When I turn around, the men are standing in front of us. They introduce themselves, but as far as I'm concerned, they're all named Kevin. They look like a bunch of Kevins.

One of the Kevins is attractive. He's a little taller than me. He's got a strong jaw, movie-star teeth. Some dark scruff. Curly hair.

"You said your name is Laurie?" he asks, leaning close to me.

"Rory," I say. "Rory."

"Rory?"

"Do you need me to spell it?"

"Could you?"

His breath smells of cigarettes.

"Do you smoke?" I ask.

"I do."

"May I please borrow a cigarette?"

"Borrow?"

"I'll give it back," I say. I raise three fingers. "Scout's honor."

"Girl Scout?"

"Oh, yes. I earned lots of badges."

"Did you?"

"Mm," I say. "I have many skills."

"Then okay," he says. "I'll meet you out back. They're in my jacket."

Mia is already mid-make-out with one of the Kevins. The other two fuss over Ashley. From what I can tell, she likes the attention. She knows she's beautiful, but she's like everyone. She enjoys the validation.

She and Seth are solid, but she did admit to me once that his compliments don't really mean anything anymore.

"He thinks I'm sexy because he loves me," she said. "He's attracted to me because he's in love with me. Almost like he has to be. You know what I mean?"

I didn't. I don't. Because I don't think anyone has ever been in love with me. It's only ever been attraction. That's fine. It's fine.

I catch Ash's eye and signal to her that I'm going out for a cigarette.

Be right back, I mouth. She returns a worried stare that I pretend not to notice.

I zip up my jacket and step out the back door onto the patio. There are some picnic tables with ashtrays, white string lights overhead.

I sit on top of one of the picnic tables and put my feet on the bench.

Kevin comes out a second later. He hands me a cigarette. He smokes Parliaments. Ian smokes Marlboros.

I know what pain is. I know how to feel it, and I know how not to feel it.

"As a Girl Scout, you should know," Kevin says, "that smoking is bad for you."

"Yeah, well, maybe I like things that are bad for me," I say.

I put the cigarette between my lips, and he lights it. A real gentleman, this Kevin.

I exhale up at the string lights. They're so bright, they burn.

"I think everyone likes things that are bad for them. Don't you?" I ask, leaning forward and tilting my head back, making my neck long.

"Do you live around here?" he asks me.

He leans against a post. It's working for him. He looks cool. The collar is popped on his jacket. The popular boys used to do that in high school.

I bet he was a popular boy in high school. Probably at my high school.

"I grew up here," I say. "I don't live here anymore. I live in the city. Manhattan."

"Oh, nice," he says.

For some reason this reaction is disappointing to me. I know the conversation isn't going to go anywhere from here. He can't keep up with me.

"You're looking at me funny," I say. This is a line. It has a high success rate.

"Really?" he asks.

"Yes," I say. "You're looking at me funny. Do I have something on my face?"

"No," he says. He's getting shy. "Sorry."

"It's okay," I say, pretending I'm shy.

Let's see if he can recover.

"You're really pretty," he says. "Gorgeous."

Ah, Kevin. Proud of you.

"You think so?" I ask after a long drag of my cigarette.

"Fuck yeah," he says.

"Yeah?"

I put my cigarette out in the ashtray and step down off the picnic table. I take two steps closer to him. Another step so my nose is an inch from his nose.

"Why don't you prove it?"

He drops his cigarette and kisses me.

It's a sloppy kiss.

Too much tongue. Too busy. He breathes heavy through his nose. His hand is on my throat, and his grip is hectic. I've got my hand on his chest, and I can feel his heart. I can hear his pulse. I can taste his adrenaline. It's sweet. Awakens my appetite.

The juxtaposition of sensations is thrilling.

The exchange is wild.

I love a no-strings random hookup. This is my sport. I'm varsity, MVP. I should be enjoying this. But it doesn't feel the way I want it to feel. The way I need it to feel.

He takes his hand from my throat and brings it to my chest. Bold.

I don't appreciate the squeezing. He bites my lip, or maybe I bite his. And the taste of blood is all it takes. My thoughts turn. My stomach rumbles.

Does he know? How fragile, how weak he is beside me? That I could bite off his slippery, clumsy tongue? That I could peel off his chapped lips? Crush his greedy fingers to dust in my fist?

He pulls away, and I open my eyes to the glint of teeth, his grin.

This grin suggests he's ignorant of danger. Suggests he assumes he is stronger. Assumes he is safe. I wonder what that's like, to assume safety.

He reaches down and begins to lift the hem of my dress.

I step back before I do something I regret.

"Thanks for the cigarette," I say.

I go back inside and straight to the bar. I order a whiskey on the rocks.

Ash comes over and puts her arm around me.

"Rory," she says, "are you okay?"

"Stellar. Where's Mia?"

"She left with that guy. Rory, I—"

"Let's get pizza and play Skee-Ball," I say. So that's what we do.

The rest of the night passes in a haze of detachment, the events rendered surreal by sadness. At some point, Ash calls Seth to come pick us up.

And then I'm in the backseat of his car, and he's got Billy Joel playing, and I say something like "You would."

Then we're back at Ash's.

"Sleepover! We can stay up all night and watch movies and eat snacks and . . ." She passes out on the couch before she gets a chance to pull it out for us.

I sit in the recliner and pull a blanket over my head.

"I could put you in the guest room," Seth says.

"I'm fine here, thanks. Hey, do you have any jerky?" I could really go for some meat.

"Jerky?"

"Yeah. Like beef jerky, turkey jerky."

"Uh, no," he says. "Sorry."

"Bummer."

I'm sitting on something. There's a small, sharp object poking into my left butt cheek. Seems like too much effort to remove it. So I don't. I don't care.

I don't care about anything anymore.

Anything or anyone.

I tried. I'm done.

I close my eyes and will myself to sleep.

XI

There's something in my nose. I open my eyes, and Luca's tiny face is there. He's got his small grubby finger shoved up my nostril.

"Luca," I say.

He removes the finger, then climbs onto my lap. He sports dinosaur underpants and what I presume is one of Ash's tank tops. It's lacy.

"Luca, I'm sleeping."

"No sleeping," he says. "My chair."

"Luca," I hear Seth say. "Luca, be nice to Aunt Rory."

"No," he says.

"Appreciate your candor."

I yawn and rub my eyes. Last night comes back to me. The hurt is there, crawling out of the shallow grave I attempted to bury it in.

I've been fighting so hard for a future, and for what? For whom?

It was a mistake, letting my guard down. Giving in to my feelings for Ian. Allowing myself to have those feelings in the first place. I should have known better. I should have protected myself.

It's on me.

Luca shoves his finger up my other nostril.

"All right," I say, shifting so I can stand. I find a plastic block under my butt.

"That mine," Luca says.

"If you really want it back," I say. "After where it's been."

He does. He snatches it out of my hands.

Something smells amazing. "You making breakfast?" I call out.

I pick up Luca under my arm and let him hang there. He giggles. I carry him into the kitchen with me.

Seth multitasks. He flips pancakes, attends to a skillet full of an egg scramble with bacon and sausage and scallion.

"You're a hero," I tell him.

"Down," Luca says.

I set him down and he goes running off somewhere, making a motor noise.

"Fun time last night?" Seth asks.

"Sure," I say, helping myself to a glass of water.

"I'm awake," Ash mumbles.

Her hair is wet; she wears a bathrobe and slippers that look like penguins. She's hungover.

"Coffee, water, Advil," Seth says, pointing to the kitchen table, where those things are all set out. "Sustenance."

"Thank you, babe," she says.

She pecks him, then sits at the table. He brings her a plate.

"Rory, coffee? Pancakes? Eggs?"

"I'll have coffee and eggs, please. Thank you, Doc."

"I love him," Ash says between sips of water. "Best husband ever."

Waking up to breakfast does seem like a pretty good deal. A deal I'll never get!

"Did you hook up with that guy last night?" Ash whispers over her pancakes. "When you went out to smoke?"

"PG stuff," I say.

"I thought you were with Ian," Seth says, setting a plate down in front of me.

"Babe, don't eavesdrop."

"We're not exclusive," I say, shoveling some eggs into my mouth. "Apparently."

"Yeesh," he says, shaking his head. "Poor guy."

I'm queasy. I push my plate away. "Yeah, poor guy. Must be tough lying to my face about how much he likes me while trying to fuck Mia Russo."

"Rory," Ash says.

"Wait. What?" Seth says, literally scratching his head.

"Nothing. I should go," I say, standing. "Thanks for breakfast. And the ride last night."

"Rory, don't go," Ash says.

I check my jacket. Make sure I have my wallet. Phone. Keys.

I have my keys, but no car.

"Let me drive you at least," Seth says.

"No, that's okay. I'm good to walk."

"It's far. And freezing. I'll drive you."

"Well, lucky for me," I say, opening the front door, "I'm warm-blooded."

I don't know how I didn't register these decorations last night.

Ash's lawn is covered in inflatables and wire reindeer and angels and wooden elves. There's a giant menorah and Star of David. There's an animatronic Santa at the end of the pathway that I'm tempted to punch.

I walk in silence. I didn't think to bring headphones. But with no music or podcast, I have nothing to listen to but my own thoughts.

Everything I've done—confronting my past, forgiving my mother, working through my anger, seeking a cure—was that really for me or was it all for him? At the time it seemed like a werewolf necessity, something I had to do to manage my monstrousness, but maybe I was just filing my teeth for him. For someone who never actually gave a damn about me.

I'm on a busy stretch of road. I pass the strip mall with the nail salon and the Dunkin' Donuts. I consider coffee but being more awake doesn't really appeal to me at the moment. What I really want is meat. The grocery store is a little farther down. I keep walking. A few cars honk at me. I must be a sight, in my leather jacket and black stockings and sky-high heels. Walking down the street at . . . what? Nine a.m.? Hard to tell because it's overcast.

When I get to the grocery store, I grab a cart and fill it with rotisserie chickens. I slog through the aisles tortured by the cheesy radio classics playing through muffled speakers.

I head over to the meat counter and say a smiley good morning to the woman behind it. I'm extra friendly to camouflage the subtle nag of embarrassment I'm experiencing ordering this much cow.

I'm waiting for steaks when my phone vibrates in my jacket pocket.

Message from Mia. Morning, sunshine! Sorry I left without saying goodbye. Had fun tho 😉

There're the little ellipses. She's typing something else.

> Sorry about the whole Ian thing. Promise I'm not interested in him at all!!

My grip tightens and I watch as her message is distorted by broken glass. Next thing I know my phone is in pieces. Pieces too small to hold. They fall through my fingers onto the floor.

I didn't just crack the screen this time. I crushed it. Brand-new phone obliterated.

"Oops," I say, attempting to discreetly kick my mess under the meat display case.

I receive the steaks and then proceed to order a rack of pork ribs. Just really working my way through the animal kingdom.

"Thanks!" I tell the woman, who, in addition to meat, is serving me some serious side-eye. I give her an affable wave before sliding away.

I turn a corner and my cart collides with someone else's.

With Matty's.

"Rory," he says. He doesn't appear too chuffed to see me. At least we're on the same page.

"Matthias."

We stare at each other, neither of us really knowing what to say.

"How's your shoulder?" I ask. He's not wearing the sling anymore.

"Okay," he says.

More silence.

Finally, he throws his hands up. "Do you have a problem?"

"Yes. In fact, I have quite a long list of problems. And you're on it! Right at the top. Congratulations."

"I don't understand why you're mad at me," he says.

I try to push my cart past his, but he won't let me.

"Will you just talk to me for a sec?"

"I have somewhere to be," I say, nudging his cart again.

"Where?"

"You got me," I say flatly.

"Rory, please. I'm really trying here."

"How gallant."

"Look, I'm not perfect."

I clench my fists. "You don't say."

He's the reason why I came back here. Whatever he did that prompted Scarlett to kick him out, it set off this whole chain of events.

I could destroy him. I want to. I want accountability. For once, some goddamn accountability. But where would that leave me? What would it solve? I can't repair damage by causing more damage. I can't do anything.

"I'm not perfect *but* I didn't do anything wrong here. This is on Scarlett. I don't know what's going on with you two, but I really wish you would talk to each other. I don't need you pissed at me."

"Uh, okay." What isn't Scarlett telling me? And why? "Now can I go, sir?"

He furrows his brow, then moves over and lets me by.

I go through self-checkout, having already had my fill of human interaction for today. It occurs to me as I buy several reusable grocery bags that I don't have my own because they're in the trunk of my car, which is back at Scarlett's. I didn't drive here. I walked. And I'm going to have to carry all this home.

I guess sometimes supernatural strength is pretty convenient.

When I get home however long later, Matty's car is in the driveway.

He's upstairs with Scarlett, painting the baby's room. The door is open. I see them, but they don't see me. I lock myself in my room with several rotisserie chickens.

I eat them in bed, finish them quickly, gnaw on the bones. My hands are grease slick. I search my nightstand for a tissue, something to wipe my fingers with instead of just using my sheets.

There are no tissues in my nightstand. There is an old receipt. I find it's not particularly effective. I crumple it up and throw it on the floor. I go to close the drawer, but something glimmers and catches my attention. My jewelry. The silver I haven't touched. The necklace that burned me. Some rings. A delicate bracelet.

I'm compelled. I still don't know what silver does to me, exactly.

What did the man at the occult shop say? Something about truth at the heart of lore?

Some lore says silver is fatal. Some lore says that it's associated with the power of the moon and that's why it has strong effects. I read somewhere that new wolves need to "baptize themselves in silver under the moonlight," whatever that means. I've also read that the silver thing is bullshit, which I guess I know isn't true. It does something.

Could it cure me? Could it kill me?

Right now I don't really care. Maybe this isn't curiosity. Maybe I'm just craving self-destruction.

I pick up the bracelet. It burns, but I don't mind this hurt. I kind of like it.

I clasp the bracelet around my wrist. It makes a very faint hissing noise against my skin.

My senses dull. My thoughts slow. It's something like relaxation. The world fades from me and I'm not sorry to see it go. I let my eyes close.

I'm ready to hibernate indefinitely.

I wake up in the bathtub with Scarlett standing over me, red-eyed, screaming my name.

"What?" I ask. My voice sounds far away.

The water overflows, sloshes out onto the bathroom floor. Scarlett turns off the faucet. She kneels on the tile, taking my face in her hands.

"What were you doing? What were you thinking?"

"Why am I in the bathtub?" I ask, blinking. The lights are bright. There's a high-pitched ringing in my ears. "Are you trying to harvest my organs?"

She scoffs, releases my face. "You were unresponsive."

"When?" I ask.

"You were locked in your room for three days. I got freaked out. I knocked and nothing. You weren't answering your phone. I picked the lock and found you passed out in bed, surrounded by chicken carcasses. You wouldn't wake up. I didn't want to call nine-one-one because, you know . . . I dragged you in here. Then I saw your wrist."

I look down. There's a vibrant pink line around my wrist. It's bubbling. Smoking. It has a hideous smell.

"I took the bracelet off, and you woke up."

"Huh," I say, blowing on my wrist like it's hot food. The silver burned through to my fur.

Scarlett sobs into a cage of her arms. "I thought I'd lost you."

"Frankly I'm surprised you care."

She looks up at me, wearing her dagger stare. "How could you say that?"

I stare back at her. "You've wanted nothing to do with me since I told you."

"It's a lot to process, Rory! And I have enough to deal with right now. I have other things going on. I can't give you all of me all the time."

"I don't want all of you all the time. I just wanted some support. Acceptance. I don't know. Something."

"And what about me? You don't think I've needed support from you? I've needed you, and you haven't been here."

"I've been here the whole time."

"You were with Ian, or Mia, or Ash, or—"

"You were with Matty!" I say, splashing her.

She leans back. "Did you just splash me?"

"Yeah." I do it again.

She wipes the water from her face and, astonishingly, starts to laugh.

So I laugh.

I don't know how long this goes on for. The two of us laughing, soaking wet. The *drip drip drip* of a leaky faucet. The pained gurgle of a drain clogged with hair. My hair. Werewolf hair.

Finally, Scarlett stands and throws me a towel. "Dry off and get dressed. We're going for a drive."

She takes me to Hillside Cemetery. A morbid, albeit picturesque, location. It's old but well maintained. There are no rotting bouquets resting on cracked headstones, no sinking mausoleums. Paved pathways lined with Victorian-era lampposts weave through family plots. A thin layer of clean white snow covers the ground. Icicles glisten in the afternoon sun. They weep from the trees, slowly returning to their former state of matter.

"I come here sometimes to think," Scarlett says, leading me down a particularly winding path.

"And I'm the weird sister."

"Did you know? That the bracelet would do that to you?"

I shake my head. "It was an experiment."

"You weren't trying to hurt yourself?"

"Honestly? Maybe part of me wanted to feel something different. Or to not feel at all."

I catch her up. I tell her about my failed trip to the occult shop, the wolfsbane under my bed that I don't know what to do with. I tell her about Ian.

"Maybe he's trying to fuck all the girls he didn't get to fuck in high school," I say.

Scarlett makes an ambiguous noise.

"What?" I ask, dribbling a small stone between my feet.

"Do you really believe her?"

"Mia? Yeah. Why wouldn't I?"

"You know how she is."

"How is she?" I ask. "Seriously. How is she?"

Scarlett sighs.

"She's like me," I say. "We flirt. We fuck around. Doesn't make us liars."

"I'm not saying she's lying," Scarlett says. "But she might have misinterpreted. I just don't think there's anything incriminating about them hanging out one time. They're old friends."

"They weren't friends."

"Acquaintances," she says. "It's Ian. He deserves the benefit of the doubt."

"Does he?" I ask. I kick the stone too far, lose it over the hill. "Whose side are you on?"

"Yours," she says, sitting on a nearby bench. There's an angel statue perched behind her, and from this angle it looks like Scarlett has wings. "Why don't you just ask him?"

"How can I trust him? He kept this from me. If it wasn't anything incriminating, why didn't he say something? It's shady."

"When you love someone, you don't just cut them off. Even if they make a mistake."

"Love? Who said anything about love?"

"Rory," Scarlett says, a tremble in her voice that makes the air go still.

I look back, and she's braiding the fringe of her scarf.

"I have to tell you something. I should have told you the minute you got here."

"You can tell me anything."

She takes a sharp breath. "I cheated. I cheated on Matty."

It's rare for me to be rendered speechless. Difficult to shock me, all things considered. But I'm shocked.

"When I first found out I was pregnant, I panicked. It wasn't planned. I felt . . . I don't know how to describe it. It was like my life wasn't mine anymore. I knew I should be happy. Matty was happy. When I was lying there in the doctor's office, staring at the little blob on the screen, I just thought, 'I've never been to Barcelona. I've never been out of the country.' I always thought someday I'd take a long holiday in Spain. Maybe do an art program. Have dinner at ten o'clock at night. Get wine drunk, smoke cigarettes. And after I'd travel around Europe, meet people. Draw. There was this other life I had in my head—this fantasy life that I didn't even realize I wanted until the possibility of it was gone. Until I was holding that sonogram in my hands on the drive home, knowing that this was my life now. Is my life. It's never going to be anything else."

Somewhere above us, clouds shift. Birds caw. The sun burns. The moon waits.

"I thought I liked where I was at. I thought I loved Matty, my work, my house. But there was this shift. I felt stuck. He was really excited about the baby, and I tried to pretend. I could feel my body changing, and every morning I woke up, I felt like . . . like everything was slipping away from me. I just wanted to feel like I had some authority. Over my life, over my body. I was at a tattoo convention in Philly, and there's this guy I know. I've met him a couple of times. He came on to me. I wasn't showing yet. I didn't sleep with him, but it wasn't just a kiss either. I went too far. And after, I felt so guilty, so stupid. Even more out of control. I wanted to tell Matty, but I couldn't bring myself to. The weeks went by, and I just didn't know how to be around him. Didn't know how to live with him, with myself. So I picked a fight and threw him out. I tried to be alone for a while, but that was bad, too. I found a therapist. It helped, but . . . I was lost. I wanted you. I needed you. To be around you and feel like myself again."

"Then why didn't you tell me?"

She finally looks up from her scarf. "Because I knew you would be forgiving, and I wasn't ready to be forgiven."

"Are you ready now?"

"No. Not really."

I go over and sit beside her, take in the view of snow-covered headstones, markers of lives, of bodies. Memories. The known and unknown.

"Well," I say, "that is pretty bad."

She buries her face in her hands. "I know."

"Understandable. Don't get me wrong. I get it. I get where you were at. Big life change. Physical change. It's a lot."

"I'm sorry I kept it from you. I tried to tell you sooner. I just . . . couldn't get the words out."

I shrug. "It's all right. But I've sure been a dick to Matty for no reason. He still doesn't know?"

"I told him. The day I got out of the hospital. Seemed an opportune moment."

"Smart. How'd he take it?"

"Okay. Better than he should have," she says, standing. "We're working through it."

"Is that what you want?"

She squints at the sky. "Once I stopped thinking about what my life wasn't going to be, I started to see what it could be. And I can still go to Barcelona someday. Let's head back. My ears are freezing."

When we get home, we go upstairs to her room and lie on her bed, not saying anything, just being together. My life might not be what I thought it was going to be, what I pictured. But I have my sister. I have Scarlett.

After a long time, she turns to me and says, "Morris sisters sure are having a year, aren't they?"

I take her hand and squeeze it. "Total shit show."

It's Christmas Eve. I know because when Scarlett wakes me up, instead of "Good morning," she says, "It's Christmas Eve."

"Is it really?" I say, rubbing the sleep from my eyes. "Damn."

"Get ready. We're baking cookies," she says. "And wearing ugly sweaters."

"Nooo!" I roll over.

"I'm kidding about the sweaters," she says, pulling off my covers. "Up!"

We spend the day at the kitchen counter, our hands covered in flour and powdered sugar, fingertips dyed with food coloring.

"Did you give this Santa devil horns?" she asks me. "We're bringing these to Joann's tomorrow. Don't make them satanic."

I pout.

After we finish icing what feels like ten thousand cookies, we FaceTime with Mom and Guy, who are skiing in Aspen.

"We'll see you soon!" Mom says. "So close, Scarlett! I can see it in your face. Almost there."

Usually, Mom and Guy come here for the holidays, but with Scarlett giving birth so soon after Christmas, it didn't make sense for them to come twice. Despite our strained relationship, I've never spent a Christmas without Mom, and her not being here has me feeling soppy and sad.

"Miss you," I tell Mom. And Guy, I guess. Guy's fine.

"We miss you," he says. "How's the weather? Get any snow?"

The call goes on for longer than it should, neither side knowing how or when to end a holiday FaceTime.

We eat dinner late. Scarlett cooks two of the steaks I got during my meat spree.

"Sorry I didn't put up any decorations this year," she says, licking some A.1. off her bottom lip. "Didn't have the energy."

"You should be sorry. I for one am outraged at the lack of holiday decor. Not one Rudolph. Not one friendly snowman. And not one little baby Jesus. A travesty. Are you listening to me?"

She's distracted by her phone. "Sorry. Ash is just wondering if we're going over tomorrow for dessert."

"Of course. It's tradition."

"She also wants to know if you're mad at her. She says you haven't responded to any of her texts."

"Did you tell her it's because I broke my phone?"

"I told her. When are you planning on getting a new one?"

"Are you going to finish that?" I ask, pointing to her half-eaten steak.

She pushes the plate across the table toward me. "You can't avoid life forever, Rory. You can't avoid Ian forever."

I pick up the steak with my fingers and shove it in my mouth. I smile at her, cheeks fat with meat.

"What's it like?" she asks. "Being a werewolf?"

I swallow. "You really want to know?"

"Yeah."

"The bite was excruciating. And after, it leaked this silvery goo. My new blood, I guess. It was weird and gross, but honestly, it was also kind of fascinating that my body was doing this weird, gross thing."

"Relate," she says.

"I did feel different, but not so different that the reality had fully set in. When I went to the distillery that first time, I still had hope I'd walk out of there in a few hours relieved. But then the moon came out. It's like being torn open. Turned inside out. I want to die during the transformation. To never feel anything again. Then there's this switch. When I'm in that form, I'm there, but it's like I'm a whisper. I'm separate from my body. In that sense, I'm powerless. But I can feel and experience what the body is like. As the wolf, I have so much power. I feel invincible. It's a rush. I can't really remember the things I do or what happens. Just brief moments, a second here and there. Then I wake up and feel like shit. Like the worst hangover you've ever had. And . . ." I look over at her. She's biting her nails. "Hey. You asked, sis."

"I'm scared, Rory."

"Of me?"

"No, *for* you."

"I'm dealing with it," I say.

A lie. I haven't exactly been proactive in my search of lycanthropy tips and treatments since my visit to the occult shop, other than essentially going into a silver coma, if that counts. I've been a bit preoccupied with my human problems.

"Don't worry about me. You're having a baby in . . . what? Two weeks? Worry about that."

"If I'm worried about you, I don't have to be worried about me. And giving birth."

"You're welcome, then," I say. "Totally worth it."

She sighs.

"We should go to bed," I say. "We need to be asleep, or Santa won't come."

We say our good nights.

I put myself to bed, but sleep eludes me. I let hours pass before I give up and kick off the covers. I go downstairs and out to the back patio. It's flurrying. I cross the patio and step out onto the frosty grass. I lower myself down. I look up at the night sky. It's starless. The moon is somewhere, I know, in a gentle phase. Letting me be. All I can see are the flurries tumbling down, down, down, down. Wet and soft and, suddenly, nothing.

The next morning, I find Matty in the kitchen with Scarlett. He brought donuts. He also got me a large pepperminty latte that's truly disgusting, but I drink it anyway because I appreciate the gesture.

I definitely have to apologize to him at some point. Admit that I was wrong. Yuck.

After coffee and donuts, he helps Scarlett out to the car, and I follow, carrying presents.

"Careful. It's icy," he tells me.

I ignore his warning and promptly fall on my ass.

"Are you okay?" he asks. His concern is genuine and sweet, and it floods me with remorse.

I try to get up and slip again. Scarlett laughs.

I flip her off.

"I'm fine," I say. If there's a bruise, it'll be gone by the time we get to Joann's.

I'm dreading seeing Joann after how I treated her at Scarlett's baby shower. I cope with my anxiety by singing along to Christmas songs on the radio. My rendition of "All I Want for Christmas Is You" is truly something special.

I try to break Matty with the high notes, but he doesn't flinch.

"You could be a professional," he deadpans when the song's over.

This gets Scarlett.

"Stop making me laugh," she says. "It makes the baby go crazy."

"Yeah?" Matty asks. He reaches over to feel.

It makes me deeply uncomfortable. It's too intimate a thing for me to be witnessing. Makes me squirmy.

They look so in love right now. So happy. It's hard for me to wrap my mind around it, with everything that's happened. That he could still love her after she betrayed his trust.

I don't understand how it's possible to live with your heart in someone else's hands. To have the capacity to forgive them if they break it.

"Last Christmas" comes on and I start dancing in the backseat.

"This is it," I say. "This is my moment."

"I can't wait," Matty says. "Please be as loud as possible."

I clear my throat. "Not a problem."

Joann hugs me and kisses me on both cheeks. I'm relieved that she doesn't appear to be holding my baby shower behavior against me.

"Good to see you, sweetie," she says. "Merry Christmas."

"Merry Christmas. Thank you for having me."

"Who is that?" says a husky voice. "Is that my girl?"

Grandma Candy. She's my favorite member of Matty's family. Perhaps my favorite person in general.

"It's me, Candy," I say, running over to her.

She's in her wheelchair at the head of the table. She wears a plaid nightgown, a red terry cloth robe, and orange lipstick.

"There she is!" Candy says. "Thank God. These people are so boring, and they won't let me have any liquor!"

"She's on heart medication," Joann says.

"My heart's broken because they ain't lettin' me drink! I've only got a few years left and I gotta spend 'em dry? Christ Almighty!"

She beckons me closer with a wrinkly finger. "Enjoy being young and beautiful. When you get old, nobody cares. They forget you're human. I've lived more life than everyone in this room, and they talk to me like I'm nothin'. Like I'm a dog. Except you."

Every year on Christmas, Candy and I hole up in a corner and talk about our exploits. She tells me about all the soldiers she's been with, the letters they would write her, and I show her pictures of recent hookups.

"He's a looker!" she'll say. Or she'll cough and say, "Why botha?"

This year is no different.

Joann's house is cozy, crowded with family. Aunts and uncles and cousins and second cousins and girlfriends and boyfriends and an assortment of children. We all loaf around and eat and laugh and drink.

"What happened to you?" Candy asks Scarlett.

"I'm pregnant," Scarlett says.

"No one told me," she says. "No one tells me anything."

"I told you, Ma," Joann says.

"Is it one or two?" Candy asks.

"Just the one," Scarlett says through clenched teeth.

"That'll be a beautiful baby," Candy says. "If I live to see it."

After dinner there's a gift exchange that I'm not quite a part of. I watch Scarlett receive baby clothes and diapers and bibs. She gets badgered on baby names and a whole bunch of unsolicited advice, including some tips on how to drop the weight post-birth. It's exhausting just to observe.

At seven o'clock, Scarlett pretends to be tired so Matty can take us to Ash's for dessert.

I haven't spoken to Ash or Seth since my unceremonious exit the other morning. I should probably apologize.

"Holy shit," Matty says when we pull up to their house, which is even more ridiculous at night. There are so many lights. So many.

"Merry Christmas!" Ash says, opening the door for us, Luca wrapped around her left leg like a koala. He wears a pair of red trousers, suspenders, and no shirt.

He gets serious when he spots Matty. He steps out and takes his hand in a very you-come-with-me manner.

"He's going to show him his toys," Ash says. "Come in. I made rhubarb pie."

She lets Scarlett walk ahead.

"I'm sorry about the other morning," she says to me.

"No, I'm sorry. I was a grouch."

She leans in close and whispers, "Have you talked to him?"

"Nope," I say, pulling all my hair in front of my face.

She understands the topic is a no-go. "If you want a drink, Seth set up a bar in the dining room. He's a mixologist. That's what he's been calling himself. He gives me these crazy cocktails to try. Can't complain!"

I say a quick hello to Ash's parents before slipping into the dining room, where Mia sits chatting with Seth, eating olives off a toothpick.

"Rory! Please tell me you don't hate me," she says, reaching out for me. Her acrylics are a festive red, color-coordinated with her dress. She reeks of that gardenia perfume.

"Course not," I say, cutting her off before she can bring up Ian. "Sorry. I smashed my phone. Haven't had a chance to get a new one."

"Damn. I can't last five minutes without my phone. Good for you," she says. "Seth, Rory needs a drink."

"Rory," he says, pretending to be happy to see me. "Merry Christmas."

"Merry Christmas. What are we drinking?"

"Rosemary martinis," he says.

"Fancy," I tell him. "Mixologist over here."

He blushes. "It's a hobby."

"I have an amazing champagne cocktail recipe if you're interested," Mia says, stabbing another olive with her toothpick. "Would be great for the New Year's party. You're coming, right, Rory?"

Ash and Seth host an annual New Year's Eve party. I'm usually back in the city by then and don't get to go, but I'm around this year with nothing else to do.

Seth gets somber. His shoulders tense; his mouth straightens. He avoids eye contact.

"What?" I ask. "Am I not invited?"

"You're welcome to come," he says. "But, uh, I invited Ian."

"So?" I say, feigning indifference.

"I don't know," he says, flustered. "I just figured you'd want a heads-up. Ash said . . ."

"It's fine," I say, finishing my martini in a single gulp. "Thanks for the drink."

"Let's go smoke," Mia says, finding my wrist.

It's healed since the bracelet ordeal, but for some reason her touch summons an unpleasant sensation. A zombie ache.

We wander out past the army of inflatables. She kicks off her heels and sits on the stone wall that separates the driveway from the neighbor's yard.

"Aren't you cold?" I ask her.

"A ho never gets cold," she says, tossing her hair over her shoulder. She digs a cigarette out of her clutch. "Only have one left. Share?"

"Sure."

"Look at me, a modern little match girl," she says, thumbing her Bic. It takes a few tries to get the flame. "Sad orphan with nowhere else to go on Christmas. Where's your mom, by the way? We chatted at the shower."

"She's coming up when Scarlett has the baby."

"Ah," she says, nodding. She shimmers. Her hair, her skin, her eyes, all reflect the thousands of blinking holiday lights that surround us. "Are you good with her? Your mom?"

I take the cigarette for a drag. "Yeah. Why?"

She shrugs. "Just with everything that happened. Everything she let happen. Was curious. Sorry. Shouldn't have brought it up."

I hold on to the cigarette. I need another drag to combat the aggressive churn of my stomach.

Once you tell someone your story, you can't take it back. I wonder if Mia thinks about it whenever she thinks of me. If, in her mind, I'm inextricable from this ugly experience I shared with her in a rare moment of vulnerability.

Sometimes, having shared this with her, having this close history, makes being around her so easy, so freeing, like gravity doesn't exist. And sometimes it feels like I've been stripped of my skin.

"My turn, my turn," she says, reaching for the cigarette. "We should get out of here. Go do something fun. Is there a karaoke bar? I could get into some sloppy Christmas karaoke."

"No idea. Look it up."

She takes out her phone and starts Googling. "I'm so relieved you're not mad at me. Let's see . . . karaoke. Hmm. Doesn't look like it."

"Oh, well," I say, staring at a wonky-eyed gingerbread man in the neighbor's yard. He looks drunk and frankly a little menacing.

"God. This town," she says, putting the cigarette out on the rock wall. "I sort of did you a favor."

"What do you mean?"

"If I told high school you that you moved back *here* and started dating *Ian Pedretti* . . ." She doesn't finish the sentence. She laughs instead. "Hand me my shoes?"

"I'm not high school me," I tell her, not bothering to conceal my annoyance.

"Oh, come on," she says, smirking. "I'm sure Ash and Scarlett are trying to sell you on some domestic fantasy. But you and me, we're not house pets."

I snort.

"Rory?" Scarlett walks toward us. "What are you doing out here? Were you smoking?"

"No," Mia says, lying for me. "She was keeping me company. We were just coming in."

We go back inside, and I choke down a piece of pie. We play a game of Pictionary that Ash and Seth get way too invested in. Scarlett falls asleep on the couch around ten, and Matty carries her out to the car.

When we get home, I stay up and play fetch with Reaper. Give him treats. At the end of our play session, to my great surprise, he curls up in my lap and allows me to pet him.

"Good boy."

Doesn't seem so bad, being a house pet.

Mia's wrong. People change. Some of us once a month.

Maybe high school me would balk at the idea, but I've never been happier than when I was with Ian. I think of Matty and Scarlett and wonder if I'm capable of forgiveness. I wonder if he'd ask for it. I wonder if he's somewhere missing me the way I'm missing him.

"'Last Christmas, I gave you my heart . . .'" I sing to Reaper. He looks back at me, scowling.

XII

I crawl out of bed late the next morning and drag myself to the Apple Store to, once again, get a new phone. I anticipate having missed messages from Ian, but there's only one from two weeks ago, from the day of the ill-fated girls' night out.

"He must know he was caught," I tell Scarlett when I get home. She takes up the whole couch, her feet up on a tower of pillows. I sit on the floor with my chin resting on a cushion.

"Or he knows about Kevin."

"How?"

"Small town. People talk."

"He would have no right to be mad at me for that, considering the whole Mia situation. He's avoiding me because he feels guilty. It's cowardice."

"Or he's upset you hooked up with someone else, which suggests nothing happened with Mia."

"Well, whatever. Doesn't matter."

She pats me on the head. "You look like a sad puppy."

"I'm not a sad puppy. I'm a fearsome wolf."

"All right, fearsome wolf. You're sitting here talking to me about it, speculating. Why don't you talk to him?"

"Because," I say, sinking down so she can't see me.

"Care to elaborate?"

"Nah. Can we talk about something else now?"

"Yeah, okay. You want some food?"

"Yes, please."

"Great, go make us omelets."

I do as she asks.

I figure the conversation is over, but later, while we're eating, she says, "You should go to the New Year's Eve party."

"You want this to turn into *When Harry Met Sally*," I say. It's our mother's favorite movie, required viewing in our house growing up.

"No," Scarlett says. "I just think you should go. Maybe it'll work out, and if not, you shouldn't let his presence stop you. Ash is *our* friend."

"Sure," I say, excavating some bacon out of my omelet. "Even if he did swoop in with some sin-absolving Harry Burns speech, then what? I say, 'Oh, by the way, I'm a werewolf. Hope that's cool.'"

"Yeah. Why not?"

"Right, because when I broke it to you, you really took it in stride."

She flicks some egg at me with her fork. "I know you have a hard time trusting people, letting your guard down. I understand why. But there are things on the other side of trust. I know, ironic coming from me. I just don't want you missing out on something special because you're scared."

"I'm not scared, Scarlett. I'm a monster. I scare. I don't get scared," I say, clearing our plates. "I'm going out for a run."

I drive to the high school, run the track for hours. I suffer the sunset, the abandonment of daylight. I suffer the tenacity of the stars, the moon's cagey accomplices. And, of course, the moon herself. Slim and tinny. I run in circles under her brutal eye, feeling the lunar cycle in my muscles, in my marrow. A tension waxing and waning.

There is so much beyond my control. Things that have happened, that will happen. My body. The people in my life, how they perceive me, what they do or don't do, if they stay or leave.

There is pain. Physical and emotional hurt. A cruel inevitability that I can't prevent no matter what I do, no matter how hard I try.

I lied to Scarlett. I am scared. Of course I'm scared. Who in their right mind wouldn't be scared? It's a nightmare out there, a great big, terrifying world. How does anyone trust anyone? We have such little control as it is, how does anyone willingly relinquish more on hope and hope alone?

Maybe I've been wrong this whole time, thinking Mom and Scarlett were weak for seeking companionship, for a hand to hold through it all. It takes fucking guts to open yourself up to someone. To love someone. To hope for their love in return.

When I get home, I take a long bath. Soak until I prune. Think.

When I get out, I don't avoid my reflection.

It's me. It's just me.

Wild and fierce and imperfect.

I kiss my fingers, then touch them to the mirror.

I spend the week in anxious limbo, unsure if I should reach out to Ian or if I should wait and go to the New Year's Eve party, see what happens.

My anxiety manifests in constant motion. I clean obsessively. Vacuum. Scrub. Do laundry. Organize the pantry.

I suspect I'm annoying Scarlett.

It's the Q-tip dust of the baseboards that gets her.

"Enough," she says. "You need to hold still. You're stressing me out."

I go upstairs and hide in my room, delve into work emails. Most people are out of the office this week, but whoever didn't take off probably regrets it now, as I micromanage while still technically on leave.

Mia messages me the day before the party to ask if I'm going.

Still undecided. You?

What else is there to do??

I respond with a contemplative emoji and leave it at that. Usually, I'm all about New Year's Eve. I always find someone to kiss at midnight. Some beautiful stranger at some exclusive party downtown with good music and expensive champagne. I wear some glittery dress and my faux-fur coat—ha-ha—and my hair in an elaborate updo. There's this energy in the city on New Year's Eve, this electricity. It's glorious.

I find the edges of these memories have frayed, gone sepia

toned. My life in the city, who I was there, it's in the past, and I feel surprisingly at peace with this.

I remember something Scarlett said at the cemetery. *Once I stopped thinking about what my life wasn't going to be, I started to see what it could be.*

I could attempt to arrange a remote-work situation or maybe branch out on my own. Freelance for a while. Find a house nearby and fix it up. Start going to Lowe's on a regular basis. Put up funky wallpaper and learn woodworking. Take up gardening. Host dinner parties for Scarlett and Matty and Ash and Seth. Make cheese boards. I could spend time with my niece, spoil her with toys.

I could go back to hooking up with random Kevins at bars if I wanted, though I don't think I will.

I could build a special werewolf shed or finish off a section of my basement with legit Hannibal Lecter–style restraints, no more flimsy handcuffs or dog crates. It isn't fair that I have to live with this, but I have to live.

I'm resilient.

My strength doesn't come from the bad things that have happened to me. It defies those things.

It'll be all right. No matter what, I'll be all right.

I close my laptop and set it on my nightstand, shut my eyes, and fall asleep.

Scarlett wakes me by knocking on my door. She opens it without waiting for a response.

"Smells lovely in here," she says, pulling back the curtains to let some light in. "What are you doing?"

"Well, I was sleeping."

"It's four o'clock in the afternoon. Are you really not going to the party?"

"Can I continue to put off the decision until the last minute?"

"It *is* the last minute."

I groan.

I guess if I'm going to try to build a new life here, I'm going to have to rip off the Ian Band-Aid at some point.

"I'll help you get ready," Scarlett says.

"Yeah, okay. What the hell?" I say, acting casual even though the thought of seeing Ian sends a fiery chunk of bile rocketing up my throat. I swallow it back down.

Scarlett does my hair and makeup, plucks my eyebrows, files and paints my nails. It's an absurdly long primping process. She dresses me in a backless, long-sleeved black minidress.

"I miss fitting into my clothes," she says when I model the finished product.

"I look okay?"

"Yes," she says. "You look exceptional."

I check the mirror. She's not wrong. "You'd never guess I occasionally kill and consume whole deer."

"What?"

"Never mind," I say, taking a swig of mouthwash.

"Do you know what you're going to say to him?"

I spit the mouthwash into the sink, run the faucet for a second. "I'm not going for him. I'm going because it's New Year's Eve and it's my best friend's party. And I know there will be pigs in a blanket. You know how I love pigs in a blanket."

"I know," she says. "Okay. Off you go, then."

"Off I go. Bye."

I start walking out of the room, which is hard, because my legs are suddenly rubber.

"Rory," she calls.

"Yeah?"

"Good luck."

"See you next year!" I tell her.

I pull up at nine thirty. The party started at seven. Inside, there are clusters of people everywhere, and I can tell by the volume of conversation that everyone's already drunk. I can smell the alcohol on their collective breath. I smell too many spritzes of perfume, too-strong cologne. There's a lack of inhibition, a lack of awareness. These people are disconnected from their bodies; their bodies don't hold them in a vise grip the way that mine does. They sway happily, free. Unaware of their surroundings. Unworried.

Someone's stomach gurgles. Someone's sweating out the tacos they ate earlier. Someone's crying somewhere; the brine of their tears flavors the air. It's the same sensory overload I experienced at the Corner Pub.

The kitchen is crowded. People stagger toward the food. I witness some blatant double-dipping.

I head into the dining room, which appears slightly less congested.

There, I find Ash in a sequined dress with puffy sleeves.

"You look like a beautiful disco ball," I tell her.

"You look *gorgeous,*" she says. "Wow. If I didn't know you, I'd think you were famous."

I give her a hug. "I'm big in Eastern Europe."

"I was worried you wouldn't come," she says. Then she whispers, "Don't look, but Ian's here. In the corner."

I look anyway. I notice him noticing me. His expression is blank.

I expect him to come over, acknowledge me in some way, but he doesn't. He returns to his conversation without so much as a nod.

"I'm going to go get a drink," I say. "Maybe think up some resolutions. I'll see you."

I turn, moving slowly to show off my exposed back. I go over to the bar. I expect Seth but he's not around, so I help myself. When I'm done pouring my bourbon, I check to see if Ian's watching me. He isn't.

I find a group of drunk people to talk to. They all find me very charming and hilarious. They laugh loudly, which is good for getting attention. I feel eyes on me. I'm the sun of the party. I shine the brightest, and it's all orbiting around me. My presence is known.

I wait for Ian to come to me, to give in, but time passes and he's nowhere, and we're now fast approaching midnight.

It's going to have to be me, isn't it? I'm going to have to make the first move.

I'm owed an explanation. I'm not going to let him ignore me. Avoid confrontation, avoid accountability. I'm going to maintain my composure. I'm going to resolve this calmly and maturely and then move on with my life as a charismatic lady/terrifying beast.

I drift into the kitchen to watch the door out to the deck. He'll go out for a smoke at some point.

I sniff out some other smokers. I chat them up. I catch Ian in my peripheral vision opening the sliders and striding outside.

"You fellas wouldn't happen to have a cigarette for me, would you?"

They don't just give me one and let me go. They decide to all go out with me. It's not ideal, but I can make it work.

"Aren't you cold?" one of them asks when we step out onto the deck.

"You want my coat?" another asks. "I could go get it."

"Such gents," I say. "No, thank you. I'm fine."

One of them offers me their lighter, but I don't take it. I look over at Ian. His back is turned.

"Excuse me. I'm going to say hi to my friend," I tell them.

They grunt as I slip away toward the back of the deck.

"Hey," I say, nudging his arm with mine. "Got a light?"

"Aurora Morris," he says like he's about to serve me papers.

"Thought you might be here tonight," I tell him. I'm looking at him, but he's staring out at the yard.

"You knew I'd be here," he says, setting his Zippo down on the banister for me. I use it.

"Thanks," I say, returning the lighter to the same spot. I take a drag. You know what? Composure is overrated. "So were you just never going to tell me?"

"Tell you what?"

"About Mia?"

"What?" He's finally looking at me, and now I wish he weren't.

"Did you think I'd never find out? You are aware she and I are friends, right?"

"I have no idea what you're talking about."

"Ah, interesting. Straight-up denial. I sort of figured you'd fess up, but you're going the doubling-down route. Interesting choice."

He leans his head back and exhales, then puts his cigarette out. "I can't do this anymore."

"Do what?"

"You don't actually want me. You blow me off. You hook up with other people behind my back. Now you're talking about Mia. What *about* Mia?"

"You went out with her."

"I took her for *a* drink after her father's funeral. She was alone. I felt bad. I have zero interest in Mia Russo."

Gotta say, the greater context of the drink would have been helpful to know sooner.

"She said you went for drinks. Said you kept texting her."

"To see how she was doing. She'd just lost her dad. Nothing happened, Rory. The night I took her was the same night I saw you."

"What?"

"When you first got back. That's why I was at the bar that night. I took Mia. She bailed early. Got all weird and flustered, then just up and left. Half hour later you showed up. Like I said, nothing happened."

"Then why didn't you mention it?"

"I wasn't thinking about it. It was inconsequential."

"That's not how she made it sound," I mumble, ashamed because I know in my bones he's telling the truth.

"When? Why didn't you ask me about it?" He shakes his head. "Don't bother answering. I know why. You're looking for any excuse. Any out. And it's fine. I get it."

"You're wrong," I tell him. "I don't want out. I want you."

The smokers are all listening. Watching. I'm keenly aware. We're putting on a real show.

Ian sighs. "I wish I could believe you. I know about Brian."

"Who's Brian?"

"The Corner Pub."

"You mean Kevin?"

"Who's Kevin?"

"I'm confused," I say. "This is all beside the point."

"Rory, it's okay. I get it. You don't have feelings for me. You never have. You never will. We're cool. If you want attention, you don't need me for it. Think you already know that."

What I want to say is *You don't understand! I do have feelings for you! The most feelings!*

What comes out is "Fuck you."

He takes it on the chin.

"Yeah," he says with a mild laugh. "Fuck me."

He turns to leave.

"Wait," I say. I grab his arm. Too hard.

When he turns back, he's wincing.

"Sorry," I say. "I'm sorry."

"Yeah," he says. "Me, too."

This time when he turns to leave, I let him go.

I look over at the smokers, who don't bother to pretend like they weren't listening.

"Fuck him!" one of them says.

"Thanks. Appreciate the support."

There's suddenly a warm hand on my bare back, pointy nails traversing my vertebrae.

"That was rough."

Mia stands behind me, unlit cigarette between her lips. She wears a strapless, skintight crushed velvet dress and a pair of tall leather boots, a chunky gold chain around her neck.

"Zero interest," she says, lighting her cigarette. "Ouch."

I don't know where she came from. I didn't see her on the deck. She just appeared.

"Don't worry. You weren't being loud. I just have big ears." She pulls back her hair to show me. "Better to hear you with."

"Sorry," I say. "That wasn't about you."

She exhales a spiral of smoke directly into my face. "I suppose I should be the one apologizing to you. Must have misread the signals. I'm clearly out of his league, so I just figured . . ." She shrugs. Gives a cool little laugh. "I could have sworn I made out with him in high school."

She looks me over, eyes narrowing.

"Aww, Rory, you're so sad. I'm not going to let *Ian* bruise my ego, and you shouldn't either. Come. Let's go get drinks."

She threads her arm through mine and leads me inside to the bar in the dining room. She steps behind it and gets out two Solo cups.

"Vodka? Whiskey?"

"Uh, doesn't matter," I say.

Everything moves too fast and too slow. There's this surrealness, this dreamlike quality pervading the party. No, not dreamlike. It's nightmarish.

"You'll never guess who's here," Mia says, pouring us cups full of Jack Daniel's. "Jay Coker. Class Flirt. Remember that time we had a threesome in his basement? On that janky pullout couch? The springs. God, I remember the springs."

"Yeah," I say, taking a gulp of whiskey.

I don't want to talk about this. Not here. Not within earshot of all these people.

"Don't tell me you're embarrassed," she says. "No shame, right? Though, isn't it annoying how if you fuck someone once, they feel entitled to you forever? Jay propositioned me and then got all huffy when I didn't immediately strip naked and bend over."

There's an uneasiness that I can't quite gauge, that I don't think I can credit solely to this conversation or to what just happened with Ian. There's something else. An ephemeral suspense. A mystery suspicion.

I look beyond Mia, trying to identify the source of my distress. The party unfolds and I experience it all simultaneously. The couple aggressively making out against the wall, the woman examining the run in her stockings, the guy pretending he didn't just spill beer on the carpet.

It's not as loud in here as it is in the kitchen, where everyone is talking over one another with their mouths full, or in the family room, where the TV is on, blasting the madness from Times Square.

I don't know where Ian is. He's absent from the corner where he was posted up earlier. There are a few people chatting there; they wear sparkly hats and hold noisemakers that I sure as hell hope they don't plan on using.

My body is trying to tell me something. Sweat seeps from me. Thick saliva spills from my lips. My left eye twitches. My ears ring. There's a kneading behind my rib cage that slowly intensifies, an angst beating against my lungs.

I sniff. There's a scent lurking underneath all the rest. Underneath the powerful colognes and perfumes, the liquor and hors d'oeuvres . . .

With stunning clarity, I recognize the scent, can assign it exactly. It belongs to the wolf that bit me.

"What?" Mia asks. "What is it?"

"Nothing," I say, eyes frantically scanning the room.

They're here. They're in this room. At this party.

"You sure?" she asks, stepping out from behind the bar, eyebrows low.

I want to tell her it's nothing, pretend I'm fine. But the panic, fear, anger . . . They're strangling me. I can't breathe.

"They're here."

"Who?" she asks.

And it's something about her tone. It's something about her expression. It's something about her perfume. Her signature overpowering gardenia perfume.

I don't smell it.

She's not wearing it tonight.

I take a step back.

"Rory."

Her boots.

I know those boots.

They're *my* boots. My vintage boots. The ones I was wearing the night I was bitten. The ones I *lost* the night I was bitten. The night I first saw Ian again, the night he'd been with Mia . . . and she bailed early, got all weird and flustered, up and left. . . .

The same night.

"Mia," I say, my voice low, practically a growl, "where did you get those boots?"

"I found them," she says. She doesn't blink. Doesn't flinch.

"Found them where?"

She rolls her shoulders back. "Let's go somewhere to talk."

"It was you!" I yell at a pitch that could shatter glass.

"We can't do this here. Just calm down. I—"

"This whole time. It was *you*!"

"Shh," she says, grabbing my wrist.

She's strong. Almost as strong as me. I break free.

"Do you really want to have this conversation here, with all these people around? Ash? *Ian*?"

My vision tints red. My teeth gnash together.

I've got her by the hair. "I don't care. I'll rip your fucking throat out in front of everyone. You did this to me. *You* did this!"

The anger I feel is otherworldly. I want to tear her head off. I want to eat it.

Someone I trusted. Someone I was close to. Someone I let in.

She's taken things from me, and I'm going to make her suffer for it. I want gore. I want revenge. I want to snatch her eyes out of her skull, to squeeze them to jelly in my hands.

"I didn't mean to," she says, wriggling out of my grip.

I'm left standing with a chunk of her hair in my fist. She presses her palm to her head, covering up a smear of silver blood.

"It wasn't on purpose. You know how it is. I lost control."

I take a step closer, and she pushes me back. I crash into the bar. Bottles clink. Solo cups go flying.

"Oh, shit, catfight!" some guy says.

"Shut up," we snap at him in unison.

He backs off.

"Don't touch me," Mia warns as I move toward her. "Don't touch me. I don't want to do this."

"Oh, well, I do. I really, really do."

"And you always get what you want, don't you?" she says.

She rears back, and I brace for her to hit me, but she doesn't. She spits at me. A wad of spit lands on my cheek. Wet and viscous, like the yolk of an egg.

The shock of it pulls me from my tantrum. The red drains from my vision, just in time for me to watch Mia take off, push her way through the crowd that's gathered around us.

There's a stunned silence. Tension thick as peanut butter. I'm too afraid to move. Too afraid to see how they're all looking at me. I can hear their hearts beating. It's not fear they're feeling. It's something else. Something I can't identify.

I lift my gaze, and when I do, I see revulsion. I see shock and pity. I see twisted grins. High eyebrows.

I'm a zoo animal, a sideshow freak.

This is her fault. It's all her fault, and she's getting away from me. She's getting away.

"Excuse me," I say, chin up. I follow the path she parted in the crowd.

I run out the front door. "Mia! *Mia!*"

Her name drags across the night like nails on a chalkboard.

I stumble down the pathway, lined with little fucking snowflakes and candy canes and smiling elves. As I walk by, the sound of sleigh bells rings out from some hidden speaker set back in the bushes. The shadows from the inflatables on the lawn loom large. How many of those things does a person need? And why? *Why?!*

I can't tell if she's hidden among the decorations or if she's gone.

"Mia!"

"I'm not talking to you unless you calm down."

I whip around. "Where are you?"

"You know how it is when the moon is full."

I follow her voice. I step into the yard, navigating around the Grinch and Snoopy, tripping over extension cords.

"It was the day of my father's funeral. I didn't realize. I didn't know. I lost track. It's so exhausting, always having to pay attention, to be vigilant. . . ."

"I don't feel sorry for you if that's what you're getting at," I say, knocking over an LED angel. "You knew. This whole fucking time, you *knew*. And you hung out with me. Looked me in the eye. You wore my boots in front of me. What's *wrong* with you?"

"There's nothing *wrong* with me," she barks.

"You obviously wanted me to find out. You wanted to get caught."

I sniff. I catch her scent and follow it back to the pathway. Where the hell is she? There are too many figures. I can't see her through the goddamn candy cane forest.

"So what if I did?" she says. "Maybe I got impatient waiting for you to figure your shit out. I didn't know for sure, so it's not like I could say, 'Hey, my wolf memory is hazy. Could you confirm our moonlit rendezvous?' I woke up the morning after and had a bad feeling. I went looking and found the boots in the woods, but no other evidence. Nothing concrete. Ash told me you were in some kind of accident, something about a bear. I wondered. Sometimes when we were together, I'd get a scent, but I couldn't tell if it was you or me. Had I known you would react like this—"

"Like what? How did you expect me to react? You did this to me, and now you're too afraid to face me."

"I'm not afraid," she says, appearing at the end of the driveway. "Like it or not, we're in this together now. You need me."

"Rory?" It's Ian. I hear the front door close behind him. "Is everything okay? Are you okay?"

I spin around. "Nope!"

His face disappears in the cloud of his exhale.

I turn back to the driveway, and she's gone. I need to go after her. I need to find her. I need, I need, I need . . .

I know it's cold only because my tears freeze to my face.

"I have to go," I tell him.

I attempt a long stride, but my knees buckle; my legs give. I collapse at the feet of animatronic Santa.

My shins are skinned, my palms. I'm dirty. I'm embarrassed. I'm furious . . . or at least I wish I were. The fury is fading and all that's left is hurt. A raw, boundless pain. It's crushing me.

"Are you okay?"

He comes around, steps in front of me. I can't look at him. I can't face him.

"Let me help you up."

"No," I tell him.

I don't cry like this very often, but when I do, I apparently sound like a Muppet.

"Please," he says. "Let me help you."

He offers me a hand.

I can't take it.

I can't.

I shake my head. "No, I can do it."

"I know you can," he says. "Just let me help."

"I don't need help! I can do it on my own. Go back inside. Leave me alone."

I get my feet underneath me. I push myself up, my bones croaking. I manage to stand but immediately topple over. He catches me.

"Rory, hey. What's going on? What happened with Mia? I heard you got in a fight."

"Why do you care?"

He sighs. "Good question."

I take a wobbly step back and am about to lose my footing when he reaches out to steady me. I get a whiff of him, his scent, and it's like coming home after a long trip, walking through the door. I inhale, and I'm home. There's nothing I want more in this moment than to have him hold me and tell me everything will be okay. Tell me I don't have to carry the weight of all this alone. But what if the house comes down on top of me?

"I'm sorry. I'm sorry I didn't talk to you," I say. "But what was I supposed to think? Mia said you took her out."

"Do you not trust me?"

"Don't take it personally," I say. "I don't trust anyone."

He puts his head in his hands, gives another frustrated sigh.

"Well, what about you, huh?" I say, stepping backward, putting distance between us. As I do, the goddamn sleigh bells jingle. "You haven't reached out to me at all. You didn't ask me about Kevin. You were just as quick to dismiss me. Did you ever stop to consider that maybe I'm dealing with shit? Serious shit. So I don't know where you get off assuming everything is about you and then telling me I'm the one after attention."

He doesn't say anything. Santa *ho-ho-hos* behind me.

"Did you ever stop to think about my life, how I grew up? All those creeps that my mom brought around. You have no idea what I've been through, the things I'm dealing with. And, yeah, I'm confident. I know my worth. I know how I present myself. But I'm not fucking invulnerable. So I'm sorry. I know I messed up. But it's not because I don't care. It's because I care so much, it terrifies me."

"Merrrrryy Christmas," Santa thunders. "Have you been naughty? Or have you been nice?"

"Yeah," Ian says. "You're right. I don't know what you've been through. But I'm not a mind reader, Rory."

"Oh, wow. News to me."

He steps toward me. The bells chime.

"What was I supposed to think? First, you disappear. Then I find out you're hooking up with guys at bars. You don't tell me anything, not about how you're feeling. How am I supposed to know if you refuse to tell me?"

Guess he's got me there.

"Because . . ." I assumed there would be a sentence to follow, but I don't appear to have one on deck.

"Because why? Why can't you tell me?"

While my brain is scrambling, the rest of me goes ahead without it. "Because I'm falling in love with you and I'm a fucking monster!"

I've done it now.

"Have you been naughty? Or have you been nice?" Santa asks. "Ho-ho-ho!"

I take a deep breath and look down at my hands. I've got something underneath my fingernails. I think it might be Mia's scalp.

"What?" Ian comes toward me.

The sleigh bells are going, or maybe what I'm actually hearing is the harbinger of death arriving to put me out of my misery.

"What did you say?"

"I *said* . . . something very eloquent and charming that made you want to be with me."

"I do. I thought I made that clear," he says. He's in front of me now. "But I can't keep going back and forth."

"I know. I'm sorry."

"Even if you change your mind. You have to talk to me. You have to tell me. You can't disappear. You can't hide things from me. It's not fair."

"But what if there are things that I'm not ready to tell you yet? What if *you* change *your* mind? The more you get to know about me. What if I've finally found someone I want to be with, and it's a swift pull of the rug?"

"I'm fucking here, aren't I?" he says. "I'm standing right here. I've been here."

"You're here now. But I can't make you stay." My mouth floods with my own tears, and snot probably. Yeah, it's mostly snot. "I hate this. I feel naked. And not in a fun way."

From inside the house, a chorus of voices starts counting down.

He wipes my tears away with his thumbs.

"Are you going to kiss me?" I ask him. "I'd kiss you but you're too tall for me to initiate. I need a step stool or something."

He laughs, lifting me up by the waist. It's a nose musher in the best way. I sink into him, and the bells become whimsical instead of obnoxious. Amazing, how that happens.

He puts me down.

"Will you take me home?" I ask him.

"I'm just gonna get my coat. Did you have one?"

"Nah. I run hot."

"Can confirm," he says, kissing me again. "I'll be right back."

When he's gone, I barely resist the urge for a triumphant howl.

"Have you been naughty? Or have you been nice?" Santa asks me.

Wouldn't he like to know.

Ian comes out of the house a minute later, carrying his coat.

"You sure you don't want this?"

"I'm sure."

We start the walk to his car. He takes my hand, threads his fingers through mine.

"This okay?" he asks me.

"Yes," I say. "But no pet names."

He laughs. "Not a problem."

We get to the car, and he opens the door for me like he always does. He starts it, puts the heat on.

"So far this has been a pretty good year," he says.

If I were to set a resolution, it would be to make this work. So next year we're together, like we are now. On our way home.

He pours us root beer in champagne coupes, and we curl up on the couch in the glow of his Christmas tree. It's a little sad-looking, since it's lost most of its needles, but the lights are nice.

"Do you want to talk about what happened with Mia?"

"Not really," I say.

He nods.

"It wasn't about you. Well, it wasn't just about you."

"I'm sorry I didn't tell you I saw her. I should have mentioned. But when you showed up that night, I just . . . She wasn't even a thought in my mind."

I sip my root beer.

"She's blond," I say after a while.

"Yeah?"

"So is your ex. I found a picture when I was looking through your books. You and some pretty blond girl. Thought maybe you liked blondes."

"I like *you*, Rory. You don't need to worry about anyone else. You've never had to worry about anyone else."

"Say that again."

"I shouldn't," he says. "But you already know. You're it."

I hold him, my anchor. His presence a salve. His scent like magic to me.

XIII

We fall asleep on the couch, and in the morning he makes coffee and eggs.

"I love your house," I tell him, looking around. "It's a good house."

"Thanks," he says. "I haven't even shown you the best part."

He takes my hand and opens a door tucked back near the pantry. He leads me down the stairs into the basement. When he turns on the light, I feel faint.

The vault. He mentioned it in passing the first night I was here, but I'd forgotten about it. It's an old-fashioned bank vault, with the thick round metal door. The door is open, and inside is a small room lined with deposit boxes. I step inside.

"Are you okay?" he asks.

The door must be two feet thick. More, maybe. There's another door, too. A set of metal bars. There's a lock on them.

"Does it work?" I ask.

"What do you mean?"

"The lock? Could you lock someone inside?"

"Are you concerned I'm going to kidnap you? Because I think I'd be the first suspect. Wouldn't take very long for someone to figure out."

"I'm serious," I say. "Does it lock?"

"Yeah," he says. "It locks. But you don't have to worry. I'm not going to put you in the vault."

I genuinely do not know whether to laugh or cry.

Is there a more perfect place for me to be during a full moon than locked in a basement bank vault?

Probably not!

Would that mean having to tell my new boyfriend I'm a werewolf?

Yep!

"This is cool," I say.

"I thought about maybe turning it into a bar," he says. "Haven't gotten around to it."

"I'm sure you'll find a use for it."

When I tell Scarlett about it that afternoon, she says, "Kismet."

I can't tell if she means it or is only saying what she thinks I want to hear. She's tired and swollen and distracted.

"When do you think I should tell him? How do I tell him? Do I bring it up casually, like 'So, do you believe in ghosts? What about werewolves?' Then, like, surprise!"

"I don't know," she says, shifting around, adjusting a pillow. "Sorry. I'm so uncomfortable, I want to climb out of my skin."

She's not interested in anything I have to say right now.

I decide against telling her about Mia. I can't stomach the possibility that Scarlett will take some satisfaction in having her dislike of Mia validated. Despite everything Mia's done, I feel a strange compulsion to protect her. I care about her. That's why this sucks so much.

I want to hate her. I *should* hate her. But it just isn't that simple.

I drove past her dad's house on my way home. Her van wasn't there.

I wouldn't be surprised if she skipped town. If I never hear from her again.

"Can you take Reaper out?" Scarlett asks me. "I can't get up."

"Sure," I say, whistling for him.

He trots in.

I take him for a walk around the block.

"Did you know I am now officially dating Ian Pedretti?" I ask him.

He doesn't care. He's more interested in sniffing garbage and eating twigs.

When we get back, I notice a small brown paper bag on the front step. Like a school lunch.

Reaper won't go anywhere near it.

"What is it?" I ask him.

He whimpers and hides behind me.

I pick it up and open it. Inside is a small glass bottle with a dropper. Some kind of serum. It's got a purplish tint to it.

There's also a sheet of paper folded in thirds. It has my name written on it.

I take it inside. I toss Reaper some treats and bring the bag upstairs to my bathroom. I sit on the tub and read the note.

Rory—

I hope you'll believe me when I say I didn't mean for this to happen. I didn't choose this. Not for myself and not for you. But what's done is done.

The vial contains a wolfsbane tonic. It helps, but you have to be careful with it. You need to build it up in your system slowly. If you take it the six days leading up to the full moon, you'll be too weak to hunt. Just a drop under the tongue. This is only enough for January but you can make more. Wolfsbane isn't hard to find.

Warning you—it's miserable, and if you miss one dose, it's basically useless. But it's something. You can take it or not. Your call.

If you decide you don't want to kill me (rip my throat out, I think you said), just howl.

XX Mia

There's an index card taped to the note. It has the recipe for the tonic, which involves a three-week fermentation process and requires rubber gloves and a gas mask, water, wolfsbane, lemon peel, and wine yeast.

I set the note down on the vanity. I examine the vial. I unscrew the lid to smell it.

It burns.

It's like acid up my nose.

I gasp, frantically screwing the cap back on.

The burning goes all the way back to my throat. Thick coughs claw up from my lungs. I can barely breathe. An atomic headache detonates between my eyes. My vision spots. I'm about to pass out.

If this is what happens when I smell it, what will happen when I consume it? When I put it in my body?

Maybe she's trying to kill me off. Poison me. The occult shop guy did warn me not to ingest the wolfsbane, said it was toxic. Though he also didn't believe in werewolves.

I get the bag of wolfsbane I bought at the shop out from under my bed and examine it, hold it up next to the vial. The petals are the same color as the tonic.

Is this legit? A fucking magic potion, an elixir I could make myself? Is this the answer I've been searching for?

If it is, why do I feel dread instead of jubilation?

It hurts to think, my head is killing me, and I've got the chills. I'm freezing; my teeth chatter. I dress in leggings under sweatpants, layer on two sweatshirts. I go down to the kitchen and drink glass after glass of water until I start to feel decent again.

"You okay?" Matty comes in through the laundry room, carrying bags of groceries.

"Not feeling great," I say, my voice hoarse.

"You don't look great."

Love to hear it.

"Need anything?"

"I'll be fine," I say. "I'm going to go hole up in my room."

He frowns.

"What?"

"Nothing. I'm just . . . I'm worried about Scarlett getting sick. If you're contagious."

"I'm not."

Matty doesn't believe me, which is how I end up back at Ian's.

"You need to start wearing coats," he says.

"That's not why I'm sick," I say. "I was poisoned."

"By the winter?"

He sets me up on his couch under a stack of blankets. I object to soup for dinner, so he feeds me steak instead.

"I have work tomorrow. Will you be okay here alone?" he asks.

I nod, and he touches the back of his hand to my forehead.

"I think you have a fever. Let me get the thermometer."

I don't think anything of it until he takes my temperature and it's a hundred twelve.

"Must be broken," he says.

"Or I'm just that hot."

He laughs. "Could be. Could be."

I fall asleep early, and when I wake up, he's already gone. I yawn and slide off the couch. I feel much better today, back at 100 percent.

I take the opportunity to explore the vault.

I examine the door, the locks. I could easily rip out the deposit boxes, but even if I did, I don't think that would help me escape.

Still, it isn't without risk. If I turn inside the vault and there's nowhere for me to direct the violence, the rage, would I hurt myself? And if I did manage to get out somehow, I'm in Ian's house. On a main road.

Mia said the wolfsbane makes you too weak to hunt. If I can handle taking it, if it doesn't scorch my insides, then maybe, maybe . . .

Maybe what? It's not a cure. All this would still require me to do the one thing I'm dreading.

How long do I have? How long can I keep this up with Ian without telling him the truth?

I go upstairs and wait for him to come home from work. I order us pizza. I have it in the oven when he arrives.

"Look, I made pizza!" I say, taking out the box. "From scratch."

He holds my face in his hands and kisses me. "I like coming home to you."

"Careful. I might never leave."

"Wouldn't mind," he says.

"I might move here."

"If that's what you want," he says. "What kind of pizza is it?"

"Meat," I say. "Ian, I am seriously thinking about staying here. Not here in your house. In town. Not going back to Manhattan."

He hands me a plate. "I might be the wrong sounding board, because I obviously want you to stay. But you used to always talk about leaving. And just a few weeks ago you said don't like being here. I know you worked hard to get to where you're at. If you wanted to go back, we'd figure it out."

"Things are different now. I'm different," I say, picking at a chunk of sausage. "I want to be here. With Scarlett, my niece. With Ash. With you."

"I can be anywhere you want me to be."

I shrug. "Maybe this is home."

"Well," he says, "I've got a great room for you downstairs."

I almost throw up.

"Ian?"

"Yeah?"

"I . . . I can trust you, right? I can trust you?"

"Yes, Aurora. You can trust me," he says.

He resumes eating his pizza, like this declaration is no big deal. I wait for him to ask me follow-ups, but he doesn't. He looks at me and waits.

"And you trust me?"

"Yes," he says. No hesitation. Just like that. Yes.

"Okay, well, I . . ."

I can't do it. I can't tell him. Not right now. Later. Another time. Anytime other than now.

"Well, I'm glad we're in agreement on that," I say.

"Same," he says. "Only, one small thing. You lied."

"What?" I ask, suffering a hot wave of anxiety that promptly soaks my back in sweat.

"I know you didn't make this pizza. It came in a box that said 'Salvatore's.'"

"That is a bold accusation," I say, climbing across the table to get to him. I slip behind him, drape my arms over his shoulders, press my mouth to his neck. "Very bold."

"I got sick just from smelling it," I tell Scarlett.

We're downstairs on the couch, and she's got her feet up on a stack of pillows that blocks my view of the TV. I just got back from Ian's, and now I regret not staying at his place. The mood around here is *tense*.

"Might be worth trying," she says.

I told her I got the wolfsbane tonic from a vendor online. She didn't ask too many questions. She doesn't want to talk about werewolf stuff. She doesn't want to talk about anything.

"I'm worried it's going to fuck me up."

"Then don't take it," she says. "Or just take a little. Maybe ask about the side effects. I don't know, Rory. I don't know."

It's a real toss-up at the moment who's the scarier sister.

"All right. Can Matty pick Mom and Guy up from the airport tomorrow? If I do try the tonic, I don't think I can drive."

"Fine," she says. "Wait. You'll be okay to come to the hospital, right? If I go early?"

"Of course," I lie. "Don't worry about it."

"I *am* worried about it. Don't tell me not to be worried. I'm worried."

"Okay," I say. "I'll be there. I promise."

"I want this to be over," she says. "I'm so uncomfortable."

"I know. I'm sorry. A few more days."

She looks at me. "I love you, but can you go away?"

"Sure," I say. I check my calendar to confirm what I already know. It's six days until the full moon. "I guess I will try it, then. Wish me luck."

"I'll check on you, okay?"

I give her a double thumbs-up and then head upstairs to the bathroom. I hold the vial away from me as I unscrew it. I've reread Mia's note a thousand times. A drop under the tongue. There's an etching on the dropper to indicate where I need to fill it to. I let some liquid out so it only goes up to that line.

I hesitate. Should I really be trusting Mia on this? She bit me and turned me into a werewolf, and either she really didn't know or she pretended not to. Why should I believe she wants to help me, not hurt me?

I have good reason to doubt, but I'm running out of time until my next transformation and I need to explore all my options.

I curl my tongue back and press down on the dropper.

I feel a slight splash.

It's boiling.

I scream, but no sound comes out. I just barely get the dropper back in before collapsing to the floor, pawing at my mouth, my extended tongue. My mouth is on fire, but the rest of me is freezing cold, like I've just fallen into icy water. I thrash around, my whole body spasming. I'm too dizzy to stand.

I clutch my throat. I can't breathe.

I roll onto my stomach and pull myself forward on my elbows, seal-crawling across the floor. I hurl myself at the door, summoning enough strength to twist the knob. I spill out into the hall and squirm to my room, desperate to get under the covers. I'm so cold. I'm so cold.

I kick the door shut behind me, not wanting Scarlett or Matty or Reaper or anyone to witness this. Drool flecked with silver blood soaks the carpet in my wake like a slime trail.

I'm too woozy to make it onto the bed; instead I pull down the blankets and burrow on the floor. I drift in and out of restless sleep.

At some point, Scarlett knocks on my door. "You okay?"

"Alive," I say, the word splitting my chapped lips.

Hours pass. Everything hurts. Everything is sore. My muscles. My bones. My eyeballs. My skin. My teeth. My nipples. My eardrums. Parts of me I didn't even know I could feel, I feel. Plus, I've got the spins.

I reach for my phone, the blankets rubbing my hand raw.

I have a message from Mia. If you feel like trash, it's working.

I can't do this. The solution can't be worse than the problem.

I call Ian. I put him on speaker.

"Hey," he says. He sounds groggy. "What's up?"

"I feel sick again," I tell him.

"Oh, shit. I'm sorry. Are Scarlett and Matty there? Do you want me to come by?"

"Nah," I say. "What time is it?"

"It's almost two."

"A.m.?"

"Yeah," he says. "You don't sound good. You sure you don't want me to come?"

"I'm sure. Just wanted to hear your voice. Hey, do you remember when we got in that fight sophomore year because I said Oasis is overrated?"

"I tried to put that out of my mind," he says. He fucking loves Oasis. "It wasn't a fight."

"Spirited debate," I say. "You like me anyway? Even though I think Oasis sucks?"

"You're wrong. But, yes, I like you anyway."

If he can get past that, then maybe the werewolf thing won't be that big a deal.

"Promise you'll never play me 'Wonderwall'?"

"I'm not going to promise you that," he says. "Won't do it."

"Fine, fine. It's late. I should let you go. My mom and stepdad are coming, and the baby is due, so this week's gonna be a shit show."

"You know where to find me," he says. "Hope you feel better. Good night."

"Night," I say. I hang up and go right to sleep.

"Hi, baby," Mom says. I open my eyes to find her kneeling beside me. "You look terrible."

"Good to see you, too."

"What can I do?"

"Actually, can I have a sandwich?"

She's back five minutes later with turkey and Swiss on a roll. She sits on the bed while I eat on the floor.

"Do you think it's the flu?" she asks me.

"No," I say. "It's nothing contagious."

"How do you know?"

"It's cramps," I lie.

"I don't miss cramps," she says. "But wait until you get hot flashes."

"Happily. I'll happily wait."

"Scarlett's really in for it," she tells me. "I remember my labor with you two. Hellish. Hellish, hellish, hellish."

"Yeah, would keep that to yourself for the time being."

"We'll see how she does," she says. "It's worth it, of course. Don't be discouraged by what you see in the delivery room. Maybe don't look."

"Good tip. I'm going to get some rest. Thanks for the sandwich."

"Come down when you're ready. Guy wants to say hello. So soon! So soon we'll get to meet the baby!"

She closes the door, leaving me alone to stew in the realization that, yes, any day now a baby will live in this house. A tiny, fragile being.

I wait until it's exactly twenty-four hours since my last dose, then force myself into the bathroom to put another drop of tonic under my tongue.

I tell myself maybe it won't be quite so bad this time.

But it's worse.

Scarlett comes into my room in the middle of the night and shakes me awake.

"Is it happening?" I ask her.

"No," she whispers. "Couldn't sleep, so I figured I'd check on you. Uh, you're wet!"

"It's sweat."

I went downstairs briefly this afternoon in search of food and to say hello to Guy, who generously cooked me a hamburger. Scarlett was napping on the couch. We haven't actually seen each other since I took the tonic.

"You look awful."

"People keep telling me that like it's useful information."

"Yeah, well, try being pregnant. People say the wildest shit to you."

I scooch back so she can sit.

"Is the stuff that bad?" she asks.

"Honestly, it almost nets even with the transformations because it lasts longer, and I have to do it multiple days."

"Mm," she says, frowning.

"It's like when you watch one of those medication commercials and they're like 'Side effects may include heartburn, nausea, bleeding out of your asshole, and demonic possession.' It's like 'Is it really worth it?' I don't know. Most lore either points to this or silver. I kind of wonder . . ."

"What?"

"The guy at the occult shop said something like there's truth in all lore but it's not what it seems. And just . . . I feel like maybe with the silver—"

"Quick reminder. You put on a bracelet and were unconscious for three days."

"But maybe if I had it on when I transformed, I'd just pass out somewhere. The bracelet burned through my skin but not my fur. My fur was fine. That could mean something."

"I'm sorry, but that's a terrible idea. Not to mention dangerous. I don't like it, Rory. Please."

"All right, all right. I'll stick with the wolfsbane and see what happens. I don't know what else to do. Maybe the vault would work, but without control over the wolf, it's a gamble. And would require telling Ian."

"When do you plan on doing that?"

"Good question."

"The anticipation is worse than the confession in my experience," she says, squeezing my hand. "If you see a future with him, and I know you do, you need to tell him. I don't know how he'll react, but I know he loves you. He's always loved you. Which is strange, because I was right there, identical and with a much better personality."

"Room for argument there, but thanks. Very reassuring."

She yawns. "I should go back to bed before Matty wakes up and panics."

"All right," I tell her. "Night, Scarlett."

"Good night, Rory," she says, but she hovers in the doorway, thumbing the latch.

"Yes?"

"I just worry about you. I need you to be safe," she says, her voice breaking. "But I do trust your judgment. I want you to know that. I made mistakes in the past, doubting you."

"Scarlett—"

"If you want to take the wolfsbane. If you want to try silver.

Whatever you want to do, I support you. I trust you. Just promise me you'll be careful."

"Cross my heart. Now go get some rest."

"I'll try," she says. "Sweet sleeping."

"Sweet sleeping, Scarlett."

After she's gone, I open my nightstand and stare at my silver. I know what it does to me in human form, but what would happen in wolf form?

I reach into the drawer and pull out all my jewelry. The silver singes my fingertips, and it takes a moment for them to stop sizzling.

I grab a pair of tweezers and use them to cautiously slide a silver medallion off its chain and onto a leather cord. I knot the cord, pull it tight. I hold it up, examine my creation. I forget where the cord is from, but I bought the medallion for myself when I got promoted. There's a small diamond in the center and there are little lines etched around it so it looks like a sun.

I take a deep breath and slip the necklace over my head.

The cord is long, and the medallion rests in the valley of my rib cage. I wait to feel something. I wait to burn. But the silver isn't touching my skin; it rests on my sweatshirt.

Maybe I'm grasping at straws. I tap a long nail on the medallion. I have no proof that it works, that the silver will save me from the violence.

Just a feeling. Just instinct.

I stay up all night, tossing and turning, sick and shivering and tortured in thought. Waffling about the wolfsbane. I'm already two days in. I'm not sure it makes sense to stop taking it now, no matter how miserable it is. Plus, seems unwise to rely on the medallion alone without knowing what affect the silver will have on me when I transform.

Hours pass, and I'm out of time to debate. I stand in front of the bathroom mirror, turning the vial of wolfsbane over in my hands. I don't want to take it. I'm quite literally poisoning myself.

But this isn't just about me. It's for the greater good.

I need to see it through. Leave no stone unturned.

"Bottom's up," I say, and as I say it, the vial slips from my clammy hands.

If my wolf reflexes were intact, I'd be able to catch it no problem. But the wolfsbane has made me achy and slow and uncoordinated, and so I'm doomed to watch helplessly as the vial bounces off the sink, cracks, then falls to the floor and completely shatters, sending shards of glass and droplets of toxic purple liquid all over the bathroom, and all over me.

There's a consuming dizziness; then my head connects with the vanity, then nothing.

XIV

There's knocking. It's so loud.

"What?" I croak.

"It's time!" Mom yells. "We're going!"

"Going where?"

"The hospital! Scarlett's in labor!"

I slip in a puddle of my own blood.

I'm dizzy. I'm weak. I'm sore. I'm barely conscious. Everything is blurry. I feel simultaneously hungover and like I'm on a bad acid trip.

"Rory?"

"I'll be there in a minute," I say. "Don't leave without me!"

I scoot my back to the wall, then push myself to stand.

My eyes are bloodshot. There's a gash on my head from where I hit the vanity. It's crusted with silver blood. Guessing it won't heal anytime soon, not while the wolfsbane is still in my system. There are small shards of glass embedded in my hands. I do my best to dig them out.

I stumble into my bedroom to grab a beanie and gloves to conceal my injuries, then slide down the stairs on my ass, taking deep breaths so I don't pass out.

"I just have to get shoes," I say to Mom and Guy, who stand at the front door.

Their faces are blurs, and I'm grateful not to have to see their expressions. I have a feeling they're pretty horrified at the state I'm in. Can't say that I blame them.

I'm wearing so many layers, I look like the Michelin Man.

I take a pair of shoes off the rack and slip them on. They're Scarlett's. Platform Mary Janes adorned with an excess of zippers.

"I'm ready," I say, shuffling to the door. These shoes are too heavy. I can't lift my feet.

"Are you drunk?" Mom asks. "Are you high?"

"I wish," I say. "Where's Scarlett?"

"She's already there. Matty's with her."

I don't remember making it into the car, but I'm in the car, drooling on the seat belt.

"We're here," Guy says, opening the door and helping me out. His hand feels slippery and weird.

I'm in the waiting room, knees to my chest in an uncomfortable chair. The lights are so bright. I pull my hat down over my eyes.

"Rory," someone whispers. "Rory."

It's Ash.

She hands me a bottle of water. "Here you go."

I gulp it down. "My angel."

"You want some more?" She pulls another water bottle out of her giant bag. I drink it.

I'm still vaguely dizzy. I take in my surroundings.

"Shit," I say. "Where's Scarlett?"

"She's in the room," Ash says. "It'll be a while. Why don't we go get you something to eat?"

She walks me down to the cafeteria and buys me a prepackaged chicken Caesar salad. I eat the entire thing, even the lettuce. That's how hungry I am.

"How are you feeling?" she asks me.

"Fine," I say, scratching my neck. "I'm just . . . really hot. Is it hot in here? I was cold but now I'm hot."

"Yeah, I can see that."

I look down. I have huge sweat stains, meaning I've managed to sweat through multiple sweatshirts.

"Uh!"

"I can take you home to change."

"I'm not leaving," I say. "I promised Scarlett I'd be here."

"We have time," she says. "Trust me."

"I don't want to leave the hospital."

"Okay," she says. "To the gift shop."

The gift shop doesn't exactly have the greatest selection. I end up getting a large green sweatshirt that reads, *I'm a Grandpa!* It's big enough, I can wear it as a dress. I change into it in the bathroom after scrubbing my face and armpits with hand soap. I'm careful not to let the medallion touch my skin in the process.

"How do I look?" I ask Ash, modeling my new ensemble.

"You can make anything work," she says. "With the hat and shoes, it's actually kind of cute."

"Thank you," I say, giving her a hug.

I put my head on her shoulder. I could take a nap right here. I just might.

She pats me on the back. "Let's go see Scarlett."

Ash leads me down a series of hallways to Scarlett's room. Scarlett's in bed, in her hospital gown, an IV in her hand. Her hair is in a neat fishtail braid. Her makeup is done. Red lip. Eyeliner. She looks at me. I look at her. I think we're having a moment.

Then she asks, "What the hell are you wearing?"

"You like?"

There are two chairs on the other side of Scarlett's bed. Mom sits in one of them. The other's empty.

"Where's Matty?" I ask.

"Getting ice," Mom says.

Ash gives Scarlett a careful hug. "I just wanted to say hi and wish you well. I'll see you after, okay?"

"Thanks, Ash," Scarlett says.

"This is the best room. I had Luca in this room! Must be good luck."

Scarlett shoots me a look.

"It'll be okay. It's not that bad, I promise," Ash says. They do our best friend handshake. "You got this."

"You're leaving?" I ask Ash.

"Yeah," she says. "They don't allow more than three people in here. Even if they did, Scarlett doesn't need an audience."

"That's correct," Scarlett says.

"Love you," Ash says, waving and blowing kisses on her way out.

"Bye, sweetheart!" Mom says. When Ash is out of sight, Mom turns to me. "I had to call her to babysit you."

"Me? Why?" I ask as the room spins.

"You can barely stand! Come, sit."

"I'm good," I say, propping myself up against the wall. I attempt a cool-guy lean.

"How you doin'?" I ask Scarlett.

She winces.

"Sorry," I tell her.

She grabs the side of the bed.

"You're all right, honey," Mom says, standing. "You're all right. Breathe through it."

I feel utterly useless.

"I'm okay," Scarlett says, still wincing. "Rory, can you get my speaker? It's in my bag. I wanted to have some music on."

"Sure," I say. When I lean down to reach for it, I get so dizzy, I almost fall over.

"I'll get it," Mom says.

Scarlett plugs her phone in, and soon there're the Ronettes singing "Be My Baby."

Mom sings along. I join in, then Scarlett. We're rusty; it's been a long time since we sang together. We used to sing all the time. In the car. While making dinner, washing dishes, folding clothes, pulling weeds. The three of us.

We still sound pretty good, I think.

When the song is over, we smile at one another and applaud.

"The Morris Girls!" Mom says.

"The Morris Girls," Scarlett and I echo.

And it's all downhill from there.

It's agonizing to watch. Scarlett writhes in bed, attempting to stifle her screams in the hospital pillow. Mom keeps telling her to breathe. Matty stands there holding ice chips, looking panic-stricken. His hand shakes, and the ice rattles around in the cup.

I can't tell if the music is helping or making things worse. Right now Scarlett is on her side, silently crying while "Once in a Lifetime" by the Talking Heads plays.

And you may ask yourself, "Well, how did I get here?"

I may, David Byrne. I may.

Mom rubs Scarlett's back. "It's all right. Breathe. Breathe."

I've been in this chair for I don't know how long. I've lost all sense of time. I've managed to soak through this sweatshirt as well. I lift my arms to find epic pit stains. Under my hat, my hair is wet and matted to my head. I oscillate between hot and cold. I chug water, hoping to flush the wolfsbane out. The dizziness comes and goes. It's making all this so surreal.

Nurses come in and out.

"Almost there!" they keep saying.

I made the mistake of asking one, "How long do these things usually take?"

I didn't get an answer.

"Rory," Scarlett says. "I want Rory."

I stand up and shuffle over.

"Just Rory," she says.

"You heard her," I say, gently elbowing Mom out of the way.

"I'll get more ice," Matty says.

"I'm going to use the bathroom," Mom announces for some reason. She opens the door, then closes it very slowly, adding, "I'll only be a minute, Scarlett honey. I'll be right here."

"Quick, give birth now while Mom's on the toilet!"

I offer her my hand.

"Why are you wearing gloves?"

"Because fashion," I say. "Obviously."

"I don't like this," she says through tears.

"No? Not a fan?"

She cracks a smile, but it quickly vanishes. "I'm scared."

"If I could, I'd do it for you," I tell her. "I mean it."

Her smile returns. "You're such a liar."

"I'm not! I really would."

She lets out a sob.

"I keep thinking about the video," she says. "Of you in the distillery."

"Hey, don't think about that now, all right?"

"I'm not tough," she says. "I'm not like you. I can't do this, Rory. I'm too scared."

She buries her face in the pillow.

I want to tell her that she has nothing to be afraid of, but I can't. Because this *is* scary. And if anyone knows scary, it's me.

I sweep some stray hairs off her face.

Mom comes out of the bathroom.

"I'm back," she says.

"Mom, the bathroom is right there. It's in the room," I tell her. "You didn't actually go anywhere."

She ignores me. "I'm here, Scarlett."

A nurse comes in.

"Let's see how we're doing here," she says.

Scarlett turns over to her back. I look away while the nurse does whatever she has to do.

"Okay," she says cheerily. "Almost there!"

Two hours later, I'm in a shower cap, a face mask, and a plastic scrub-poncho thing. Mom and Matty are not. The nurses gave them only to me, which is telling. My pit stains are apparently that offensive.

"I look like I'm going to Niagara Falls," I say.

Scarlett takes a shallow inhale and cries out through clenched teeth.

"Okay, Dad, I'm going to ask you to hold right here, thank you." One of the nurses instructs Matty to hold Scarlett's foot.

For someone as open as myself, I find it surprisingly disturbing how many people are currently gathered around my sister's vagina.

Mom is asked to hold Scarlett's other foot.

I am not assigned a task.

"Okay, Scarlett," the doctor says, "it's time to push. I'm going to tell you when. I'm going to say 'Push,' and then I'm going to count to ten, okay? And you're going to push for that ten count, okay?"

"I can't," Scarlett whimpers. "I can't."

"You can do it, Scarlett. Ready? Big breath in. Okay . . . push! One, two, three, four, five, six, seven, eight, nine, ten. Okay, good, good."

Nope. Nope nope nope.

I don't know where to look.

"Okay, you're doing great. I need you to take a deep breath, and then I'm going to need you to push again, okay?"

I expect the baby to come every time she pushes, but she keeps doing it, and nothing seems to be happening. The moment keeps repeating and repeating. The only things changing are the song that's playing and how loudly Scarlett moans over it.

"Okay, good, good, Scarlett. So, I'm not going to cut you; I'm going to let you tear naturally. The more the baby's head stretches it out, the better, okay?"

I've never heard a worse sentence in my life.

I look at Mom, but she won't meet my eye.

"I can't do it anymore," Scarlett says. "I can't. Please."

She looks so exhausted.

"You can. You can do it."

The more time passes, the more the tonic sick fades from me, and everything becomes more terrifying. More exciting. More real.

"Almost, almost. One more, Scarlett."

She lets out a scream so ear-piercing, so bloodcurdling.

And then . . .

"Here she is."

Scarlett gasps.

The nurse places the baby on her chest. There's a moment of silence. Even the baby's quiet. Scarlett looks down at her, wide-eyed.

"Hi," Scarlett says.

The nurse wipes the baby's face, suctions out her mouth and nose.

Still no crying.

"She's quiet," Scarlett says. "Is she all right?"

The baby gives a little squeak, then starts to wail.

"Oh, my God," Matty says, wiping his eyes with his sleeve. "Oh, my God."

Scarlett looks up at me. Her expression is pure awe.

"She's so precious," Mom says.

"Good job, Scarlett," one of the nurses says.

She offers Matty the scissors to cut the cord. He does it.

Another nurse puts a little hat on the baby's head.

I forgot. I'm so used to being reminded how ugly a place the world can be, I forgot it could be beautiful, too.

Later, Matty and I take a trip down to the cafeteria, just the two of us. I'm not sure if this is the right time to apologize as we sit across from each other in awkward silence, sharing dry sandwiches and vending machine snacks. But I'm feeling gooey and optimistic, so I decide to go for it.

"I'm sorry for how I treated you. For assuming the worst about you."

"In the past," he says, opening a bag of Combos.

"That's it? I dislocated your shoulder. You've been so good to Scarlett. You didn't deserve it. I was wrong and I'm sorry."

He shrugs. "You didn't know."

"You're really going to let me off that easy?"

"Kind of my thing," he says. I don't detect any bitterness. He tosses a Combo up and catches it in his mouth. "Ready? We should get back."

The room is far less chaotic than it was a few hours ago. No nurses. No Mom, who went back to Scarlett's to get some sleep. It's just me, Scarlett, Matty, and the baby.

"I see she's inherited your sense of style," I say, pointing to the hat.

Instead of the pastel hat the hospital gave her, she's now wearing a black one. She rocks it. I look at her squishy little face. At her tiny nose, pink lips.

"Oh, she's so cute," I tell Scarlett. "We're in trouble."

"Look. She's got some hair." She peels back the hat to reveal a puff of fine dark hair.

"You made that!" I say.

"It was so hard," she says. "Why does it have to be so hard?"

"For us ladies to prove how strong and amazing we are so we can continue to be overlooked for leadership positions and receive less pay."

"That's your aunt Rory," Matty whispers to the baby.

"Does she have a name yet?"

"We wanted to wait until we met her," Scarlett says.

"And?"

"We're thinking Lennox," Matty says. "Lenny for short."

"Cute and a little edgy," I say. "It suits her."

"You want to hold her?" he asks.

My stomach flips. I look at Scarlett. "Really?"

"Here," she says. "Support her head and neck."

"You trust me?"

"Yes," Scarlett says, "I trust you."

I take a deep breath and reach out for her. I carefully slide one hand behind her head, the other under her body. She's so scrawny. There's nothing to her.

I cradle her in my arms. She looks up at me with her goopy dark eyes. She's taking me in. Considering me. It's so clear that's what's happening, that she's sizing me up.

"Very cerebral, this one."

"She's serious," Scarlett says.

"Weird they come with personalities."

"Didn't we?"

I look down at Lenny, who still appears to be on the fence about me. I gently swipe my finger against her fuzzy cheek. I whisper, "I've got you, kid. I've got you."

She closes her eyes and falls asleep in my arms.

I don't sleep. I haven't slept in two days, and I'm in a state beyond exhaustion.

Scarlett's being discharged from the hospital. Matty's taking her home, and Ian's coming to get me.

He shows up with flowers.

"For me?" I ask.

"For your sister."

I gasp. "My *sister*?"

"I mean, for Lenny."

I gasp again. "My *niece*?"

"All right, just take them."

"We can drop them at Scarlett's. I'd say you could meet Lenny but she's sleeping."

"Another time," he says. "Hey, I like your sweatshirt."

"Thanks," I say. I forgot I was still wearing this. "Quick, let's go before my mom sees you."

"Would that be bad?"

"Ian!" I hear.

My mother.

"Ian, so good to see you. Oh, you brought flowers!" she says. "How thoughtful. Such a gentleman. And so tall!"

"Mom."

"Hi, Ms. Morris."

"Cyndi, please," she says. "This is my husband, Guy."

"Nice to meet you," Guy says, giving Ian a firm handshake.

"Likewise."

"We're all just so thrilled the two of you finally got together. You'll have to come by the house," Mom says. "Or the four of us can all go out for dinner."

"Would love to," he says. "Looking forward to it."

"You will live to regret that," I tell him as we cross the parking lot. "So, do you mind if we stop at Scarlett's for a sec so I can change?"

"Change? Why?" he asks, opening the car door for me. "I just told you how much I liked your 'I'm a Grandpa!' sweatshirt."

"I know. I just think it might be too sexy."

"I hear what you're saying, but I would have to disagree."

He takes me to Scarlett's. I put the flowers in a vase and grab a change of clothes. Then he takes me back to his place. I shower. He feeds me a cheesesteak and then tucks me in.

"I missed you," I tell him.

"I missed you, too."

I sleep through the rest of the day, the night, the next morning. I wake a little after one o'clock, wait for Ian to get back from a lesson. He takes me out for a late lunch. We go to the diner. We used to come here as teenagers in big groups late at night, order disco fries and Happy Waitresses and drink black coffee. It feels like homecoming to be here. It's nice.

"She didn't even cry when she was born," I say between bites of corned beef hash. "It was . . . I don't even know how to describe it."

"What song was playing?" he asks. "More Talking Heads?"

"Actually, no," I say, thinking back. "It was 'Do You Realize??' by the Flaming Lips."

"Damn. Great song," he says. "What a way to come into the world. To the Flaming Lips."

"Yeah," I say. While we're on the topic, I figure I should ask. "Do you want kids?"

He chokes a little midswallow. He reaches for his water. He takes a sip, then adjusts his glasses.

"Um," he says, "I don't know. You?"

"No. I don't think it's"—*How the fuck do I phrase this?*—"uh, conducive to my lifestyle. But I wasn't sure if it was important to you. Having kids, I mean. If it was, I didn't want to spring this on you at a later date."

I feel my face go flush.

He looks at me for a moment, then starts to laugh.

"What?" I ask.

"Nothing."

"No, tell me. Don't be mean! You asked for communication."

"I know. I'm sorry. It's just surreal to be here with you having this conversation about the future. To be with you at all, actually. Surreal."

"What do you mean?"

"I'm fucking lucky, is what I mean."

I hope he always feels this way. I hope he always looks at me this way.

"Can I be honest?" he asks.

"Please."

"Babies freak me out," he says. "They're so small."

"They are really small. I didn't know they came that small."

"I'm not saying I don't like babies."

"Right. You're saying that you hate them. You hate babies."

"If you tell your sister—"

"If I tell her what?"

"Never mind," he says. "Never mind."

"That you hate babies?"

He sighs.

"You chose this," I say, leaning across the table to kiss him. "You chose me."

"I did," he says. "I do."

We get in the car and start driving back to Ian's. It's dusk, the sun sinks behind the trees, and the snow-coated branches glitter in lingering daylight. The sky is a vibrant pink.

I notice my reflection in the side-view mirror. I'm smiling. I reach up to feel my face, to hold the smile in my hands.

We pull up to a stop sign. There's no one coming, but he doesn't roll through like I would. He follows the rules. He's good. He's so *good*.

He turns.

We're on Cutter Road. Not far from where I was bitten.

I've been on this road since. Many times.

So why this sudden sickness?

I'm queasy. My heart beats fast. It's getting louder and louder, the sound blaring inside my head.

"I feel weird."

"You're probably still tired," he says. "We can take it easy tonight."

I crack the window. There's a smell in the air. A ripeness.

"You okay?"

I watch mist seep through the trees.

"Rory? You need me to pull over?"

"What day is it?"

"Saturday," he says. "Why?"

A chill chokes my bones. I take out my phone.

I must have lost track of the days. It's tonight. The full moon is tonight.

I look through the windshield.

It's now.

"Pull over," I say. "You have to pull over."

"All right. Are you okay?"

The car's still moving when I open the door and fall out into shallow snow.

"Rory?"

"Stay in the car!" I start running. "Promise me you'll stay in the car!"

"What? Rory?"

"Please! Don't follow me! Stay in the car!"

He's not listening. He's following me. He's following me into the woods.

"Where are you going?"

"You have to stay away from me! Please!"

"I can see you get sick. It's fine," he says. "I'm not going to leave you alone."

"Ian! Will you just fucking listen to me! Stop following me!"

"Why are you running? Can you hold on? Damn, you're fast."

It's getting darker and darker. I'm running deeper into the woods. The terrain is treacherous, the ground sheathed in ice and snow. He's behind me still. There isn't much time left. There isn't much time.

I turn around. "Ian, please. Listen to me. Don't follow me. Go back to the car. Lock the doors and drive away. Please. *Please.*"

"Rory, you're freaking me out. I'm not going to leave you."

I look up at the sky and see the faint brag of stars.

He means it when he says he isn't going to leave me. At least, he means it in this moment. The last moment before he knows.

"Ian, listen to me. I wasn't attacked by a bear. I was attacked by a werewolf. And now I am one. I know how that sounds, but if you don't get the fuck back in the car, I'm probably going to kill you."

I don't wait for his reaction. I don't have time. I keep running.

I don't get far.

The moonlight hits me. A spotlight hot on the back of my neck.

I scream.

My hands go to the top of my head, where the skin splits as my skull warps. But now the moon is on my hands, and they break loudly.

"Rory?"

He's here. He's standing a few feet from me, watching. The look on his face. It annihilates me.

It's impossible to form words. My screams will not bend.

My neck unfastens. It snaps back and I collapse, my limbs twitching as they contort.

I attempt to hide my face, turning away as my jaw detaches, as it begins to extend into a hideous snout. My nose is severed from me, rapidly elongating. My mouth ruptures, my lips now pulled thin and taut. I don't want him to see me like this. No, no, no, no. I don't want him to see this face, this form.

But it's too late.

The pressure in my eyes. That's how I know I'm almost gone.

"Ian! Run!"

The final scream expels my teeth. My blood roars in my ears, and then it's the howl slicing through the night.

I blink.

I look down at hands that aren't my hands. I close them into fists. Open them up again. I lift my palms, let them explore my snout. I discover coarse fur. A wet nose. Hot breath.

There's a hunger raging in my gut. A slimy drip of saliva slowly descends from my gaping jaws. For a second, the hunger razes everything else. All thoughts. All sight. All sounds.

For a second, there's only this. The space between my teeth.

"Rory?"

The hunger is a vice. It's closing in, begging me forward. Begging me to feed. He's in front of me, and I could feed on him easily. So easily. Rip him open.

But then my fingers find my neck. The leather cord. The medallion. With the expansion of my body, the silver now rests directly on my fur, at my heart. It shimmers in the moonlight, turns the fur beneath it metallic. I watch as it spreads, radiating, blooming over me.

Suddenly, the night is pearlescent. The air sweet with snow. My thoughts come back to me. I come back, like a memory. Like a good dream. My breathing slows. My hunger wanes. It's in my control.

I am in control.

I give a whimper of relief.

"Rory?"

I hang my head to show I'm not a threat, stagger backward. I feel transcendently calm but precariously unsteady. I lean against a tree. I stare at my fur as it shines. I am pure silver.

"What the fuck . . . ?" He doesn't sound afraid. More confused.

I sniff for his fear, but I catch another scent instead.

Another animal.

Another . . .

I hunch forward, adopting my predator posture.

"Shit," Ian says.

My thoughts are mine, and it's my word, but it's not my voice that speaks it. It's the wolf's.

"Ruuuunnnnnn!"

A scathing howl echoes through the night. Only it isn't coming from me.

A shape emerges in the mist, high on the hill, through an arch of mangled branches. A ravenous panting scares the woods silent. A crimson glow pierces the haze, and then the moon lolls forward, illuminating the threat.

"What the fuck!" He needs to run. Why hasn't he started running?

It's her. It's Mia.

She creeps, body low, head high. Sharp, pointed ears, a long frothing snout, teeth like ivory daggers. Starving mad.

There's a flit of fur, a sudden shuddering of branches.

Ian turns to me. It's enough, the moonlight. Generous enough for me to see the brilliant blue of his eyes. And cruel enough for me to see.

It's too late for him to run.

She's on him.

A giant gnarl of fur. A spine curled too far over. A head rearing back. A luster, the sheen of teeth.

I push off my hind legs to cut between them, a growl burning my throat.

Mia lifts her head with a snarl. A sudden burst of pain blurs my vision. She's got me. She's eating me. Chewing my shoulder, chewing down to the bone. With her teeth, the strength of her jaws alone, she throws me into the air. I land facedown and she climbs onto my back, forcing me down into the snow, crushing me. I'm sustaining too much damage. She's got my arm now. It's pulled back at a frightening angle. She heaves into my ear, and I understand.

It's eat or be eaten.

"Hey!" A rock whizzes overhead. "Hey!"

It's Ian.

He's okay.

At least for now.

Mia's head swivels, and she's after him.

I struggle to stand. I'm afraid I'm not strong enough. I'm afraid the silver has made me weak. That *I* am weak, and only the wolf is strong.

In the distance, I see them. They're doused in moonlight. She chases him onto the road. She's closing in.

A sound reigns over the night.

This time, it comes from me. It's all of me. All my rage, all my pain, all my strength, all my love. When I howl, I howl with everything I am, every fiber of me, in every form, every phase. Past, present, future.

There is no me and the wolf. I *am* the wolf. This body is mine; it belongs to me. I'm here inside it, in control.

I'm on my feet. I run.

And goddamn, I'm fast.

I'm on her. I pull her away from him, her neck in my jaws.

I taste the faint tang of her blood.

If I were to clamp down, bring my teeth together.

If I were to feed.

Rip out her throat, rip out her spine. Mash her bones. Lick her dust, let what remains dissolve on my tongue like a snowflake.

The frenzy threatens to take me back. Take over.

There's a loud humming. An engine. I look up, see taillights fading into darkness. Ian driving away.

Distracted by the car, I lose my grip on Mia and she breaks free, swiping at me, opening a deep gash on my snout. She hits me again, and I meet the pavement. My skull ricochets, neck twists. Silver blood squirts from my mouth as I yank my head back in the right direction. But I have no time. She wrestles me into the woods, pins me down.

I get an arm underneath me and push, bucking her off me. She hits a tree with a nasty crack. Crumples forward.

I approach her slowly, cautiously. We're in a clearing, and the moonlight is strong and true. I watch as she stirs, as she lifts her head. She shoots forward with lethal speed. We claw at each other. My jaws overflow with blood and fur, and I can't tell if it's my own, if it belongs to me or to her.

I get her down.

Above us a cloud drifts over the moon, and without it I can't tell where I end and she begins.

Mia. My friend.

I sniff, and there's a trace of gardenia. Her perfume.

The scene around me becomes grievously clear.

Look at what the world has done to us and look at what we're doing to each other because of it.

I release her, and she howls in anguish. She attempts another strike, but I dodge her. I can see her anger. Feel her rage.

"Mia," I say. "Stop."

She lunges at me, her teeth grazing my fur, drawing blood. She barks.

"Stop!" I growl.

But she won't. I know she won't. She doesn't want to. She's going to force me to make her.

This time, when she comes for me, I'm ready. I bring her down, sink my nails into her.

I don't want to do this, but she's not giving me a choice. I press my blood-slick snout into her chest. Her heart beats fast not with fear but with defiance. With hate.

I bury my face in her side.

I take a bite.

The taste is bitter. She whimpers underneath me.

I spit her from my mouth.

Still she struggles against me. Gnashes her teeth.

I keep her pinned there until she stops resisting. Until she relents. Until the destruction is over. Until the sun comes up.

XV

I squint into vague daylight.

I'm not the wolf anymore. What I am is naked, facedown in the snow.

I must have fallen asleep, but I don't know for how long.

A twig snaps somewhere behind me, and a moment's panic dissolves when I see it's Mia walking toward me, wearing matching sweats.

"Here," she says, tossing me an oversized hoodie patterned with the *Playboy* bunny logo.

I slip it on, adjust my medallion so it rests over the top.

Mia props herself against a tree. She looks terrible. She claps a hand to her mouth, then turns her back to me to vomit. When she's done, she wipes her lips on the sleeve of her sweatshirt and says, "That never gets any easier."

"Mm. Uh, care to explain to me what the *fuck* happened last night?"

"So aggressive," she says, rubbing her temples.

"You tried to kill me. You tried to kill Ian."

Ian. The look on his face when he saw me transform. I close my eyes, and it's all I see. When I open them, still there. Shit.

"Well, what were *you* doing out with him in the woods last night?" she asks. I stutter, and her lips curl. "Appears I'm not the only one who got distracted on a full moon by Ian Pedretti."

"This is twice now you've almost killed someone."

"Almost. But I didn't."

"You bit me." I put my head in my hands. "Why are you being like this?"

"Like what? I gave you my wolfsbane. You're welcome, by the way. I didn't have enough time to brew another batch."

"So what? That's an excuse to eat people?"

She rolls her eyes. "You're just mad I scared your boyfriend off."

"Maybe you don't remember, but I had your neck in my jaws last night. Don't press me."

"Ooh, big bad," she says, pulling a pack of cigarettes out of her sweatpants pocket. She lights one and takes a long drag. "I didn't know you two would be out here."

"Did you even try? Last night. Did you make any attempt to stop yourself from going on a rampage?"

She shrugs.

"Really? That's it? That's all I get? A shrug?"

"I didn't have a plan."

"You don't say."

"Back off. I haven't been at this for that long. I've only got eight months on you."

"What happened?"

"What always happens," she says. "Went home with the wrong guy."

She pulls down her sweats to show me her bite. Hers is on her hip, but otherwise it looks just like mine.

"Never really heals, does it?"

"Nope," she says, untangling a dead leaf from her hair. "At least he left a note. That's how I knew about the tonic. And I had the van, so I could drive out to wherever. Remote campsites, middle of nowhere. Take the tonic. Wait out the moon. I thought I was handling it. Then I come back here."

She takes another drag.

"He's dead," she says. "My dad. Died in his sleep. Everything he put me through, and he gets to go out peacefully, warm in his own bed. No guilt. No consequence. No nothing."

She sighs, wipes away some silent tears. "I was like you at first. After I was bitten. Bitter, upset. But lately I've been thinking, 'What if it's more of a gift than a curse?'"

"What are you talking about?"

"Aren't you fucking angry? Don't you want to tear it all apart? I spent too long being powerless. I won't go back to that."

"Mia . . ."

"I'm done, Rory. I don't want to take the wolfsbane anymore. I don't want to suffer, sacrifice my strength. Why should I?"

"I need a cigarette."

She tosses me the pack. I take one and light it with the Bic wedged inside the foil.

"Silver," I say, showing her my medallion. "If you wear silver, you can control yourself during the full moon. No suffering. It's, like, this synergy. It's—"

"And what if I don't want to control myself?"

"What if I'm not giving you a choice?"

"Yeah? What are you gonna do?" She leans back against the tree, crosses her arms over her chest. "What kills me is you of all people should understand."

"You can't free yourself of pain by causing pain. If you don't take measures to control yourself, all you'll do is cause pain. There's no relief in destruction. I think you know that."

She closes her eyes. She's quiet for a while. Tears stream down her face, fall into the snow. "But it feels so good, doesn't it?"

I look up at the sun, rising, rising. "You can't stay here."

"What?"

"You have to leave, Mia. You can't stay here."

She scoffs. "That's rich. You think I want to be here in this shithole town? Date someone from high school? No fucking way. I'm too big for this place. I thought you were, too."

"I want proof. Send me a postcard or something."

"You want to be pen pals? Adorable."

"I need proof that you're far away from me and everyone I care about."

She sneers. "There it is."

"I care about you, Mia. Despite everything, I still do. But I don't trust you anymore. You're a fucking loose cannon, and I can't risk it. I'm asking you. Wear silver. Take the wolfsbane. Do something to make sure you don't hurt anyone else. And you're right. I can't make you. But I will make good on my threat to rip your throat out if I ever see you anywhere near Ian, or Scarlett, or my niece, or if you set foot in this town ever again."

She lifts her chin. "If you say so, sunshine."

"Are you hearing me? Do you understand?"

She lights another cigarette. Inhales. Exhales.

Then she raises her pinkie.

I trudge toward her, hook my pinkie on hers. "Remember, this is legally binding."

"Fine. But I'm keeping the boots."

I release her finger, take a step back.

"Did you really not know that you bit me?"

"Why bother asking? I thought you didn't trust me anymore."

I nod. "You're right."

"I didn't know," she says, "if I wanted it to be true or not."

She grabs me, pulls me in before I can wriggle from her grasp. We share a strained embrace, and then she lets me go. "No one will ever understand you like I do. Not even your sister. We're bound forever, Rory. Remember that."

It's one final look, and then I put her behind me.

"I'll be waiting for that postcard." I walk away, the ground crunching under my feet. "Drive safe."

I want to run straight to Ian's, but considering I'm barefoot, wearing nothing but a *Playboy* hoodie, I go back to Scarlett's instead, sneaking through neighbors' yards, hoping they don't see me creeping and call the cops. Or animal control.

When I get inside, all the lights are off, the curtains drawn. I figure Lenny's sleeping, so I tiptoe through the living room, careful not to make a sound.

"Rory?"

I jump.

Scarlett's on the couch breastfeeding Lenny.

"You scared me," I whisper. "Hi."

"Where were you? What are you wearing?"

I sink to my knees and rest my head against the arm of the couch.

"It was a full moon last night," I whisper. "I was with Ian."

She gasps, then winces, looking down at Lenny.

"He knows," I tell her. "He saw."

"He saw?"

"Yeah. But, Scarlett, it worked."

"It did? The wolfsbane?"

"Silver," I say, lifting the cord to show her the medallion.

"Really? That's . . . It's . . ."

"It's fucking magic," I say. "Think I'm finally coming around on the supernatural."

"Wait. What happened with Ian? Is he okay?"

"That's what I need to find out. I'm going to change and go over to his place. I'd call him but I'm pretty sure I left my phone in his car."

"What do you mean, need to find out? You don't remember?"

I give her the short answer. "It's complicated."

"Rory."

"You want anything while I'm out? Need anything? Food? Supplies? Someone's house blown down?"

"Aurora. I'd go with you, but . . ."

"It's okay, Scarlett. I'm fine. I'm tough, remember?" I peek at Lenny. "She needs you more than I do. But not by that wide a margin."

"Good luck."

I run upstairs and change into jeans and a sweater. I should probably shower but I don't have time.

What if he got hurt last night? What if Mia did damage?

I play back the series of events. I was with him. I transformed. He saw me. Mia showed up. I remember everything, but it all happened so fast. And I keep coming back to that moment when he saw me transform. When he first saw me in my second skin.

He knows now.

He knows.

I get to his place, and he isn't there. No car. Lights off. Door locked. I knock. No answer. I listen, press my ear to the door. I peer in the window. There's nothing. I would be able to sense if he was in there. I'd be able to catch his scent.

The panic sets in.

I drive through town, looking for him. Past his parents' house. Past Ash's. The grocery store. The liquor store. The hospital parking lot. The bus station. 7-Eleven.

He's nowhere.

The panic shifts into full-on crisis.

I drive around for hours, until the sun sets, and I realize there's nothing more I can do but retreat home with my tail between my legs.

Any hope of quietly slipping away for a private meltdown is immediately vanquished when I step inside. I find a full house. Scarlett and Matty and Lenny and Joann and Mom and Guy. Guy made seafood paella and insists I join them for dinner.

We eat in the dining room. Matty holds Lenny and the way he looks at her is art.

I feed Reaper a shrimp under the table. I much prefer him as an ally.

Mom and Joann go back and forth trading stories while they

plow through a bottle of red wine. They engage in a playful debate about whom the baby resembles more, Matty or Scarlett. They attribute specific features. The nose, the ears, the lips.

"I, personally, think she looks like me," I say.

Scarlett picks at her food. She excuses herself halfway through dinner and doesn't come back. I find her dozing on the couch. I sit beside her.

"I'm so proud of you," I whisper in her hair.

She opens an eye.

"Sorry. I didn't mean to wake you."

"I wasn't sleeping," she says. "Resting."

"Have you slept at all?"

"A little."

She holds my hand. "Did you talk to him? To Ian?"

"Couldn't find him," I say, my heart in my throat. "Don't worry about it. Are you doing all right? Be honest."

"I'm wearing mesh underwear," she says. "It's essentially a diaper. It hurts to sit. Hurts to stand. My nipples hurt. Everything hurts. I'm past exhaustion. And I feel this cosmic peace, this crazy joy. But I'm also sad."

"Sad?"

"It's hormones. I know it's hormones, but still . . . I'm so sick of these wild hormones. I just want things to be normal. To feel normal. I know that's not going to happen. Not anytime soon."

"Normal is overrated," I say. "Take it from me."

"I'm proud of you, too, you know," she says, resting her head on my shoulder. "You're the best sister I've ever had."

"Same. Hands down."

Lenny cries in the other room.

"You can have Matty bring her to me," Scarlett says, sitting up and adjusting a pillow. "She's probably hungry."

"All right," I say, getting up. "So weird you made a human."

"I know," she says, grinning. "And such a good one, too."

I grab my vape pen and sneak away, not wanting anyone to see me and offer their company. I'm hoping to sulk in solitude.

"Are you going out for a smoke?"

It's my mother.

"No," I lie.

"Yes, you were," she says, picking up her coat. She throws it over my shoulders. "I know you like to be a rebel, but you don't need to spite the cold."

"Thanks, Mom."

"Love you, baby."

"Love you, too."

She opens the door for me, then closes it behind me, giving me my moment alone.

I sit on the steps and take a drag. My gaze follows my exhale across the yard and out to the street. Across the street.

Where there's a car parked.

Ian's car.

Only he's not in it.

Because he's coming up the driveway. Smoking a cigarette. He's in the same clothes as yesterday. He's got his head down, but I can see that his glasses are broken. There's a crack in one of the lenses.

I stand up. "Hey."

"Hey," he says. He doesn't make eye contact.

"I was looking for you," I tell him. "I went everywhere. I'm glad you're okay. You are okay, right? Are you okay?"

"I've been driving around, looking for you," he says, his voice so low, I can barely hear him.

"You . . . you want to go for a walk?" I ask. "I'm not . . . It's not a full moon. So . . ."

"Uh, yeah," he says. "Okay."

We walk along the sidewalk in complete silence for a few blocks.

"I would have called," I say. "I didn't have my phone."

"It's in my car." He lights another cigarette. His hands are shaking.

"Look, I'll just give you the out," I say. "I understand. Nobody goes into a relationship thinking, 'Hey, so what if they turn out to be a supernatural monster?' So I just want you to know that if you don't want to do this anymore, I get it. It's not what you signed up for."

"Signed up for?"

"I was planning on telling you," I say. Now that I've started talking, I can't seem to stop. "Well, not at first. That's why I wasn't being responsive. I thought maybe I'd just spare you, but then it was too hard for me to be away from you. It's all new to me. I was back and then I saw you again and then I got bitten and then we kissed on Halloween and then I had my first full moon. And then—"

"Rory."

"I'm trying to explain."

He's looking at me now. His eyes are bloodshot behind his glasses. "There's no explaining. What happened last night, what I saw, there's no explaining that. There's no rational explanation."

"I know there isn't. I know that," I say. "I know it makes no sense, Ian. But the logic doesn't really matter. It's real. It's my reality. I have to live with it. And I don't blame you if you don't want to. Live with it. After last night, which, by the way, I'm really sorry about. I'll pay for your glasses."

"Let me just . . ." he starts. He takes a breath. "So you're . . . ?"

"A werewolf."

"Every-month-full-moon kind of deal?"

"Yep," I say. "Every month, the night of the full moon. Yeah. Just that night."

"I don't . . . I can't. I'm trying to . . ." He sighs.

"I'm sorry," I say, scooping up a falling tear with my tongue. I'm too afraid to face him. Instead, I stare up at the black sky. "When I turn, when I'm the wolf, there's just this violence. This hunger. And I've been trying to figure out how to control it. Manage it. And I did! I figured it out last night. I was in control. But I wasn't prepared. I lost track of the days. I didn't mean to put you in any danger. That's the last thing I'd ever want. That's not how you should have found out."

"There was another one."

"I didn't invite her, trust me."

"What? Invite who? Who was that?"

"It's not important."

"They tried to kill me."

"I took care of it."

"What do you mean, you took care of it?"

"She's leaving and she's not coming back. I'd never let anything happen to you."

"But it did happen."

"Are you hurt? Did you get bitten?"

"No, but it was fucking close." He rubs his head. "This is so fucked, Rory."

"I know, I know. I'm sorry. I've been trying to wrap my head around it and deal with it and sort things out. I didn't want to keep it from you, but I didn't know how to tell you. And I thought if I told you . . . I thought this would be over. I was afraid I'd lose you."

"You didn't tell me because you thought I'd break up with you?"

"Yeah," I say. "I mean, why wouldn't you? Like, I get it. If you don't want to be with me anymore, that's fair. Understandable. I wouldn't blame you."

He gives a sober laugh. "I don't care."

"What do you mean?"

"I don't care," he says. "That you're a werewolf. I don't care."

"You don't?"

"No."

"It doesn't bother you?" I ask. "That once a month I turn into that thing in the woods?"

"It should," he says. "It definitely should. I've been driving around all day, and I was trying to figure out what I was thinking and feeling, if I'd lost my mind. If I really saw what I thought I did. But more than any of that, I was just hoping that you were okay. That was the most important thing. I was more concerned with that, with you, than anything else. So, yeah, it doesn't change how I feel about you."

"Really? Not even a little?"

"Well . . ." he says.

My breath catches, and he laughs.

"Hey!"

"No, not even a little. I don't know what that says about me. But it's like you said. There's no logic. Logic isn't really at play here, though I do have some questions. A lot of questions, actually."

"I don't know if I have answers. I wish I did. I don't know what a life with me will look like, Ian. I don't want to hurt you. Ever."

"Rory, I've been in love with you since the sixth grade," he says. "When I saw you at the bar that night in October, I thought, 'Really? Still?' We hadn't seen each other in years, and I was right back. A lot has changed. A lot *will* change. But turns out I'll always be in love with you."

I pull my eyes away from the night. I look at him. When he's in front of me, there's nothing else. He's all there is. "Well, that's a relief."

He laughs. "Oh, good."

"Good."

"You want to shake hands now?"

"No. No, I don't want to shake hands."

We turn toward each other. I get up on my tiptoes. He leans down, and I tilt my head back.

"Can I kiss you?" he asks.

"Just be careful," I whisper. "I have such sharp teeth."

He kisses me anyway. Not careful. Not afraid.

I kiss him back.

Not afraid.

Rory—

Hello from the Lone Star State from a lone star.

I'm liking it here. A lot of wide-open space. Great barbecue.

Delicious snacks. As for the things I don't like... well, same as everywhere. There sure are a lot of pigs, if you know what I mean.

Don't worry. I'll be a good little wolf. Keep my promise.

For now.

Scarlett's baby is fucking cute, at least in the pictures she posted. Seems like everyone's happy & everything's boring.

Doesn't it make you miss me, just a little?

XX Mia

PS If you ever change your mind & feel like gnashing your teeth, come find me....

ACKNOWLEDGMENTS

To Lucy Carson, the most incredible agent, thank you for everything but especially for believing in me. To Jess Wade, the most brilliant editor, thank you for your insights and for always guiding me in the right direction. To Claire Zion, Alexis Nixon, Jessica Plummer, Miranda Hill, Katie Anderson, and the entire team at Berkley, please know I marvel every day at how lucky I am to work with all of you. I'm grateful every day for your faith and talent and hard work. Thank you!

To Molly Pohlig and Clay McLeod Chapman, to Jenna Lyn Wright, and to Stephanie Kent, Jai Punjabi, and Amble Johnson. Thank you for your inspirational talent and for your sweet encouragement when I needed it most.

To my family, I'm so thankful for your support. Shout-out to Ryan Shepherd and Alison Cerri—your presence in the book world is a gift.

To Courtney Preiss, thank you for your enthusiasm, patience, and friendship.

And to Nic, you know I couldn't do it without you.

Before I set off writing this book, I read *The Body Keeps the Score: Brain, Mind, and Body in the Healing of Trauma* by Bessel van der Kolk, MD, and *She-Wolf: A Cultural History of Female Werewolves*, edited by Hannah Priest. These books helped me shape Rory's story, and I extend my deepest gratitude to their creators.